# Once I Knew

VICTORIA LYNN

© 2022 by Victoria Grzybowski

Published by Glory Writers
10545 78th ave.
Allendale, MI 49401
www.glorywriters.com

Victoria Lynn is a credited author with The Glory Writers.

Printed in the United States of America

Library of Congress Cataloging-in-Publication Data

ISBN –
Paperback: 979-8-9857294-0-5
Hardcover: 979-8-9857294-1-2
Ebook: 979-8-9857294-2-9

This is a work of fiction. Names, characters, incidents, and
dialogues are products of the author's imagination and are not to
be construed as real. Ny resemblance to actual events or persons,
living or dead, is entirely coincidental.

Cover Design by: Victoria Lynn Designs in conjunction with The
Glory Writers for Glory Writers Press
https://www.victorialynndesigns.com/
https://glorywriters.com/

First Printing

*To my girl, my sister, my cheerleader, my first knight, Alexandria, writer of words and carrier of dreams.*

*This one is for you. You're my Malcom and a Violet of the first order. Climb aboard Captain X.*

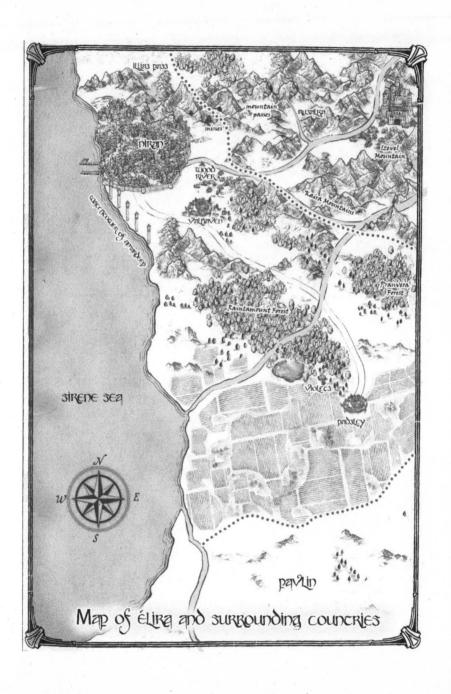

Map of élira and surrounding countries

# Table of Contents

"It is for freedom that Christ has set us free. Stand firm, then, and do not let yourselves be burdened again by a yoke of slavery."

GALATIONS 5:1 NIV

# One

## THE BODY IN THE WOODS

DIRT UNDER HER fingernails, the gentle breeze in her hair, and the sound of the wind rustling through the leaves like a soft hand stroking the fabric of the earth soothed her senses; it all culminated into one of the most comforting feelings in the world. Violet Frell loved tending the fields. She felt safe here. Content. In control. It was her happy place.

After loosening the soil with her fingers, she scooped out the dirt, making a small hole before reaching for the tiny seedling she had been tending indoors until it was strong enough to brave the elements on its own and be planted outside. She lifted the tomato plant from the tiny pot it had called home and settled it gently into the prepared hole in the ground. Pushing the dirt close around its stem, she smiled and hummed to herself before brushing a stray strand of half-curled hair out of her eyes with the back of her hand. She could feel some mud transfer to her face, but it didn't bother

1

her. It wasn't like she could rid herself of the smudge on her face now with her hands completely covered with the grime. She would use her apron and the lake to wash away the remaining traces of the garden when she was finished.

She closed her eyes and sat back on her heels as another breeze blew by and tickled her face with its gentle fingers. Despite the calm around her, the weight pressing on her mind gathered like a nuisance in her heart. So much turmoil was happening in the world beyond her village. The outside world had always been just that...on the outside. Yet with each passing day, she couldn't help but admit the truth: it was getting closer.

The young prince was finally set to take the throne. It was rumored that his spoiled attitude was the reason the kingdom had fallen into the hands of the chancellor, Enguerrand, from which the present tyranny was springing forth. As the regent, he had taken control of the throne until the prince came of age at twenty-one...which was this year. Those who valued their way of life only whispered of the regent's tyrannical rule. To be heard speaking ill of the new ruler could bring a punishment swift and life-altering. She had never experienced it firsthand, but she had heard stories of those forced into the army or labor for the crown, their possessions seized, or rarer yet, their children taken into slavery to the bordering kingdom of Rusalka. While Rusalka was governed by a king who praised and used slavery, her home kingdom of Elira was not one that sanctioned such servitude...at least, not yet.

Violet sighed. Thoughts of the pain outside her village walls plagued her even in her sanctuary.

She shook her head, trying to clear the depressing cobwebs

2

from taking up residence in her mind. Turning back to her plot of earth, she sank her fingers in once again to loosen the soil when a vibration beneath her knees startled her. Stretching her fingers out flat to feel the thuds more clearly, she strained her ear to catch even the slightest sound.

Thundering hooves.

Bolting upright, her brown skirt and flax-colored apron falling and billowing around her, she looked toward the woods. Their looming evergreen shades danced and swayed in the slight breeze. The tall trees towered over her little glade, tucked away in their midst, a hideaway carved out by her ancestors. The lake bordering the far north side of the property glittered with the last rays of the setting sun. A small movement in the distance caught her eye amidst the misty green hue. A large horse plowed through the underbrush and sent the birds scattering and clamoring out of the way. The stallion's black mane flowed behind him, matching his equally dark body. His head was high in fright, ears laid back.

She gathered her skirts in her hands and rushed toward the edge of the forest to head him off, the trees reaching high overhead and blocking out the sun as she stepped into their shade. As she drew closer, she realized that he was saddled.

And without a rider.

Violet stepped in front of the charging steed's path, raising her arms to ward him to a stop. Her heart raced, and she gulped for air to catch her breath. The horse saw her and snorted, throwing his head back as he half-reared and stamped his foot so close she worried for her toes. But he didn't run. He was wary, and she could see the white's of his eyes. She cooed under her breath. His ears came forward, and he breathed

3

heavily, nostrils flaring, as she held out a slow and gentle hand toward him.

"Easy, boy. I'm not going to hurt you." Violet barely spoke above a whisper.

After a tense pause, he stepped forward and touched his nose to her hand. She rubbed the sweaty muzzle and slowly worked her hand up his face. Showing him her other hand, she moved it toward his neck. Softly petting him, all the while crooning sweet platitudes, she glanced at the saddle.

Her pulse froze. A royal saddle. It had the crest of the king on it: a lion and a crown surrounded by thorns.

A tremor coursed through her. A kingsman so close. The stories that had been haunting her mind while she worked rushed to the forefront, and she fought to catch her breath. Until the blood suddenly rushed from her head.

There was blood on the saddle.

Gathering the reins in her hand and leading the horse beside her, she could sense its skittishness. Gripping tighter, her knuckles whitening, she followed the trail of broken branches and twigs the horse had made on its frightened dash through the forest. Brush crackled beneath her step and the damp, earthy smell of the forest floor filled her nostrils with its heady and sharp scent. The blood on the saddle made her nerves tighten up like the balls of woolen yarn that Granny wrapped too tightly. The cool breeze tickled her skin with its gentle fingers, and the shadows cast by the elm and pine created caverns of shadow that tried to hide from the light that filtered through the thick canopy above.

Magical little rays of that light captured dust motes here and there, casting a foggy atmosphere upon the hush of the forest, broken only by the chatter of the leaves. It would be beautiful if it weren't so sinister. There was a lump in her throat, and she tried to swallow it, but to no avail. A dry twig cracked beneath her foot, deafening in the silence. The horse snorted and jerked, and her pulse jumped.

"Shhh..." She comforted the animal with a soothing coo and a soft pat to the neck. The stallion settled, but Violet could tell he was still nervous. His nostrils flared and though she could no longer see the whites of his eyes, the constant twitching of his head betrayed the beast's uneasiness.

She knew enough about animals to know that if the horse didn't feel safe, she shouldn't feel safe either.

A bird flew into the air off to her left, and she gasped, startled, looking in that direction. Her foot caught on a fallen log, and she sprawled out on the muddy ground. The horse half-reared and let out a nervous whinny over her stumbling fall. A slight dizziness gripped her, almost as if she didn't know which way was up in the green hued wavering shadow and light, as she tried to untangle herself from the sticks, rubble, and creepy crawlies of the forest floor.

She glanced over her shoulder, half-entangled in her skirts, and almost fainted at the sight of a white face with closed eyes lolled over the very same log she had tripped on. Shoving away from the body in a panic, she scrambled to her feet and stepped behind the horse for protection without even thinking about it. Sensing her fear, he maneuvered in a hop-step away from the body. Gulping in deep breaths, she peered around her living shield and tried to calm herself. The form had not moved.

Once her pulse had calmed a bit, she stepped toward the

5

man, thoughts racing. If this was the horse's rider, judging from the blood on the saddle she had noticed earlier, he had to be severely injured.

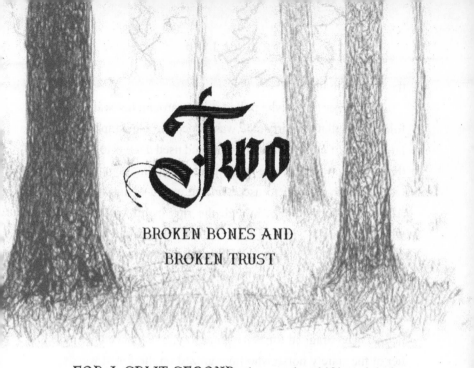

# Two

## BROKEN BONES AND
## BROKEN TRUST

FOR A SPLIT SECOND, she wondered if he might be dead. In which case, what did one do with a dead body in the woods? One did not simply report it to the local authorities. These days, misunderstandings with the Kingsmen were so commonplace that they might just be inclined to think that she was responsible for this man's death. Especially if he were one of their own, as it certainly appeared with the leather armor and the king's coat of arms on his shoulder piece.

A sudden movement on the part of the corpse made her gasp. A moan escaped his cracked and bleeding lips. With all hesitation leaving her body, she knelt beside the injured man and adjusted his oddly positioned head to a more comfortable angle which allowed her to view his wounds properly. His clothes were muddy and stained beyond use, littered with an overabundance of holes and tears. His rather thick, but short, mop of brown hair was caked with mud and leaves, matted in the back with blood.

Untying her apron, she pulled it from around her waist and folded it so that the dirty side was folded in. She wrapped the large piece of cloth around his head and used the ties to ensure that it stayed in place. She made a quick examination over the rest of his long form to ascertain the extent of his injuries. Abrasions were visible through the rips in his clothes and when she caught sight of his left foot, she grimaced. It lay twisted at an odd angle, and a clear picture of what had happened came into her mind. He had lost his seat from the saddle, whether he hit his head before or after that, but by the shape of his ankle and the wounds and rips across his body, he had been dragged for quite some way. She glanced behind her at the stately horse who now grazed on the forest weeds, completely oblivious.

She bit her lip. How was she, a mere slip of a girl, to get this rather long and lanky man atop a horse that she herself would need assistance to mount?

Without panicking or giving a second thought, she looked around the forest floor and made a plan. She gathered a few small but sturdy pieces of wood and used them as a splint for the man's leg. Placing one on either side of the misshapen foot, she tied them down with the shawl that had been wrapped around her shoulders. That done, she set to work.

Dragging the longest, straightest branches she could find, she bound them to the sides of the horse's saddle just above the stirrups. Shaking her head in an attempt to get her outspoken Granny's voice out of her head at the impropriety of it, she untied, then stepped out of, her skirt. The hem of her patchwork petticoat was muddy from the garden and the woods. She ripped out the seam of the skirt and pulled the gathers out of the waistband until it was one long strip of fabric. Fastening it to the two logs extending from the horse's royal-crested saddle, it formed a makeshift travois to carry him home.

Slightly out of breath, she leaned her hands on her knees and took a few deep draughts of air. But she dare not tarry here. The sun had been moving steadily toward the horizon while she had been hard at work, and one never wanted to be caught in the Raintamount Forest past dusk.

Pulling the horse's head closer to her, she tied him tight to the fallen tree that was wider around than three of herself. She didn't want him spooking again.

It took a good bit of time, and while she was strong, half-dragging and half-lifting a grown man even a short distance was strenuous at best.

With great relief, she succeeded in maneuvering him onto the travois and started on the journey home. The sun was just now casting its last rays over the forest floor, and the thickening gloom and growing chill made her skin crawl. They needed to get out of the forest.

Leading the horse and constantly checking back to make sure that her patient was still safe made their journey take longer than she had hoped; it was nearly pitch black when she reached the forest edge.

"Halt! Who goes there?" A gruff voice bellowed.

Her heart rocketed into her throat.

The swaying, soft yellow light of a lantern swung closer and closer to her feet, and she swallowed against the bitter taste in her mouth. Blinking, she shied away from the light as it was thrust toward her face. The sudden and possibly over-dramatic thought of death being near made her knees shake and threaten to give way. Squinting her eyes against the brightness, she dreaded what she would see when she opened them. A kingsman? Even worse if he was the one who commanded the guard over their village.

"Violet? What on earth are you doing out this late? Don't you know you could be detained for being out past curfew?"

Her shoulders relaxed at the familiar voice, and she opened her eyes, relief coursing through her body so quickly that she sank to a seat on the already dew-dampened ground. "Mr. Bennett. You have no idea the relief I feel at seeing you!" Her voice quavered. Mr. Bennett was a neighboring farmer, and she could not be more pleased that he was the one who met her on this clandestine errand. Anyone but a kingsman.

"I don't know that relief is what I'll bring, though I am glad I can be of service. But do answer my question, what on earth are you doing out here at this time of night? Surely you should be getting back home! A kingsman could stumble across you, and then what would you do? They do not take kindly to those who stay out late, and an unaccompanied woman such as yourself should be a good deal more careful than most."

"I know, and thank you for your concern. But would you be so kind as to be of assistance? I found this man in the woods. He is injured; I couldn't leave him for dead."

Mr. Bennett spooked at a cracking twig and stared off into the dark distance, as if trying to discern if his own life was in danger in that moment. Turning back to her, he drew in a sharp breath and fidgeted with the lantern. "What stranger? What happened?" He took a few steps toward the horse, who snorted uncomfortably and stamped awkwardly in trepidation. Her neighbor held the lantern aloft, but the minute he caught sight of the king's insignia on the saddle, he nearly fell over in his attempt to get away from the horse and the injured man being pulled behind it.

"Are you daft? What do you think you are doing? Are you trying to kill us all?" His words came out like whispered daggers, the edge of his voice so sharp she could easily picture it cutting her skin. The horse sensed the uneasiness of the man's voice and body language and sidestepped, rocking the travois and eliciting a groan from the stranger nestled there.

"Mr. Bennett, please. I beg of you! I can't possibly lift him myself. Please. Come back to the house and help me move him inside. I won't say a word if asked. I will never give up your name if questioned!" It was a weak proposition. Even she knew that. Most were not strong enough to withstand torture...and the Kingsmen had been known to push farther than needed.

Shaking his head, he stepped farther away, all but turning to run right then and there. "You are on your own, Violet. If you choose to trifle with your life and that of your poor, defenseless, and crippled grandmother, then that be upon your own head. But I will have nothing to do with it. I have a family and a farm to support, and I cannot very well do that from the stocks...or a noose." With this cold premonition, he turned and fled. The golden lantern light, her last warm comfort, bobbed away into the darkness with the hasty footsteps of a man who lacked conviction or the bravery to walk in it.

The horse snuffled and nuzzled her shoulder.

The darkness, bereft of any warmth and light made her wish

to cry. She sniffed and swallowed back the tears, setting her shoulders and squinting into the darkness. Despite the ominous forebodings from Mr. Bennett, she couldn't leave the man out here to die alone, even if that meant meeting an untimely end herself. She clenched her jaw, chirping to the horse and pulling on his reins. They must get home. She prayed that they would not meet another kingsman. One was enough for today.

# Three

## WEARY HEARTS AND IRKSOME FEARS

THE FLICKERING, orange light of the fire inside of her cabin bounced and wavered across the windows with such an inviting warmth that Violet, bereft of her sacrificed skirt, desperately needed. She shivered against the cold night wind that whistled past the small barn and sank through her clothes to chill her skin. A rustle in the woods lining the back of the cabin made her pull the horse's lead harder and rush them to the front door. Miracle of all miracles, they had made it home without meeting anyone unsavory, and she wanted to keep it that way. Tying the horse to a hitching post that was a bit decrepit due to the fact that it was rarely, if ever used, she burst into the cabin, startling her grandmother from her seat before the fire.

"Violet, dear! What on earth is the matter?"

Violet thought she had schooled her features a little better than that, but apparently Granny had seen past her look and into her heart, as always. "Everything is all right. I just need your help." She kept her voice level so as not to send Granny into a panic. If she wasn't careful, one of her grandmother's episodes could easily take this night from bad to worse. "I found someone in the woods who is hurt, and we need to take care of him."

That caught Granny's attention, as Violet knew it would. The old woman's white hair was in disarray beneath her cap, and her wrinkled face lit up with interest and determination at the idea of someone who needed help. Her grandmother wasn't always the most mentally stable or aware, but give her someone to take care of, or a hardy task to accomplish, and she could problem solve with the best of them.

Violet grabbed the lantern off the kitchen table and took the old woman's hand, leading her out of the cabin to the travois behind the stallion.

"What a beautiful horse!" Grandmother made a move to step to the animals side, but Violet held her fast on their course.

"No, we need to tend this man. I'm concerned that if we don't get him help soon, he may die."

"Oh my!" Grandmother exclaimed as the light from the lantern fell on the kingsman's pale face. "Quickly, Violet, we must get him inside."

Sighing with relief and grateful that the need to focus on a task had pulled her grandmother out of the childlike trance she seemed to live her life in, she handed the lantern over and stooped down. Untying what had once been her skirt from the long sticks she had used to create the structure of the travois, her fingers worked at the knots that had been tightened with

14

the weight they carried. Her back ached from tending the garden and fields all day and then the treacherous work in the woods. Muscles spasmed with the stress of the entire situation, and deep inside, she wished that she could forget all about this man and live her life as if he had never existed. Unfortunately, this situation was far from easy, and that was certainly not the way she operated.

She paused for a moment to stretch out her back before she commenced with the difficult process of getting a grown man, who was thoroughly unconscious and compared unfavorably to a rag doll, through the cabin door and into a bed. She leaned back, her hands placed at the base of her spine to try and get the best possible stretch, looking down at the kingsman as she did so. Nothing moved. Her heart stopped, and she fell to her knees beside him, placing a hand on the leather of his vest. His chest didn't rise as it should have, and she wondered if, after all of her labors, she had brought him home only to have him die on her doorstep. An overwhelming urge to burst into tears made her throat tighten as she leaned her face over his, hoping to feel hot breath on her cheek. She rubbed hard on his chest with a fist and was rewarded with a slight twitch and gasp from his pale lips.

Sitting back on her heels, she threw her head back and drew a breath of relief. Her lungs ached from holding her breath. Shaking her head, she straightened. She needed to get him inside.

Gathering fistfuls of the fabric while stooped over with the weight, she dragged him to the doorstep. It was hard work, and she strained with each step, her fingers screaming with the effort of holding onto the fabric. Out of breath, she fell to

15

a seat on the step that led into the house.

"Up up up! We must get him inside!" Her grandmother fluttered her free hand in an upward motion, and the lantern bobbed about in the other.

The urgency in her grandmother's voice and actions set her tense nerves even more on edge. "Shhh…" she soothed, looking to the outskirts of their farmyard, hoping and praying that there wouldn't be a patrol of kingsmen about. It rarely happened that they were about at this hour—most were secure in the pub in the village, drinking away their sanity—but the periodic patrol went out for a romp, and occasionally there were tales of women assaulted or children dragged from their home and made to watch a man get beaten for being out after curfew or for not paying the exuberant taxes. Her stomach clenched. *Lord, please, not tonight.*

The thoughts of what happened to Joy Carpenter down the road made Violet's blood run cold, yet it strengthened her resolve. The poor girl had been found wandering the road, beaten and worse after being out late to fetch a wayward cow. Violet felt as though she could hardly blame Mr. Bennet after such an incident in their very own community had taken place only a short while ago. With a groan, she grasped the man beneath the arms and, putting her back into it, heaved him through the door and across the floor. Knowing if she stopped at this point, she may never finish, she stepped backwards up onto the low cot that her grandmother used in the far corner of the room and hoisted him up, laying his back onto the bed.

Sweat falling down her face and into her eyes, she stepped down and carefully swung his feet up and onto the bed, minding the broken ankle, adjusting him so that he lay

16

straight. She almost collapsed onto the floor until she heard a soft whinny from outside the open door. She sighed, slumping her shoulders, and rubbing her left with her opposite hand. She would be sore tomorrow, but animals needed to be cared for too.

Her grandmother already had a cloth and basin in hand and was sponging the dirt and blood away from the man's face.

Violet hauled herself up the ladder to the cabin's loft and knelt in front of a wooden chest that had once belonged to her parents. The small half-loft was occupied by the supplies for their handiwork and their food stores, quite low on provisions as of now, but it would be filled up with their harvest before winter came. Hesitating a moment before lifting the lid, she remembered the last time she had been in this chest, right after her father died. She swallowed against the painful memories and pulled it open. Stealing her heart against the flood of emotions that swamped her mind with the mere smell of the sage and rosemary that had been packed inside with the contents, she yanked out a long tunic and soft, worn linen trousers from the trunk. Slamming the lid, she retreated down the ladder. She set the clothes down at the foot of the bed for her grandmother to use before she dragged herself outside.

The black horse nuzzled her shoulder and whuffled in her hair, his long curly mane getting in her face. She rested her hand on his head and scratched between his eyes. With his massive head over her shoulder, she rested her now throbbing forehead against his neck, and he dropped his lower, almost as if he was embracing her. The tears started and burned at the edge of her lashes. It had been a harrowing few hours and the feeling of support, even if it were just from an animal, made the emotions swell and seek release. But she needed to stay in control. She drew the crisp night air into her lungs, cooling herself from the inside out, and she shivered.

Gathering up the reins in her hand, she led the magnificent beast to the barn. Unhooking the makeshift travois only took a few seconds, but there were sundry other things that needed to take place. Stripping the horse of the saddle, reins, blanket, and saddle bags, she folded everything up as tightly and neatly as she could. Hauling them up to the small haymow and settling the belongings in the corner, she swiped some hay over them. No sense in leaving them out in the open should any kingsmen visit the farm, and if the man inside her home woke and asked them of her, she would fetch them. They would be underfoot in the house. She gulped back at the anxiety creeping around her throat when she hauled the saddle up the ladder and tucked it away in the corner as well. She ran a hand over the king's crest embossed into the leather. If only the man who now wielded that seal was as kindly and wise as the king for whom it had been created.

Sighing, she swept a pile of hay over it and clambered back down the ladder. Her muscles screamed, and she gritted her teeth as she gave the horse the rub down he deserved and hauled a bucket of water for him to drink from the well at the back of the house. She left everything in order with her cow and the horse tucked safely in their small, but adequate, stalls before trotting back to the house. The fire of energy inside of her was burning to a low smolder and she was running on fumes. Grandmother had gotten the man out of his clothes and dressed him in Father's things. His torn and tattered kingsman's clothes were in a pile on the floor. Swallowing hard at the sight of so much blood and dirt covering them, she threw them into the fire. They were far from repairable anyway.

She washed her hands in the basin in the kitchen corner and watched the flames lick at the clothing. They burnt through the linen quickly once they caught. Shaking the water from her hands, she dried them on the cotton towel and hung it neatly to dry, focusing her hands on the predictable and controllable actions she could manage.

Their humble cottage was a small and simple place, but it had always been home to her, and she loved it dearly. The large straw tick bed rested in the far-right corner; a bedside table, a chest of drawers and another wooden chest at the foot of the bed grouped the sleeping quarters. The fireplace was centered in the back wall of the house, giving off even heat around the room. In front of it sat two chairs: Granny's rocking chair and another for Violet. The kitchen was in the front left corner of the building, and the oven, another fireplace for cooking, as well as the washbasin stand and a table that doubled for preparation and dining, rounded out their humble abode.

She rolled her head, and tried to relax her shoulders that felt like they were strung so tight they might as well have been touching her ears.

She had no idea how many laws regarding how to treat or deal with kingsmen she had broken in the last few hours, but she was sure it was more than a few.

Shutting and barring the door, she rested her forehead against the wood to gather her strength. She didn't want any unannounced intruders. The world was not exactly the safest place these days, and any extra moments of awareness or warning could go a long way. She leaned against the door, feeling the exertion and toil of the day coupled with the fear and stress of the last few hours weighing her down like a sack of potatoes hung around her neck.

She tried not to think of what could happen if it was made known that she was harboring a kingsman. Friends and neighbors would be scared and too concerned with their own safety to be trustworthy, and she knew not what the Kingsmen would do if they found out. Was harboring a kingsman without telling the authorities a hanging offense? What would be considered inappropriate? Her mind spun with the things she thought she should do, but nothing felt right. She should wait until the man regained his senses before she made a decision on who to tell. Whatever the outcome later, she was far too tired to do anything about it now, and it was past curfew. Heading into town now would surely put her in the stocks at the very least, and in line for a beating at the worst. She would simply have to wait for the morrow.

"Come and give me a hand, dearie. This head wound doesn't look good."

Violet begrudgingly opened her eyes and shot a glare at the bed. This man was causing her more pain and aggravation than she had thought possible from one person. Blinking hard at the sight of him, she took a few steps closer to the bed. He looked completely different with all the mud and blood cleared away from his face. His dirty clothes now replaced with soft items from her own father's wardrobe, and his finger-width, military-cut brown hair was washed and pulled away from the nasty wound that curved around the side and back of his head. He looked even more pale without the coating of blood, and she feared even more for his survival. It seemed as though there was little life left within him.

"Please, Lord, don't let him die now. Not after all that. And what would I do with the body?" she whispered her prayer as she placed one of their straw pillows beneath his injured leg and pulled the blanket over top of him and up to his chin.

"Don't speak of such things. He won't die." Granny handed her a clean cloth she had just wet in a second basin of water. The other was full of dirt and stained red with his blood. "When is your father coming home?"

Violet's heart sank, and she closed her eyes for a moment in an effort to keep back the tears. Nothing unnerved her grandmother like seeing her strong and able-bodied granddaughter burst into tears; it was an occurrence Violet did her best to keep few and far between. Keeping Granny stable was one of the most important tasks in Violet's life. She turned to her grandmother and took her by the arms, noticing now that she was trembling, and her eyes had that far-away look in them. She was grateful for the moments of lucidity that Granny did have, but it made the moments where she seemed to lose her mind even harder to witness.

"It's going to be okay. Papa will come home soon. Let's go sit by the fire; you need to rest."

The old woman dug in her heels for a moment and shook her head, trying to pull away from Violet, a nervous look in her eyes. "I need to wait for Richard! He said he was going to come home!"

"Shh-shh…" Violet rubbed up and down Granny's arms, keeping her voice soothing and calm. "He wants you to wait for him. Come, sit down. You look so tired. Rest and wait for him. All right?"

Warily, Granny allowed Violet to lead her to the rocking chair in front of the fire. Violet settled an afghan over the old woman's knees and ran a soothing hand over the white head, removing her cap and smoothing the sides of the soft hair back from her sweaty face. "Just rest." She kissed the top of Granny's head and felt the tight muscles of the old woman's shoulders relax beneath her fingertips. Her head leaned back against the wooden headrest of the rocking chair and lolled partially to one side.

Turning, Violet let the tears out and two of them chased each other down her cheek. It was desperately hard to see her grandmother like this. She had never been the same after the day Father never came home. Just another reminder of the terrible tragedy that turned her world upside down. She swallowed and fought the resentment that gathered in her chest toward the kingsman. His uniform reminded her too starkly of what she would much rather forget.

Sighing, she took the clean cloth back up in her hand and started sponging the blood away from the wound, trying to get a better look at how bad it actually was. A strike to the head tended to bleed quite heavily and usually wasn't as bad as first assumed once cleaned properly. She winced and drew air between her teeth when she saw the depth of the wound and the true size. She glanced at his face. It was so pale. She prayed under her breath that the man would make it through the night.

There was no way she could go for Master Fendrel tonight, even in this dire strait. Master Fendrel was the doctor of the village and would do far better patching up this wound than she. She hoped against hope that she would not have to send for him. She knew it would be far safer if they kept the kingsman's presence in their home a secret. She trusted Fendrel with her life, but it only took one slip of the tongue and they could all be sent to prison, perhaps even to death if they suspected her of hurting this kingsman. There was no evidence, no proof, and no witness that could prove she had found him by happenstance in the woods. Her rescue could easily be construed into a plot or vicious attack. The Kingsmen often jumped to worst case scenarios and swayed conclusions from their own dangerous perspective. They thought the people were rebellious and had to be kept in line. And with the current tension between those within the king's service and those without, it was a better plan to keep things as quiet as possible.

Violet carefully wrapped his head in bandages and sat down, finally able to rest, her body screaming for it, but unable to still her mind. She hoped he would make it through the night.

# Four

## TREACHERY AND SACRIFICE

VIOLET STARTLED AWAKE, jerking her head up straight, when a moan met her ears. Wincing, she cried out at the pain in her neck from sleeping cockeyed on the hard wooden chair beside her grandmother's bed, which currently held the injured kingsman. Light from the early morning sunrise brightened the windows and cast a golden hue across the cabin's floor.

Violet squeezed her eyes shut and reopened them, trying to extricate herself from the feeling of being cocooned in cotton. She stood and stretched her back when another moan came from the bed. She rushed the two steps forward and bent over the man. He writhed in pain, and she jumped, her heart flying into her throat and pounding heavily in her ears. His eyes were still closed, but he moaned again, thrashing the other way and almost out of the bed.

Her heart still pounding harder than she wished, she placed

25

both hands on his shoulders to keep him steady. His face was dripping with perspiration, dampening the bandage around his forehead. He was burning with fever.

"Manure," she whispered under her breath like a curse. Grabbing one of the basins still on the bedside table, she took it to the kitchen, filling it with water from the kettle that always rested on the trestle beside the fire. The steaming water, though incredibly hot, was clean and sterilized, and that was what mattered most. She set it aside to cool and dipped her cloth in the bucket on the floor. At least this water would be cold, and she could use it to bathe his face.

Granny stirred from her seat on the rocking chair in front of the now dying fire as Violet flew past.

While mopping the man's face, she was frightened when his eyelids fluttered as he continued to thrash about. The moaning grew more intense. Violet struggled to keep him as still as possible, all while swabbing at his face and neck. His movement couldn't be good for his wounds and would only aggravate them further. She felt so helpless. Her resolve waned, and she knew she was inept to handle this much longer. If she tried, his life might be forfeit. She needed to get Master Fendrel. She had hoped they could do without, but there was nothing for it now. Who knew how long this kingsman had been in the forest before she found him? Hopefully not long, as any further delay in his treatment could be the difference between life and death.

"Here, dearie; try this."

Violet startled again at the sudden nearness of her grandmother. She hadn't even heard her up and about as she had been so engrossed in taking care of the feverish man.

Annoyed with herself for being so jumpy, she stepped aside for Granny, who held a cup of tea in her trembling hands. Violet set down the cloth she had been using and quickly took the cup from the old woman. It was only half full and smelled incredibly potent.

"What is it?" Violet sniffed at the tea and contemplated how she was going to get it into the man's mouth without spilling it all over him and the bed.

"It will help him rest. It has valerian and willow bark."

Violet grimaced. She remembered the times when she had been forced to take willow bark tea as a child when she was ill. It had definitely not been the most pleasant tasting concoction she had ever put in her mouth. "How?"

Her grandmother handed her a spoon and stood beside the bed, placing her frail hands upon his shoulder in an effort to hold him down. As much as a frail, old woman could, at least.

Violet spoon fed as much to the kingsman as she did to the bed clothes, but by the time she had gotten the last of the half-cup gone, he had started to calm down. He still moaned and rolled his head back and forth, but the full-body tossing and turning had abated somewhat.

"I need to get Master Fendrel. Will you be all right if I leave you here with him?" Violet asked as she dashed some water on her face and pulled on clean petticoats, a skirt, and tucked a crisp blouse into her waistband.

"I'll be fine. You get the doctor. This lad needs him." Granny rested a hand on the man's head and ruffled his close-cropped hair with her fingers. Granny was the perfect person for the job. While she sometimes seemed to lose her mind, she was capable of keeping it together a good half of the time and was the most nurturing and careful person Violet knew. Somehow, God always gave grace when it was needed, Granny would be perfectly herself as she did what she did best: caring for the sick or wounded.

Violet hustled out the door, throwing a cloak over her shoulders as she did so. The cool, crisp spring breeze tickled her face, and the scent of the dew and freshly-turned earth set her blood to dancing through her veins. Holding the cloak close to ward off the chill, she trudged up the road for the near thirty-minute trek into the village of Padsley. When she reached the outskirts of town, she pulled her cloak even tighter about her shoulders and kept her eyes on the ground. Entering the domain of the Kingsmen was always a nerve-wracking experience. It almost seemed at times as if they were on the prowl, waiting to see whom they might devour.

She was nearly to Master Fendrel's cottage when a pair of leather boots, folded over on top near the knee, stepped into view.

"Oi! Ey now, 'ere's a pretty one."

Her heart fell into the bottom of her shoes. *Lord, keep me safe.*

"She is pretty, at that," came another voice. A second pair of boots came into view.

Violet stepped forward as if to go around, keeping her eyes down. Somehow, making eye contact often only added another level of inflammation to the situation. "Excuse me, sir."

"Ey, no, you don't, me pretty." A rough hand grabbed her shoulder, and she tried her hardest not to shrink away from the grasp. "'Ow bout a little kiss, eh?" A raucous laugh issued

28

from the man's throat.

Bile rose in her throat, and she resisted the urge to spit on the vile man's shoes. She brought her eyes up, knowing that they were probably flashing with righteous indignation as she felt the waves of heat flood her cheeks and flow down her arms. She locked eyes with the middle-aged kingsman in front of her, and her blood well-nigh boiled. She hated those sharp, near-black eyes and the memories that flooded in when she saw them.

He seemed uneasy at her piercing gaze, and he turned his head to spit to the side.

"Please, let me go." She dared to speak, and while she wished her voice could have been scathing in its delivery, it ended up trembling beneath the weight and pressure of holding back the anger that coursed through her heart and soul.

"I'll let you go when I'm good and ready and not a moment before." With a glint in his eyes, he took off his glove and traced a warm finger down the side of her face. She stiffened, and he smiled with a wicked grin. He tilted her chin up, and she just stood, straight as a board, her jaw clenching until she felt a pop in her head by her ear. "Give me a kiss, and I'll let you pass."

She swallowed hard against the bitter taste in her mouth. *Lord, please!* A commotion down the street drew his attention away, and the other kingsman took off running, his hand on the dagger hilt tucked in his belt. "Oi! Drake, let's get a move on!" The kingsman who held her captive gave her a pointed look that signaled his intentions and grabbed her chin in his hand. "Maybe next time then, eh?" His face and voice held a suggestive tone as he gave her a look from her head to her toes and back to her eyes. He pinched her chin hard before letting go, as if to make sure she knew he was the one in charge. He stepped away and dashed after his fellow, leaving her trembling like a leaf about to fall in the middle of the street.

Her feet were barely doing their job as she stumbled along, dragging in shuddering breaths that did little to calm her tumultuous insides. She barely registered knocking on Fendrel's worn front door.

"Violet, quickly, come in." Strong hands wrapped around her shoulders and drew her through the cottage door. She moved as if in a trance, her body shaking and her mind blank. "Here, drink this." A cool drink was thrust into her hands and guided up to her lips. She took a drink of the water and sat down on the chair placed behind her. She blinked hard and shook her head, setting the cup down and wrapping herself in her own arms, dragging in a deep breath.

"Are you all right, my dear?" Master Fendrel crouched in front of her, resting a comforting hand on her knee.

She nodded, took another deep breath, and tried to calm herself. But her body wouldn't listen and continued to tremble, though much improved upon what it had been. She would just need to give it time.

"Marcus, fetch me that blanket."

"I'm all right." She stood, then reached a hand out for the back of the chair to steady herself. Perhaps she had moved too hastily in her effort to prove herself well. She glanced over at Marcus, who sent a sympathetic smile her way, one that was far from reaching his eyes. Her dear friend, Marcus. He and Violet had grown up together, and it was only in the last few years that he had been apprenticing with Master Fendrel. His wavy reddish-blond hair flopped onto his forehead, and the freckles splattering across his face somehow made him look more cheerful than he already was, which was incredibly difficult. If there was one thing about Marcus it was that he had the most joyful heart mixed with the most compassionate spirit and could make just about anyone smile, even in the worst of times.

Marcus hobbled over to her with the help of his crutch, leaning heavily on its support for the few steps it took to gain her side. It must have been a hard day today. She could tell by the strained lines on his forehead and the extra amount of weight that he put on his crutch, despite the smile that graced his lips.

"You all right, Vi?"

She nodded and let him pat her on the shoulder. She wasn't much of one for physical affection, but for some reason, Marcus was one of the few people she let into her tightly-walled world. "I need your help, Master Fendrel."

"Is it your grandmother?" He instantly started packing instruments into his leather satchel with all haste, worry furrowing his brow.

"No, it's not—"

A pregnant pause grew between them following Violet's cut-off sentence, and Marcus was the first to break it. "What's going on, Vi? Are you in trouble?"

She turned to him and took his hand. "I would love to tell you, but I don't want to put you in any more danger than you already are. I will let Master Fendrel decide if it is important that you know." She gave him a long look, hoping that by her seriousness she could convince him not to press further. But by being so mysterious, she might open the door for more curiosity than was safe. Marcus had already suffered enough at the hands of the Kingsmen. She didn't want him involved in any way, to protect him. She also didn't want him to go through having to mentally process what she was doing. If anyone had a right to hold a grudge against a kingsman, it was Marcus.

He held her gaze for a long moment before he seemed to decide to let it go with a resigned sigh. "All right. I trust you. But, Vi, be careful."

She nodded, exchanging a look that only he could understand. There was more than just childhood fondness that bound the two of them together. Their shared life experiences bonded them in more than a few ways, and often, it was as if they could speak to each other without the use of words. There was a trust between them that much pain, and many years together, had grown and fostered.

"Well, let's go tend this mystery patient of yours. Marcus, pray we don't meet any kingsmen on the way." Fendrel gave him a nod and set his hat atop his head before opening the door for Violet.

She gulped. If only he knew stumbling into one along the way wouldn't be the only opportunity for meeting a kingsman.

"Yes, sir, that is always my prayer." Coming from Marcus, that meant more than just the words. The young man was one who meant what he said, and offering a prayer was never an idle gesture. Perhaps it had something to do with the fact that he couldn't walk through life as fast as most, but there had been a devout relationship with the Lord that had been

32

fostered from his lack of mobility and weak health.

Violet pulled her cloak closer around her and stepped out the door, followed by Master Fendrel. She did her best to keep to the shadows and alleys on her way out of the village. Master Fendrel was silent on the walk out of town. She knew he was mulling over what might be before him; she could tell by the determination on his face. He couldn't have known that she was doing her best not to cry and feeling like she had taken a mental mud bath after the encounter with the kingsmen in the street. She felt disgusted and disgusting under the supercilious gaze of the malefactor. She was grateful that Fendrel respected her silence, even though he probably had more than a few questions he wanted to ask. They fell into an easy and comfortable pace.

By the grace of God, they made it all the way home without incident. With the turmoil she was already in, she didn't know how she would handle herself if another meeting like the prior one took place.

Taking a deep breath, Violet flung open the cottage door. The kingsman was still on the bed where she had left him, and he seemed quite restless again. Granny was bent over him, trying to spoon feed him some more of the tea that she had made.

Master Fendrel didn't even flinch at what must have been a confusing sight as he stepped toward the bed and gently moved Granny aside. "Thank you, madame; I'll take it from here." He started his swift and careful examination of their restless patient while Violet drew her grandmother away and into the kitchen area of the cottage.

Sitting at the table, Violet rested her head in her hands, her elbows on the surface in front of her. Her grandmother set a cup of tea before her and started humming as she puttered about the kitchen.

Violet paid little attention to what she was doing. There was so much else occupying her mind at the moment, chiefest of which was what to tell Master Fendrel. She didn't want to leave him in the dark on the matter, but she also didn't want to entrust him with a secret that he either did not want or, at the very least, did not ask for…one that would put him in danger.

She took a deep breath to still the trembling in the pit of her stomach. She knew not if her own actions were the right ones. Had she made the right decision? She tried to think of it in general terms. If she had found anyone in the woods, she knew that she would never leave them to die. She would have to go against everything within herself to deny the responsibility of taking care of an injured or wounded fellow human being.

But when she put it in terms of the kingsmen…she shuddered. If it had been the kingsman Drake lying there, unconscious and wounded, covered in dirt, blood, and leaves… In her heart, she wished that she could have left him there and let him rot. But she knew that no matter how vile the person, she could not refuse the common decency of saving their life and caring for their wounds. It was what her Savior would have done, and after all He had offered her, how could she refuse to live in a manner worthy of that sacrifice?

She supposed with all of that, she must have her answer. But it still left her quaking inside. Doing the right thing did not always mean it was done without fear. So much of her life and the lives of those around her—her family, friends, and the other villagers—had been adversely affected by a kingsman in some way. How would she explain and keep this from hurting herself or those whom she dearly loved?

Perhaps she ought to say that he wasn't a kingsman at all. After all, she had hidden his things, and no one would be the wiser. She took a sip of her tea and choked. She forgot to remember that the kingsman himself would have something to say when he came to his senses. She groaned and buried her head in her hands. It would all come out eventually. What on earth was she going to do?

She hadn't even noticed that her grandmother had placed a wooden plate with some toast and a few eggs on it in front of her. She picked up her fork. How could one be hungry without an appetite? Her stomach turned over, but she knew if she didn't eat, she would be even hungrier later.

Her eyes strayed to where Fendrel was examining the kingsman's leg. She swallowed hard and looked back at her plate. She didn't know what to say to him about the man's identity, and at this point, unless he asked, maybe it was better not to say anything.

"Violet, I need your help to set this leg."

Violet quickly stood, washed her hands in the basin, and stepped to his aid.

His slightly wrinkled face was deep in concentration, eyes never leaving his patient. "I need you to get up on the bed behind him and hold him beneath the shoulders. He is probably going to buck when I set this leg, but it must be done. I'm sorry to ask you to do it, but I have no other—"

"I can do it," she assured him, despite the fact that it was most assuredly going to be a bit uncomfortable. With only

35

slight hesitation, she helped Fendrel lift the unconscious man to a sitting position, his head lolling forward. She climbed into a position behind him and wrapped her arms under his and around his chest, his head rolling back on her shoulder. She tried not to cringe. The man needed her help, and she was going to extend it, no matter the cost. There was little point in turning back now.

# Five

## INTO THE DEPTHS

"ONE, TWO, THREE!" Fendrel gave the man's leg a sudden jerk, much harder than Violet had expected, and the grinding sound that followed, as well as the massive moan from deep within his chest that reverberated through hers, made the room spin, and she blinked hard.

"Violet, are you all right?" The words were echoey and sounded far away, but she knew they were from Fendrel.

She nodded, even though she couldn't exactly see straight. She blinked a few more times, and her vision focused enough for her to realize that Fendrel was wrapping the leg and ankle tight. "We will need to keep this elevated so it doesn't swell anymore than it already has." He grabbed the one pillow that Violet had already placed under the man's leg last night. "Do you have any more pillows, my dear?"

Violet nodded and shrugged out from behind their patient,

laying him down gently on the pillows. He moaned, and his eyelids fluttered, stealing her breath when she thought for a moment he might awaken. He didn't, but it gave her heart a terrible jolt. The idea of him awakening and seeing her and his ensuing confusion at the current state of affairs made her want to sink into the floor.

Violet climbed to the loft and snatched the few extra down pillows, made with feathers they had collected from their own chickens. They were a part of her meager collection of household goods she had been setting aside for her future wedding date. She didn't give the sacrifice a second thought. The man needed them more than she did at this juncture, so there was no use trying to save them.

She couldn't wait till the kingsman had a name. It did no good to call him a kingsman. It wasn't really a fact she wanted to advertise. She sighed as she climbed down the ladder. It wasn't easy what she was doing. Not by any means. There were so many obstacles and perceived dangers around every corner, but she knew it was the right thing to do. Hadn't the Lord said to "love your enemies"? She didn't know about loving them: truly loving them, at least. Honestly, that would probably never happen, but she could do her best and take care of this man who needed her help sorely. She just hoped that he didn't try to kill her and her grandmother for their efforts when he woke.

Fendrel tended the man's head and the wound, grimacing as he peeled back the bandage.

"Will he get well?" Violet asked as she gently lifted the splinted and neatly-bandaged leg to place the extra two pillows beneath it.

"I hope so, for all our sakes. This wound is quite bad indeed, but the fact that he is still responding, even if it is only to the pain right now, is a good sign. I would have very little hope if he made no movements and was unaware of everything. But time will tell. We will know more when he wakes. This fever does not bode well however. Once I clean and stitch this head wound, hopefully we will be able to get that under control." Fendrel gave her a glance over his shoulder as he held the two edges of the wound together after threading a needle. "Do you want to tell me what happened and why this stranger is in your house?"

Violet gulped, her heart stilling in her chest. "Do you want to know?"

He looked at her for a long moment, his gaze probing, yet kind, compassion etched into his features as he seemed to contemplate the weight of her words. When he spoke, his words were measured, gentle…and reassuring. "You don't have to carry this alone, Violet. I understand you wanting to protect me, Marcus, and any others, but perhaps it would be good for you to tell at least one person. If you don't want to, I will not blame you, but I want you to know I can handle it and that your best interests will always be at the forefront of my thoughts and actions. My dear, I know it's not easy being…alone."

Tears started to her eyes. She knew exactly what he meant. He didn't have to say another word, but he was right. Sharing the burden might make it a little lighter and he knew as well as she did that her grandmother could carry little, if any, of it. His compassion moved her, and she was grateful for those like Fendrel who had come beside her after the loss of her father.

"I found him in the woods. I was gardening when his horse dashed out of the forest, fully tacked up. I tried to calm him after I caught hold of him and that's when I noticed the blood on his saddle. I tracked his path back through the woods and found the...." She merely nodded her head toward the man on the bed. "Lying there, injured and unconscious. He hasn't woken up since. But..." She hesitated, wringing her hands in front of her. Dare she go on?

"It's okay, Violet. I can take care of myself. And more importantly, God can take care of all of us."

"He was wearing a kingsman's uniform." The words fell from her lips like the dam had suddenly been released, and they tumbled free.

Fendrel's hands only hesitated for a split second before he resumed his work of stitching up the wound. He nodded. "What did you do with his things?"

"I hid them. The horse is in the barn."

"I hope you hid them well? Though that might be of little import if he wakes with all his faculties."

"I hid them as well as I could for now."

There was a pause as he continued his tight, even stitches. Without looking up or stopping, his soft voice encouraged her. "You did the right thing, Violet. Your father would be proud."

Violet had a harder time fighting the tears this time. If there was anything in the world she had ever wanted, it was for her father to be proud of her. Her earthly one, of course, but even more so her heavenly One.

They were both silent while Fendrel finished his work by stitching up the large gash on the man's head. The kingsman looked so much better just from the simple fact of having a

40

proper bandage and less fabric wrapped around his head. Fendrel dabbed at his own face with a clean rag to remove the sweat that had beaded there during the stitching.

"Well, for now, try to keep his fever down with sponge baths. That tea Granny has been giving him should also be helpful. Keep that up. Make sure you keep trying to get him to drink water as well. He needs to be drinking as much as you can get in him. Any and all liquids he will take will improve his condition considerably, even though it makes it far more difficult with him being unconscious. I hope the fever will come down quickly. You let me know if you need anything at all. Maybe take the back alleys to get to my place this time. Or ask one of your neighbors to come fetch me."

Violet winced. "I'd rather not involve anyone else until I know what to expect. But you're right. I'll be more careful. If that's even helpful these days." She sighed.

She walked him to the door after he had gathered his things and washed his hands. "Thank you. You have no idea how much of a help you have been." Her voice lowered with gratitude and repressed emotions. "And in more ways than just taking care of our patient."

He nodded, his kind eyes resting on her face. "Anything for Richard's daughter. Make sure you take care of yourself, too, Violet. You've been given a heavy load and you will do little good for those in your care if you are worn out yourself."

She nodded and smiled, though she didn't know how well she would be able to follow his directions. She just prayed that he would make it home safely.

The darkness was overwhelming, but he felt as though he had succumbed to it so long, he couldn't fight his way back again. But the pain…the crushing weight of it kept nagging at him, dragging him back into the light. He didn't want to return. In the depths of the darkness, there was no pain. Nothing. Just the dark. And the quiet.

He heard voices, felt an intense amount of pain, but after, he was soothed, and he felt himself slipping away again. There wasn't much in him that wanted to hold onto the light. It was easier to let it slip farther and farther away. So, he let it go and sank back again into the depths.

Violet did her best to handle the day-to-day chores of the farm, but while she was out tending the garden, her hands buried deep in the soil, she couldn't help but worry about what would happen if the kingsman on their bed were to wake up and demand to know where he was.

Her one comfort was that with the fever and the injuries, he wouldn't be much harm of any sort to either her or Granny. But that was her only comfort. Practically, as the provider and main worker of the household, it wasn't as if she could just put her life and her chores on hold to take care of him.

There was a garden to finish planting, now a horse to take care of, and the cow to feed, milk, and take to and from the pasture. She glanced over at their cow, Bertha, and drew a sigh of relief. She was grateful that they had been able to procure Bertha as a calf from one of their neighbors last year. She had been a runt, and they had purchased her for cheap, but under the care and tender ministrations of Violet and her grandmother, they had fed and raised her to be a perfectly normal and healthy milk cow. Bertha's calf of this year had brought them a good earning at market, and Violet was incredibly pleased at the small pouch of coins that she had been able to stash away in the box beneath her tick mattress.

Taxes were steep, and those who refused to pay were treated shamefully, and more times than not, their lives were never the same. Many had lost family members to forced servitude, restitution had swept out any savings or hopes at making a living, or they themselves were beaten and coerced into what could be called little else than slavery, either working in the mines to the north, or pressed into military service.

Things had not always been this terrible. The king who had ruled before Chancellor Enguerrand took the reins had been kind and wise. But that was seven years ago, and she remembered little else before the death of her father, aside from how much happier times had been then.

She sighed and took a harder dig at the dirt, hoping to take out some of her aggression on something other than the kingsman who resided in her house. He and his kind had been the living face of the chancellor who ruled in the stead of the prince with an iron fist and no compassion. While many rumors had spread of the prince's selfish lifestyle, the people wondered if he was ill-equipped or if he simply did not want to rule. She didn't know how it was possible that all the kingsmen could be so down-right terrible. She had yet to meet one who was kind, or good, or compassionate. But if the chancellor was so terrible, and the prince had not a care in the world for his people, it was probably little wonder that they hired soldiers with the same belief system and lack of respect for humanity as themselves.

"Hello, Violet."

Violet's hand trowel flew into the air, and she whipped around, her long hair, tied up in a kerchief to keep out of her way, swinging over her shoulder as she did so. Some strands caught on her face and obscured her vision for a heart throbbing moment of panic before she recognized one of her neighbors' daughters, Alma. Her pulse was nearly pounding out of her neck, and she suddenly couldn't catch her breath. She clapped a hand to her chest.

"Oh my goodness, you startled me!" She gave a little laugh that came off as nervous, even to herself, and she stood, dusting at the dirt on her apron.

"I'm so sorry. I didn't mean to!" Alma laughed with her and prattled on, but Violet heard next to none of it. It wasn't often that she had visitors, but when she did, she usually offered for them to come inside and sit a while. There was much work to be done on the farms, and it would have to be winter before anyone had much time to socialize. She noticed that Alma swung a basket covered with a cloth back and forth in her hands, and Violet plotted how on earth to handle this situation, all without alerting Alma to the fact that she had a stranger in her house. She didn't need to tell her it was a kingsman, but just the fact alone that she had a strange man, injured and unconscious, that no one knew about in her house... Violet

44

had a hard time not wanting to run in the opposite direction from this situation. The rumor mill was alive and active, despite the hard times that had befallen everyone, and now more than ever, one's very life could depend upon what information was shared and what wasn't.

"Alma! What do you have there?" Violet interrupted the poor girl mid-sentence, a plan beginning to form in her mind. Alma was a talker, but if Violet could just figure out what she came for and get her to leave, they might all live to tell the tale another day.

"Oh! This? I brought a basket of eggs over because Mother said you had told her that your hens aren't laying much yet. I know it's hard to make much of anything delicious without eggs, and I also know that when your chickens are young like yours are, they tend not to lay much of anything. You know, I always wondered why it took so long for them to get going. One batch of chickens we had took many more months than the ones we have now or have had since, and I always wondered if maybe we didn't feed them enough, but you know, now that I think about it, I happen to know we fed them just as much—"

"Why, thank you so much!" Violet loathed interrupting others under normal circumstances, but that was quite literally the only way to get a word in edgewise with Alma, and somehow the girl never did seem to mind it very much. Perhaps she had come to expect it, as constant interruptions were to be anticipated in large families, of which Alma was the oldest. Violet reached over and took the basket from the girl's hands and smiled. "That really is sweet of you."

"Can I stay a spell? I finished all my chores early and

Mother said it wouldn't be any trouble if I stayed a bit. She is trying to get Elise to manage more responsibilities and take care of the younger ones, and that never happens when I'm home, you know. I always do so much of it that she doesn't really have a chance to practice. But I—"

"Actually, now really isn't a good time." Violet glanced over her shoulder at the cottage, painting what she hoped was a look of concern on her face. She leaned over to Alma and whispered her next sentence. "Grandmother has had a really bad day today and...she's not quite all right in the head, you know?" She then pretentiously looked over her shoulder again as if making sure that Granny wasn't lurking behind some bush to overhear her. She tried not to cringe at her own theatrics. She might be laying it on a bit thick.

"Oh." Alma's eyebrows scrunched together. "I didn't realize she had days that bad. Why didn't you say something? You poor dear! I don't know how I could stand to have a family member like that. It must be awful hard on you, and all alone too."

Violet tried not to cringe at the patronizing tone of Alma's voice. "I do all right." Why on earth was she being defensive? She really did wince now but this time at her own snippy tone. "I mean...that is to say, we really do just fine."

"O-of course." Alma stuttered, but then took a deep breath. "Anyway, you know maybe Mother has some herbs that would help your grandmother! I know she always seems to do quite well with them and—"

"Thank you anyway, Alma, but I really should be getting inside to check on her. We have Master Fendrel to keep a close watch over us these days. Granny hasn't lacked for

46

anything with him on guard over her health." Violet said it with as much decision she could muster. She had long since given up hope that her grandmother would ever return to a normal state of mind, and she had made her peace with that. There was no sense in others holding out false hope, or worse yet, coercing her into latching onto it. Much had been attempted in trying to right the wrong in the poor woman's mind, but there wasn't anything that could be done. In the physical, at least. Because to all intents and purposes, her grandmother was healthy as a horse. Her mind just didn't seem to track the way others did; she seemed to have her mind stuck in the past.

During her bad spells, she would relive the day her son never came home and the day that Violet had to tell her how terrible a death her beloved and only son, Richard, had met. It was not a day that Violet herself wished to relive, but it seemed as though she was forced to, time and again when Granny begged and begged for her son to come home.

"Oh, look at that; it's getting a bit dusky out. Perhaps you should head home. You know, you really shouldn't be walking about outside, but especially not in the dark. The Kingsmen are not lenient to anyone they come across past curfew."

Fear lit in Alma's eyes, and Violet regretted her words. She hadn't meant to scare the girl, but honestly, there was a very real threat, and Violet didn't want anything to happen to her. Not like what had happened to Joy. She shuddered. Their village and the outlying countryside had seen much pain in the last few years. And they had heard it was worse closer to the border, the Kingsmen's power even more overbearing and excessively watchful. There had even been raids from the bordering country of Rusalka upon their borders, claiming women, children, and helpless men and ransacking their belongings, wares, and stores. There had never been raids under the king's rule, but they had become more and more frequent of late, their enemies emboldened by their success. And somehow the Kingsmen had either seemed unconcerned at the turn of events, or perhaps just allowing of it. She shuddered a second time.

"Again, thank you for these eggs. I know we will all get much enjoyment out of them."

"Why do you say all? Isn't it just you and your grandmother?" Alma's brow still pinched as she turned to go.

Violet stopped suddenly. "Yes, of course. Though there is a strange cat that comes by sometimes, and we give him our scraps." She laughed awkwardly and shrugged.

Alma nodded, though she still looked confused. "Of course. Well, take care of yourself, Violet! You and your grandmother will be in my prayers."

"Thank you, dear." Violet waved as Alma picked up her skirts and traipsed off to the road.

Violet's tense shoulders collapsed in a heavy sigh. She really was grateful for the prayers. And it seemed that they needed them now more than ever.

It was getting dark outside, and she knew Granny would need help getting supper ready. She stretched out her back with her free hand, then gathered her small tools and the seeds she had been planting. It was a heavy load trying to take care of an invalid who couldn't do much for themself while simultaneously trying to stay on top of the chores and other tasks that needed to be done on a daily basis. They endured much toil and heartache to eke out their meager existence. She shook her head. "Lord, continue to help us. We need it now more than ever."

She was washing her hands in the house, explaining to Granny across the room that Alma had left them eggs, when a small squeak from her grandmother made her whip around, sending dirty water flying across the floor.

"Violet, dearie. I think he's waking up."

Violet's stomach lurched, then felt like it dropped into her shoes, and her head spun. "Lord, help us."

# Six

## BURIED MEMORIES

THE KINGSMAN CRINGED and shuffled his shoulders, then lay still on the bed. Violet tried to draw a breath, but it seemed frozen in her lungs. When his face contorted in pain, she rushed to his side, drying her hands on her skirt as she did so. She stood over him, breathless, while a moan escaped from his throat. Her stomach flipped at the thought of the amount of pain he must be in.

His eyelids fluttered open, and he blinked a few times as his eyes adjusted to the light.

"Who is that?" His voice croaked. He swallowed hard against what must be an incredibly dry throat. Violet reached a hand under his head, trying not to tremble, and held the glass that had been on the bedside table to his lips. He swallowed gratefully and winced again as she laid his head back down on the pillow. "Who are you?" He blinked a few times, squinting up at her.

"My name is Violet." Her own voice croaked on the words. She swallowed back against the lump in her throat. Though he had asked the question, he didn't seem at all interested in the answer.

"Where am I?" He looked around the room, his focus seeming a little shaky. She could see it in his eyes, the way they didn't quite seem to focus on anything in particular.

"You are at my home. I found you hurt in the forest, so I brought you here, to my cabin to care for you. You have been unconscious since I found you, which was two days ago."

He seemed very confused. His breathing grew more rapid, and his eyes darted around the room, to their faces and back again, as if trying to find something of familiarity to latch onto. She had seen that look before. When her grandmother was having one of her spells and couldn't remember who or where she was. Nothing seemed to make any sense to her and it was as if her memory fled for the time being. Violet always felt so helpless in those moments.

The kingsman caught her gaze, and the level of fear and panic she could detect on his face alarmed her. "Who are you?" he asked again.

His brain was a blank slate. He couldn't remember what had happened to him, where he was, or why he was there. The things that he did know was that he was in an immense amount of pain, his leg was throbbing, and his head pulsing painfully as if someone was pounding a heavy object from within. The small cottage where he lay was a one room affair and though simple, he thought it was tidy and neat. His vision was blurry, and he struggled to focus on what was going on around him. His main concern was that he had no idea what his own name was. Something like that should be easy to remember, no matter where he was or what had happened to him. His breathing ratcheted faster, and he tried his hardest to keep it under control, but for some reason the panic became more intense the harder he thought, and the harder it was to concentrate on retrieving those lost facts. He pulled himself up onto his elbows with a groan and tried to fight the overwhelming dizziness and the blackness that clouded the edge of his vision.

"Hey, you need to rest. Just lay back." He blinked into the face of a beautiful young woman, her light brown hair curly, streaked with blonde, and falling around her face as she bent over and laid her small hands on his shoulders. He fought it for a second, but he was incredibly weak and couldn't seem to hold his own against even her slight pressure.

"Where am I?"

"You are in my cottage. I'll tell you the whole story if you'll just lay back and rest. Could we get some more of that tea, Granny?" She glanced over her shoulder, and he followed her gaze to see a small old woman, white hair frizzed out beneath her cap and a stained apron covering the front of her brown dress. He glanced around the rest of the house, but they were the only ones about. He was trying to make sense of his location, but it wasn't anything he recognized or remembered.

"Do I know you?" He asked finally, wanting to put his mind to rest on what he could.

She shook her head and helped lift his head while holding

53

a cup to his lips. The tea that she made him drink was bitter, but there was something in her face that told him that she brooked no argument. "You don't know me. At least, I don't remember having met you before." Her voice was monotone, controlled, short, but her hands were shaking slightly. It was as if she were trying to prove that she was calm, while hiding the opposite beneath her measured words and movements.

"How did I come to be here?"

"I found you in the woods; your horse had thrown you, and you were unconscious. Your leg is badly injured. I brought you back here and have taken care of you since. We had the— well, nevermind. You are on the mend now. Do you—that is to say, have you any memory of..." Her words grew more unsure and then trailed off entirely.

There was something in her eyes he didn't quite understand, and he wanted to know what it was. Uneasiness, perhaps? Fear? Why would she be scared of him? He hardly had enough strength to hold his head off the pillow, let alone hurt either her or the old woman. But he really ought to answer her question.

"That's just it, I don't remember anything. And..." He kept his voice low, anything above softly breathed words set his head to pounding harder. Anxiety and frustration pressed on him, the weight tightening the muscles in his neck. He hated admitting this. He didn't want it to be true, but he had thought as hard as he possibly could and the only thing he had to show for it was a splitting headache and a growing sense of panic at the thought of what he was about to say. "I don't know who I am."

Something flashed across her face, and she turned

suddenly, wiping her hands on her apron and picking up the cup to return it to the other side of the room.

When she came back, her face was set and blank again. He didn't really know her at all, but he felt as though she were trying to control some deeply hidden emotions. He was a perfect stranger to her, but it was a mystery, and he wanted to know the meaning behind it.

"You don't remember your name?" Her voice was measured and soft.

He tried for a moment to think, but nothing came of it except a flash of pain, and he hissed through his teeth. "No."

A look of concern washed away the blank stare that had been on her face, and she held a hand to his forehead. "You don't feel warm anymore. Looks like the fever has broken, thank God." She sighed. "Granny." She turned to the old woman again who had been doing and saying nothing but twirling her apron string around her finger. "Could you please get a basin of the water from the kettle and some clean rags? Fendrel said to clean and rebandage the wound, and we have yet to do that today."

She turned back to him. "I apologize if this hurts, but it must be done if we hope for you to get better." Her words were so monotone, and there was little to no expression upon her face, her green eyes solid in their gaze fixed right above his head.

He cringed and shut his eyes as he felt her fingers start undoing the bandages around his head. The apparent wound on the back of his head where she now tended would explain the headache, blurry vision, and perhaps even the memory loss. He didn't know how he knew it, but he knew that being struck on the head could result in such things. He thought hard for a minute, trying to ascertain where that thought had come from. He only moaned with the effort, and he felt the woman pull her hands away quickly.

"I'm sorry. Did I hurt you?"

He opened his eyes and even though it was cloudy and difficult to see, he caught her eye. "No, I'm sorry. I was just trying to remember something. Do you think I can't remember because I hit my head?"

"Possibly, though it might be a good idea to get Master Fendrel out here to take a look at you."

"Who?"

"Oh." She continued working on his head, her quick, fluid, and gentle movements telling him that she had done this before, possibly many times. "That would be our village doctor. He came out to take a look at you, and he was the one who stitched up your head and set your leg. I would feel a lot better about everything if he came out and examined you again to see if there is anything he can do to help you."

"Thank you."

"What?" Her hands stopped, and he looked up to catch a look of shock on her face.

"I said, thank you. For everything. You didn't have to take me in. I know it must be difficult for you, having a stranger about, and all the work you have gone through to help me—" It was getting harder to form words; they sounded farther away even though they were coming from his own mouth. "You have been...taking care of...me." His eyes grew heavy, and it was almost as if his mind and his body had stopped working together.

"You really should rest. Close your eyes. You need some

sleep." That note of concern was the one thing his mind latched onto in her voice.

He closed his eyes. Maybe just a short rest.

Violet wasn't sure if she should be concerned or relieved when Master Fendrel confirmed her suspicions that the kingsman's memory was missing.

"It can be more common than you realize with head wounds." He assured her with a fatherly pat on the shoulder as they whispered at the doorway while the man slept on the other side of the room. "He might never get it back, or it might come back tomorrow. We just won't know until it happens."

Violet felt the weight of the world on her shoulders and the panic doing its best to choke the life out of her. She fought it, pulling Fendrel out of the house and shutting the door behind them. "So, he doesn't know that he is a kingsman?" She still spoke in a whisper, even though there was little to no chance that the man could hear them from the other side of the door.

"No."

Violet turned and bit her lip, pacing back and forth.

Fendrel took her arm gently. "Violet, you need to breathe. You are going to wear yourself out with this amount of stress. You need to be careful, but you also need to relax and trust that God will work it out."

"God hasn't exactly told me whether or not I should tell the man about who he is and who he serves. I don't know who to trust, Fendrel. What if I tell him, and he loses it? Suddenly remembers everything and decides to kill me and my grandmother for our trouble? What if he reports it to the other local kingsmen? You know Commander Drogo will not let this go unpunished. They will look to make an example of me. Drag me through the square and blame me for his injuries. You know they will. They've done it before, and they've done worse for less." She gasped for a breath, desperately trying not to get hysterical, but the lack of sleep, the stress of the situation, and the constant worry about saying the wrong thing or saying too much was getting to her.

"Violet, breathe. Come, sit down, child." He led her to the log that rested on its side as a chopping block for the firewood. She sat down heavily, wrapping her arms around herself in an effort to still the racing of her heart and her fast breaths. "Hold still. Let me get you some water." He set his bag down and turned to go into the house.

"You don't need to." She stood quickly. "I can do it."

"Violet, for the sake of mercy, just sit down and let someone do something for you for a change." Fendrel's words were firm, and his eyes flashed with determination when he pushed her back into her seat with a strong, but gentle, hand to her shoulder.

While he fetched the water, Violet worked on schooling her breathing to be even and slow. She bent forward, resting her elbows on her knees and her head in her hands. She rubbed her scalp, lifting the hair away from it and giving it room to let some of the cool breeze cool her hot head. Fendrel was right in some ways. She was worrying too much.

But was she? This was a lot more than she would have ever thought she would have to deal with. She really didn't want to die. And she certainly didn't want to put anyone she loved or cared about in danger either.

Fendrel came out of the house and handed her a cup. "Violet, I am serious now. I want you to take care of yourself. You need to rest, and you needn't be in a constant state of panic, or you are going to put yourself in your own sickbed. And it won't make one lick of difference if the man in there knows if he is a kingsman or if the next harvest is going to make it in or not." Fendrel's quiet seriousness stilled the storm in Violet, and her mind contemplated his words. She drew a shuddering breath, looking to the horizon and catching the treetops of the forest in her gaze, their uppermost leaves reflecting the light from the lowering sun and glimmering in the breeze.

"You're right." She swallowed hard. "I'll try." This wasn't going to be easy.

He nodded and patted her on the shoulder. "Good, girl. Now, make sure you get plenty of sleep, and once that fellow is good and ready to get moving, you put him to work. I honestly don't know how you have done it all these years by yourself, keeping this farm running and you and Granny fed, but you need help, especially with another mouth to feed. He seems like he would be more than willing to help."

"Fendrel." She paused and leaned in to speak softly. "He thanked me." She stared at the front of her house, the firelight inside flickering off the gathering shadows that crowded around the corners of the cottage, and the long dark shapes the trees in the forest cast stretched across the ground as the sun sank lower in the peachy sky.

"And why does that surprise you? You've done an awful lot for the man, my dear."

59

She swallowed and rubbed her temples with her fingers. She could feel a headache brewing there. "He's a kingsman. I've never heard the words 'thank you,' 'please,' or any other such nicety come from their mouths. They take what they want, and they don't express gratitude for it."

"You think all kingsmen are the same?" Fendrel's voice sounded like he was smiling, and Violet looked up at him.

"Why wouldn't they be? They were recruited by the same man, and were all trained and expected to have a certain code of ethics during their training. Why wouldn't they all be the same?" Every kingsman she had met was evil or some varying shade of it.

Fendrel just smiled and stooped to pick up his medicinal bag. "You might be surprised, Violet. The Lord works in mysterious ways."

"I don't see how that can be true when it comes to kingsmen."

"Just keep calm and remember that the Lord has it all planned out."

"That's what people said when they took my father to the capital." Violet almost regretted the words that flew out of her mouth, sharp as daggers the moment she said them. Though, truly, she only regretted the way they sounded. Because even though she shouldn't have been defensive or harsh about what she said, it was true. People had said that oh-so-many times after her father had been marched off in chains, tied to the back of a kingsman's horse. And that situation had ended in a more painful way than she could have ever imagined.

Fendrel sighed. "I'm sorry, Violet."

Violet felt the tears rise, but she pushed them back. "No,

I'm sorry. You have been nothing but kindness, help, and love to us, and I-I'm sorry." She stood, penitent before him as he waited to leave.

He touched a hand to her chin and lifted her face so she was looking at him. "You carry much pain, Violet. But it is a pain that I cannot heal. You must ask your Heavenly Father for that healing, and you must accept it. Only He can right the wrongs and heal the wounds that you carry." His fingers left her chin and gave her a fatherly touch to the shoulder. "Goodnight, my dear. Remember to get some rest."

Violet nodded and watched him go, hugging herself and rubbing her arms as the air turned chill with the gathering dusk. She prayed that he would make it back to the village safely and out of sight of kingsmen.

She thought about what Fendrel had said. He might be right. She hadn't thought it could be an option to live without the pain she carried on a daily basis. She shook her head and cut off her train of thought. It was too much to think about, and she would much rather leave those memories buried deep inside, walled within her emotional fortress. It hurt less that way.

The girl named Violet handed him a bowl with some soup and a spoon. He was grateful for all she had done for him. After the doctor had filled in a few details that she had been reticent to mention, he was even more thankful for what she had done over the last few days. Dragging him all by herself out of the woods, to her doorstep, and getting him into the house without anyone's help...he was honestly quite impressed but also curious as to why she would do so much for a perfect stranger.

"Thank you."

She gave him a quizzical look, as if she didn't understand what he had said or perhaps why he had said it, before nodding and returning to the kitchen to get her own supper.

Reflections danced off the glass of the windows, as it was too dark to see out. The firelight and some of the candles made the cottage glow with a golden hue that was both soothing and warm.

He wished he knew what on earth to do with himself. He had found no distinguishing mark upon his skin. Nothing jogged his memory, and Violet had said that she had found him with nothing but the clothes on his back. She had said it so decidedly. When he asked where they were, she had told him they had been so mutilated, torn, and bloodied, that she had burned them.

There was nothing. Not one thing that could tell him who he was or where he came from. He looked at his hands. They seemed pretty nondescript to him. No scars and very little in the way of calluses. There was one of the latter between his thumb and first finger on the palm of his right hand, but that was it. Was he a farmer? A shopkeeper? A squire or a kingsman? What had he done before now to distinguish himself and make a living? He had no knowledge or skill that came to mind. He glared at his broken leg. And with this injury, he was an invalid and couldn't even help the ones who had given up so much to take care of him. As soon as he was able to move around, even a little, he would start helping; he had to earn his room and board.

He had seen how much they had given up for him. He was in their one bed; Violet often slept on the floor by the fire at night in order to tend it and keep it going, and her grandmother slept in a small cot that rested on the floor in the corner, too small for them to share. Violet worked day in and day out, from before dawn to long after dusk. He didn't know exactly what she was doing, but she often came in at the end of the day with hair flying about in many different directions, her hands filthy and her apron covered in mud. He hadn't asked her what she had been up to yet, but then again, she didn't exactly invite conversation. She was quiet and withdrawn, and when she spoke with him, she seemed to be walking on eggshells, as if unsure what to say to him. He sighed. But then, she didn't talk much in general anyway. When Master Fendrel had been there to check up on him the last two times, she hadn't said much of anything during the visits and had only followed the doctor outside for a few moments.

In short, she didn't seem to communicate even with those closest to her, much less him.

He tried to refrain from pounding a fist into his forehead. He was so frustrated with the lack of remembering. There were so many things he wanted to know. So many things he wished to remember. His name being the most important. It was difficult going through life without a name, and while it could be done, it made for some rather awkward situations.

Violet startled him by pulling a chair close to the bed and sitting down in it. Her back was ram-rod straight, and she wouldn't meet his gaze as she folded her calloused and cracked hands together in her lap and looked at the wall past him. "We need to talk."

# Seven

## A NEW IDENTITY

A SLIGHT NIGGLE of worry interrupted his thoughts. "About what?"

"You. People are going to ask, and for your safety and mine, we need to have a story that we both know and can explain. That way, people won't be confused and if the—" She gulped. "If the Kingsmen ask us, we must be ready with an explanation."

"But neither of us know who I am or what happened." He was at a loss to understand what they could possibly tell anyone if they themselves didn't know. "And what do the Kingsmen have to do with anything?"

She blushed and took a minute to respond, the words hesitatingly tripping from her tongue. "The Kingsmen do not take kindly to people moving around. They like to know where you reside so that you can be taxed accordingly. It would be frowned upon if I had a random stranger living in

65

my house. We aren't exactly allowed to take in strangers. Wayfarers, tramps, and gypsies aren't—well, let's just say they aren't looked upon kindly."

"What do they do to them?"

She fumbled for words, and tears rose in her eyes as she glanced at Granny across the room. The old woman sat, knitting needles in hand, rocking to the rhythm of her own humming.

He was confused and concerned.

"Let's just say that they aren't treated well," Violet finally said.

"What does that mean?"

Exasperated, she stood and started pacing, her eyes fixed on the ceiling. "They either put them in prison, turn them into slaves, or service them. That's all for those who can't pay the outrageous traveler's tax. And that is most, if not all, of them."

She wouldn't look at him, and he could tell that this was agitating her and making her nervous because she went to the door and made sure that the bar was secure. He didn't know what 'service' meant, but the other two sounded terrible, and if it was as bad or worse, he couldn't imagine the injustice.

She stormed back to the bed, this time standing over him. Her breathing was rapid, and she still wouldn't meet his gaze. "Listen. You are my cousin, visiting from Ravendale. It's far enough away that no one should think to verify that information. And...what do you think of the name Obed?"

He rolled the name over in his mind several times. For some reason, it felt right. Almost as if that could have been his real name. He identified with it immediately and was more than pleased to carry it as his own. Though, he couldn't really understand the tears in her eyes. "I like it. But can we think of a different story?"

"Why on earth? What's wrong with it?" Exasperation colored her tone. She was being a bit prickly tonight.

He had better put this just the right way in order to get past it, but he didn't want to be her cousin. Even if it was just make-believe to keep them out of trouble. She was too beautiful... "We look nothing alike. How about I am from Wood River, and I am a friend of your uncle, here to learn how to farm?"

She gave him a sharp look. "Fine. Though your story has more holes than mine."

Holes he could deal with, but being relegated to the place of cousin he could not.

"And your injuries. Might as well keep it as close to the truth as possible. Your horse threw you on the way here. That will also explain the presence of your horse." Her face fell, and she stared at the ceiling, heaving a sigh. She brought a hand to her forehead and rubbed her temples with her fingers. "We'll probably be taxed on that too now." Her voice was soft, but he still caught what she had said.

"I don't know how, but when I am well, I want to be able to help you all I can. I know I'm a burden. I'm sorry, but I am grateful. If there is ever anything I can do to help, please tell me."

She gave him a long stare, her eyes betraying the fact that she didn't believe him. He desperately wondered why she was so distrustful. Was it something that he had done or said before? Why did she treat him as if he were the most dishonest person she had ever laid eyes on?

She gave him a nod. "I need to go take care of the animals. I'll be back. Granny, do you need anything from the barn?"

"We're almost out of sage; could you bring me in another bundle, dearie?"

Violet nodded and wrapped a tattered shawl around her shoulders, crossing the ends over her chest and tying it behind her back. She picked up a bucket near the doorway. "I'll be back in a bit."

He watched her go, then rolled his new name off his tongue. "Obed."

"Do you need anything, dearie?" He opened his eyes, startled by how Granny had made it across the room so silently that he hadn't even noticed.

"Thank you, but I'm all right. Though, I do have a question."

"What is it?" She sat down in the chair by the bed and pulled the needlework she'd been busy with from her apron pocket and began unwinding the yarn, pulling out two sharp looking needles.

"Why does Violet act so...cold and distant?"

Granny just blinked at him over her flashing needles. "Maybe one day you will understand." She looked down and stitched faster.

He was surprised, but also not. He knew that Granny wasn't quite...all there. It had been obvious during the first breakdown he witnessed as she had panicked and begged Violet to bring home Richard. He knew there was a story there, especially since he had seen Violet's face after she had calmed her grandmother down and gotten her to sleep. The look of pain and sorrow that had washed over the young woman's face when she thought no one was watching intrigued him, but it also scared him at the same time. He wondered what on earth could have caused so much trauma to bring up so much raw emotion.

Violet was surprised over the next few weeks how quickly the kingsman mended. Though, now she should call him Obed. The name was one that had come from the deep recesses of her mind, and one that she had regretted offering the moment it had left her tongue.

When she was around five or six, her mother had been with child. When both she and the baby died, her father had wished to name his son, and Obed was what he had chosen. She hadn't realized she still remembered. She had been quite young and there was little that she could recall about that time. She remembered her father's tears, her mother's cold, white hand, and the perfect, tiny, porcelain face of her still-born baby brother.

She wished she hadn't offered a name of such import to a stranger, let alone a kingsman.

She hadn't spent much time with the man. He had been in the house, mending, while she had spent most of her time outside getting the garden and the wheat field planted before the spring rains. She had also been single-handedly taking care of the animals.

Not being used to help, she was fine on her own and wouldn't be accepting the offer, even though he did so what

69

seemed like every other time she came anywhere near him. He was barely able to hobble out to the outhouse without help, let alone do work of any kind.

She was grateful that her work kept her out of doors most of the time. Having to see him, let alone interact with him on a regular basis, was incredibly difficult.

He still had no idea about his identity; the thought that she might let it slip, or that Granny would say something, Violet could not control. She also worried that Granny herself didn't understand the importance of keeping their knowledge quiet. There was the constant fear that at any moment, he would remember something that would bring him back to his senses and become the kingsman she knew him to be. Fendrel had told her there was the chance that he was a kind man, and he certainly seemed so in his current state of mind. But that couldn't be trusted. She thought for sure that once he remembered who he was, he would embody what she knew all kingsmen to be like: cruel, careless, and wicked.

The fear was getting to her. She knew it was. She hadn't been able to sleep well in weeks. Her head had taken to constantly pounding, and despite the massive amount of work to be done, all she felt like doing was curling up on her little mat by the fire and falling asleep for enough hours to bring her back to her normal, cheerful, rested self. But every time her head hit the pillow, no sleep came for the worrying. No matter how hard she tried, she always tossed and turned, nervous, anxious, and overwhelmed at the possibilities of the dangers that presented themselves at every corner.

She knew she was taking a risk when she brought home the kingsman. She had endured days and weeks of thinking of everything that could possibly go wrong and every scenario, most of which ended with either her or her grandmother, or both, dead, or at the very least shattered beyond repair. She had worked tirelessly to keep this family together, to keep them afloat, to keep them out of the clutches of the Kingsmen, the tax collectors, the debtors, or thrown to the mercy of her neighbors. So far, she had succeeded, and she didn't want to see all of that washed away in one moment.

But the secret was burdening her. The weight was almost too much to bear at times, and she felt a physical weight on her shoulders every hour of the day.

Time would tell how much he would remember, if anything at all. She hoped to high heaven that it was the latter.

Obed leaned against the wall, propped up on his crutch, and watched her hang the laundry on the line. He couldn't seem to take his eyes off of her. Her face had yet to look upon him with anything more than tolerance, and he wondered at that. He had never done anything to her to cause any animosity, was there something that he had said or done in his delirium? Perhaps he had known her before his injury? Though she had seemed to deny that vociferously, and whatever her motive or reactions, he thought that denial to be true. Violet had only told him the truth, so he had no reason to doubt her word.

He wished he knew what was bothering her. For some reason unknown to him, he really wanted to understand why she would have brought him into her shelter. He couldn't understand why a complete stranger would be so giving as to

71

take in someone she didn't know and give them the best of everything when it was painfully obvious that they had very little to give in the first place. He might not know anything about his past, but he was incredibly observant of his present. Violet and her grandmother had very little in the way of clothes, and what they did have, while serviceable, was drab and well-worn. The furnishings around the house were simple, plain, and the only thing of any detail was the mantle above the fireplace where a rather crude, but still lovely, 'R' was wound around an 'M' with stems and leaves twined around them. It was one of the few fancy things that existed in the house, and with the way that Granny kept it dusted and the way Violet looked upon it with what was akin to reverence every time it caught her eye, he knew it must have some sort of sentimental value.

Violet Frell wasn't exactly the most approachable person, but if she ever lowered her walls, he had a slew of questions he had compiled in his head to ask her. It was highly uncommon, or at least he thought it was, for a young woman to be on her own in such a fashion and with a dependent, at that. Violet was beautiful, young, and obviously a very kind, caring, and hardworking individual.

He wondered why she wasn't married. It seemed that a woman who was such a catch would have long since found a husband. Maybe it was the grandmother? Though he didn't understand that. Granny was an endearing person; she was loving, kind, and tender. Even though he knew that her mind didn't seem to be working all that well, he felt it was of no consequence in comparison to the amount of love and kindness that she had showered upon him. He wished he had a grandmother. But then again, maybe he did? But how could he know if he couldn't remember?

He pounded his fist on the windowsill. He hated that his mind was failing him. Granny wasn't the only one with broken faculties. His seemed to have completely vacated his body at times, and it was one of the most infuriating feelings to have his mind fail him. No memories. No recollection of who he was, who he had been. No images of family, faces, places, or anything in between. He clenched his jaw as a feeling of failure overcame him. He so desperately wanted to remember.

# Eight

## KILLED FOR LESS

VIOLET HIKED THE large basket that was suspended from her shoulder with leather straps higher on her back and drew in a deep breath, trying to slow the fast beating of her heart and the throbbing in her chest. She tried not to gulp for air, knowing that always made things worse. It was a long walk from the farm with a burden of any kind, but she wanted to reach Padsley quickly. Her basket was full of wares, mostly knitted and woven items that Granny had worked from the wool they had harvested from their sheep. There was also some of the early produce from the garden. The wares were for bartering and selling at the market, and when she returned home, it would be just as full of necessities and supplies.

The bi-weekly market was generally an event that she looked forward to. It was always an opportunity to pay a visit to old friends, get around town, hear the latest news and fellowship. The joy of the outing, however, had been slowly stolen over time until it was the last thing she thought of with enjoyment. The amount of kingsmen in town had tripled, and their vigilance and belligerence grew increasingly oppressive each day.

Anxiety crept its cold fingers around her heart and squeezed, making her stomach feel tight and unsettled, and the muscles at her neck tense.

Everyone felt it. Those in the market who had been her closest friends had started speaking in whispered tones of tales of broken homes, people hurt by what was going on in their world, and the politics of the chancellor. It was as if the market had become a whispered courtroom full of judge and jury as they all spoke together of the accused. She didn't disagree with the sentiments her neighbors raised, for the most part, but she did hate the feeling of existential dread and overwhelming heaviness that weighed her down after hearing them.

She took another deep breath and let all the air out of her lungs as she topped the hill and saw the village below. She needed to focus on some positive things. She grew excited because she would be able to see Marcus. It had been a few weeks. His deformities prohibited him from visiting the farm unless Fendrel borrowed a cart. The walk was far too much for him. He had attempted it once, but had been in so much pain he had ended up spending the night on her bed, while she took to the floor, and Fendrel had brought a cart in the morning to fetch him.

His pain affected her deeply. Though he would never know how much, it had scarred her heart, and the wound had festered. They had grown up the best of friends, and seeing him cut down at such a young age, never to recover fully and with many of his life's dreams impossible…it had destroyed a small part of her heart.

The town buzzed with a nervous energy that she could feel the moment she stepped through the gates. People bustled about, but instead of a cheery coziness about their doings, the familiarity of a group of people who lived, worked, and played together...there was a tense silence and a stern, set look to their faces. Words did not need to be spoken to feel the trepidation and fear that pervaded the atmosphere.

She refrained from asking Galeron, the textile merchant, what was going on when she emptied her basket of woven goods on his market table. He didn't even smile at her, just gave her a nod and the few coins due her. She remembered a time when this thin rail of a man had found it his heart's greatest desire to bring joy and mirth to those around him. His tongue had been quick with a jovial, witty repartee that had kept everyone around him on their toes or doubled over in laughter. Tears started to her eyes as the realization struck home again: what a great change had come over her people.

That is what made this all the harder. These were her people. Her friends, comrades...they were like family, and to see the change that had come over them all was just another painful reminder of the oppression that had become normal in Elira. Her blood boiled as she dropped the coins into her pouch and tucked it under her sweater, in its designated pocket that was attached to the belt around her waist. If only someone could step up and make the change that was needed. They couldn't live under this tyranny forever. They wouldn't survive. Not these people around her, or the whole country of Elira.

"Have a good day, Galeron." She smiled at him, hoping to

bring some joy back into his morose face. He looked at her with a blank stare, a slight bit of confusion sparking in his eyes. Almost as if he wondered why she tried to be so cheery. He only nodded in response and turned to greet his next customer.

Feeling a bit hurt and not a bit less confused than she had been before, she hurried on to her next stop. The sooner she made it through her errands, the sooner she could drop in to visit Fendrel and Marcus. She so desperately needed their healing company. It was the same wherever she went, and her heart burned with the questions that were assuaging her brain. She needed to know why there was this extra fear and silence on the part of the villagers. She often detected such feelings, but this was different somehow. Heavier.

In her hurry, she turned a corner, some of the apples she had bought spilling out of the top of her basket and rolling across the cobblestones of the street. Frazzled and annoyed with herself for having bruised the perfectly good produce, she chased after them, not even looking where she was going. A hand grabbed her around the collar and pulled her out of the way just in time as several kingsmen atop their horses trotted through the middle of the street, the beasts' hooves completely obliterating the apples or anything else that might be in their path.

"Get back to your business!" Shouted a gruff voice. She barely heard it above the ringing in her ears as she was crushed against the muddy brick wall of one of the shops by a body larger than her own. She heard and felt her basket crunch in the fray. Intense pain seared her arm, and gray hazed around her vision as adrenaline soared through her body.

78

Before she knew it, the kingsmen were gone, shouting threats and other directions to the people in the streets. If they were attempting to bring order out of the chaos, they were doing an ill job of it.

Two massive hands grabbed her shoulder, and she looked up, and then up some more into the dark eyes of the blacksmith, Everard. "Are you all right?" His usually deep, rich voice was barely louder than a whisper, and she saw what must be her own fear mirrored in his black eyes as he looked deep into hers.

"I—I think so." Her voice squeaked as it came out and she choked against the dryness of her own throat, bringing up her arm to cough into her elbow. It was then that she noticed the blood running down her arm from where she had been skinned by the rough bricks of the wall. Her entire arm where she had been slammed into the wall was skinned, her sweater torn, and her arm bleeding. It was starting to sting, now that the adrenaline was wearing off.

His eyes flickered as he looked right and left before reaching into the pocket of his leather apron, rumored to have been made from the hide of an entire cow. He pulled out a cloth rolled into a ball and shook out the crumbs that must have been from his lunch. He carefully and swiftly wrapped it around her bleeding arm, and she winced as he did so. The stinging was more intense now that she wasn't under the spell of her shock.

"I'm sorry I pushed you into the wall." His voice was so deep it almost seemed to make the ground around her tremble with vibrations.

"No." She reached out a trembling hand, willing it to stop

shaking as she did so, and placed it on his massive arm. Her hand barely spanned half of his forearm. "Don't be sorry. Thank you for saving me. I don't know what came over me. I'm so sorry to have put you in that position." For some reason, she felt the urge to cry coming over her. She would not. She forced back the tears.

"Are you sure you are all right?"

She didn't believe she had heard him string so many words together in a conversation before. He had been quiet ever since she had known him. Her father had always been able to connect to something in the man, and she knew him as one of her father's dearest friends. Though she hadn't really seen much of him since his death. She nodded. "Don't worry. I'm heading to Fendrel's as it is."

He nodded. Gave her one more searching look with those piercing black eyes and disappeared around the corner.

She sagged against the wall. She hadn't wanted to make him feel bad, but she was weak from the encounter and the realization of how close she had come to being destroyed beneath the hooves of the kingsmen's horses, or if not that, railed upon by the men themselves.

Mustering up what little strength she had, she hurried through the streets, alert to what might be going on around her. She heard kingsmen's shouts in the distance, and the occasional wail or cry from a villager made her blood freeze. What on earth was happening?

By the time she made it to Fendrel's, her legs were weak, and her head pounded hard with the effort she had exerted.

When he opened the door, she collapsed inward, shutting it hard behind her as she fell against the wooden door frame and burst into tears.

It wasn't but a few moments before Fendrel had an arm about her waist, her basket off her back. She was already mopping up her own tears and blubbering an apology as he helped her into a seat at the table.

"Take deep breaths, my dear. That's it. Deep breaths..." Fendrel's soothing voice penetrated her scattered mind, and she started to breathe easier while he coached her. Marcus was there on a chair across from her, holding her hand that rested on the table and gently stroking it to the rhythm of her exaggerated and slow breathing as she attempted to calm herself. She didn't often lose control, but when she did, it wasn't for long. She had too much mastery over her own emotions to let herself fall too deeply into them.

She winced and hissed a breath through her teeth as Fendrel peeled her sleeve away from the abrasions on her arm. "I'm sorry, my dear, but I fear Granny will have to mend this sweater." He took some sheers and carefully cut up the length of her sleeve. Her gut rolled, and she tasted a bitterness in her mouth at the pain in her arm as he worked at peeling the fabric back. Marcus pushed a glass of water toward her, and she gratefully sipped it, letting the coolness of it coat her throat. She never had been one to handle pain well, and she was struggling through the nausea.

Fendrel whistled through his teeth as he examined her arm. "You bashed this one up good, I'm afraid. Marcus, fetch some sterile water from the kettle and some of those linens that we boiled this morning." He worked carefully at her arm.

After a few moments, she groaned and leaned heavily against the table as she started to feel lightheaded. Marcus pulled his chair closer and held her up with his hands at the front of her shoulders.

Violet dragged heavy breaths through her nose and blinked a few times as the haziness closed in around her vision. Fendrel and Marcus exchanged a glance, but she hardly noticed as she felt herself slumping against Marcus's hands.

"What happened to you, Vi?" Marcus's voice was soft, concerned, but also pointed. She knew he was trying to distract her from the pain. And she was grateful.

"I turned a corner and was being careless." She spoke in measured tones, slowly, trying to organize her thoughts since her mind didn't seem to want to cooperate. "Some apples fell from my basket, and I wasn't even paying attention. I went for them as they rolled in the street. I was so stupid. I didn't see that some kingsmen were coming toward me. Everard pulled me out of the way, but I got pressed between him and the wall as the kingsmen passed. In the rush my arm was crushed against the brick wall." She hissed in a breath to punctuate her story as Fendrel dug a little extra deep with his cleaning. She let loose a few elementary curses before she could even stop herself, then instantly apologized.

Marcus's grin was all she could see through the haze. "I didn't know you had the mouth of a miner, Vi."

She wanted to smack him, but a glare would have to suffice as she felt her face heat. She was ashamed that she knew those words, let alone had let them slip. The miner's were known for the most foul of mouths in the kingdom. Though, she didn't know as she blamed them. Being in the dark and dank pits of the mines was enough to drive anyone to some desperate measures. Their language was probably a defense mechanism against a world that would drive most mad.

"I'm sure we will all forgive her as I know the Lord does. One doesn't always have perfect control of one's mouth or actions, especially while in pain. I have to admit that I've heard much worse."

"Just because they weren't the worst that they could be doesn't mean I'm not ashamed I've said them." Violet ground out through gritted teeth. She winced and pulled away slightly.

Fendrel's grip on her arm tightened. "Sorry, lass, but some of these pebbles are ground in quite deep, and I don't want to leave them there to fester."

"Don't." She tried not to gag. "Feeling it is enough. I don't need to hear about it." She swallowed against the retch that tried to clamp down on her throat.

"It's a good thing you aren't a doctor, Vi. You definitely didn't miss your calling on that one." Marcus' smile lit up the room and took a bit of the edge off for Violet. But the worry behind his eyes and that annoyingly adorable smile made her heart squeeze. Something was wrong. But now was not the time.

"I'll have you know I'm perfectly fine helping with wounds as long as they aren't my own." She growled.

He merely chuckled in response.

"Almost done. This section was a little more difficult." Fendrel dipped his rag in the now soiled water one last time and dabbed a little harder against the top of her shoulder.

"Oh no." She squeaked and felt herself falling toward Marcus before everything went gray.

Violet awoke to the smell of vinegar in her nostrils. She sneezed and startled awake.

"Easy. Not too fast."

"Did I pass out?" She asked, blinking to clear the fuzzies from her sight.

"You sure did." The smile and amusement in Marcus's voice was unmistakable. She punched him in the arm with her good hand.

"Ow! What was that for?"

"For being amused by my inability to handle intense pain."

He glared at her for a moment, the twinkle in his eyes betraying his true feelings. He fought the smile on his lips before he took his hands off her shoulders from where they had been supporting her. He pushed away from the table and started to stand up, but she grabbed his hand and tugged.

"What?"

"What's going on?" Her voice was urgent. "What are you not telling me? Why is everyone so on edge?"

Sighing, he shook his head and pulled away, pain in his eyes. He limped across the room to put the handful of clean bandages that Fendrel hadn't used away in the wooden cabinet against the wall.

Fendrel rounded the corner from the kitchen, wiping his hand on a towel. "There's been word from the capital. The prince is missing. They haven't even found his horse. He was out with a scouting party when he got separated from the group. They haven't been able to locate his body."

Violet's head reeled. "Body?" Images of the broken kingsman lying on the forest floor filled her mind, and she thought she might actually vomit this time.

"There are a lot of rumors floating around, and no one really seems to know what to believe," Fendrel continued, placing a hand on her shoulder. "Some say that he was kidnapped for ransom, or even taken by a rival kingdom. Some say that he was attacked by a wild beast. The worst of it is that the Kingsmen have been told to be on their guard and look out for any suspicious activity." Fendrel looked deep into her eyes, his gray ones full of meaning that only she would understand.

She swallowed hard.

What could be more suspicious than a kingsman who didn't remember who he was residing in a villager's home? What if the kingsman was part of the posse that had been with the prince? What if he had been the prince's bodyguard, who had been taken out so that they could get to the prince? She had run through the scenario so many times, but now it seemed even more likely to have happened than before. "Where—" She gulped. "Where was he last seen?"

"Compton."

She drew a breath of relief. That was at least a day's journey from here, longer if you were going at the military's measured pace. But the worry didn't leave. It was entirely within the realm of possibility that the kingsman who was living at her house was in some way related to this incident. In which case, it was paramount that no one ever knew where he truly came from. Her decision to refrain from telling anyone of Obed but Fendrel had been a good one, and one that she was grateful she had made. She glanced over at Marcus, who still stood

85

organizing the medicine cabinet. She understood his worry and trepidation. He had lost so much at the hands of the Kingsmen and their new ruler. They both had.

A frantic knock at the door sent Fendrel striding toward it.

"Please, Master Fendrel, it's Mya." A frantic farmer stood, dirt streaked on his face and sweat beading on his brow and wetting his shirt. "She's in child pain, and it's early. The midwife told me to fetch you. I'm worried." He was trembling.

Fendrel turned, but Marcus had already hobbled over with his medicinal bag. The older man took it, looked pointedly at Violet and tilted his head forward as if he were telling her something of great import.

"Make sure you keep that wound clean." He tilted his head farther down to look at her over his spectacles. "And I mean very clean." His voice was even, measured and stern.

She nodded, and he was gone.

Fear wove around her heart. She stood quickly, her chair squeaking as it skidded across the floor in her hurry. "I need to go home."

Fendrel's words echoed in her ears. *Clean.* He had meant more than her wound; she was sure of it.

There was something she needed to destroy so that no one ever found it.

# Nine

## BY ORDER OF THE REGENT

VIOLET WAS OUT of breath and not a little lightheaded by the time she made it home. Her basket wasn't as heavy as normal, but she had been in such a hurry that filling it the rest of the way with the things they might need was far less important than getting home and taking care of what she knew could put them all in danger.

Marcus had been disappointed and confused by her hurried departure. She could tell he had been hoping they would have some time together to talk, but Violet could wait for nothing.

She stumbled through the doorway, startling Granny from nodding sleepily over her knitting and causing Obed to start from his restful position on the bed. She dropped her basket in the kitchen, sneakily snatched the tinder box from the top of the mantle, and stuffed it into her pocket. She hurried back to the door.

"What in tarnation? What's going on? Richard?" Granny

stood shakily from her rocking chair and turned toward the door.

It had been a long day, and Violet's emotions were at a fever pitch. She almost lost control and burst into tears right then and there, disgracing herself before Obed. "He's not here, Granny. I don't want either of you to leave this cabin until I get back. Under *any* circumstances." She looked pointedly between the two, first one, then the other, holding their gaze and making sure that they knew how serious she was. "Do *not* leave this house. Do I make myself clear?" Her voice was firm, but it wavered at the end.

They both nodded solemnly, probably a bit too startled to argue.

She nodded and hurried toward the barn. She had to burn everything.

Her hurried entrance into the barn startled Bertha and the horse. They jerked their heads up and made their respective animal sounds. Apparently, they were more than comfortable expressing their opinion of her disturbing their peace and quiet.

Violet hiked up her dress and clambered to the loft.

Dusk was already starting to gather like a shadow over the firmament of the sky, pooling in the corners and filling odd colors and shades around the sun. She needed to have the fire done and out by dark. Curfew was strictly enforced, and though some thought themselves safe out here in the farmland where houses and families were fewer and farther between, there had been raids and ambushes from kingsmen who had stumbled upon, either by luck or evil happenstance, a family not quite settled for the night. The tyrants had taken the "fee" for missing curfew of their own volition. Violet often wondered if any of it went to the ruler as it was supposed to, or if the Kingsmen simply took what they wanted and cared for nothing else.

She gathered as many things into her arms as she could, but a cold, hard, heavy metal medallion slipped out of her arm and hit the floor with a clanking thud that made her jump and cringe.

She dropped the other things and scooped it into her hand. Wasn't that the king's crest? The lion who stood rearing within a crown and surrounded by thorns was embossed into the golden, but blackened, medallion. The thought of the danger that they were in struck hard again, and panic built in her chest. No one could ever know who the man they sheltered under their roof really was.

"Lord," she whispered breathlessly as she regathered all of the items into her arms. "I don't mean to tell You how to do Your job, but please don't let Obed's memory ever come back. I don't want to die, and I don't want to bring that upon Granny. She might survive the kingsmen, but she wouldn't survive the repercussions of losing me." Tears blurred her vision, and she struggled to keep them at bay so she didn't trip on her way down the ladder with her arms full of the kingsman's belongings.

Or rather, previous belongings as the case was now.

For a moment, a smidgen of doubt darkened her thoughts as she prepped the pile to burn, placing straw and kindling beneath the items. Should she really burn every shred of what might be tied to Obed's identity? It was an incredibly sobering thought, and one that she wasn't prepared to deal with in this moment. She rubbed the flint together, creating a few sparks that lit the hay. She blew gently, encouraging the ember to grow into a flame. The blue light of the fire glowed orange as it picked up speed. She watched it slowly eat at the straw, then catch on the bark of the kindling. Some of the documents started to burn at the edges. She blinked and set her shoulders. There was no turning back now.

Obed held the wrap of yarn for Granny, the circle strung between both his hands which he held out in front of him. She was muttering to herself as she wound the yarn unraveling from his hands into a ball that was currently the size of his fist. Somehow, it magically and swiftly grew, and he was fascinated and somewhat mesmerized by the process of turning, rolling, and winding that she was accomplishing with her wrinkled and frail hands as they sat before the fire.

He wondered what had Violet so worked up. She wasn't exactly the cheeriest person; in fact, she seemed quite morose most of the time, with a quiet nature, but he had come to realize that her mind was working hard behind the thin, straight mouth that rarely smiled and the eyes that were too dark and hooded for a woman so young. Her green eyes were large in her wide face, but they were curtained off with a past he knew nothing about. She kept much to herself and was working out of doors more often than not. She seemed to never take a break. She had a perfect plan for everything; if something took her longer than expected—the repair of the roof, for example—she seemed to grow incredibly frustrated, and even though she kept most of it inside, he could see the bottled up tension in the rigid set of her shoulders and the clenching of her jaw.

If he had to boil it down as one thing, he would say that she liked to be in control of things. It didn't take long to realize that about Violet Frell. That, and she had a strength about her that fascinated him. She always seemed to know what to do next and how to go about it, which more than intrigued him at this moment in his life when he had no recollection of where he was from or who he was, let alone what he was going to do next.

There was a bit of distrust that was beginning to grow in his mind toward her. What if she knew something and wasn't telling him? It seemed unlikely; she had given him no reason to distrust her. But he was so desperate, and she ought to see how much knowing who he was meant to him. Why wouldn't she tell him the least bit about who he was? She must know something. He knew she did, and he should ask her outright. Another thing he had learned in his short time with these two women was that Violet was terrible at hiding her trepidation when telling someone something that wasn't entirely true.

He had seen it upon occasion when she was comforting her grandmother by insinuating that her son would return. There was an unease in her face as she put off the woman's questions by telling her to "wait and see" or "not yet."

He felt for her. Now she not only had one person who was slowly losing their mind, but two. He sighed. He wished that he could help her in some way, but Violet didn't seem the least inclined to trust anything to him.

With a thud, the wind swept the door open and slammed it

against the wall, making him jump. The sound reverberated in his skull, and he winced. Dusk was gathering, and while he had only existed here for a few weeks, even he knew that being out after dark could bring a severe punishment if caught.

Violet stood in the doorway, her light brown hair, streaked with light from long exposure to the sun, was tousled by the wind, curly wisps framing her face. Using her elbow to shut the door, she held her dirt-covered hands close to her. She hurried to the basin in the kitchen, and he could tell that she was out of breath.

"Where have you been, dearie? Is your father going to come in soon? Dinner was ready ages ago."

He saw Violet's shoulders sag as she slowed in washing her hands. She used a forearm to brush some of the hair out of her face. "He's not coming home, Granny."

"Oh, is he staying the night in town?"

Violet hesitated. She dried her hands slowly, her chest heaving. Obed still couldn't see her face, but he could tell she was trying hard to control herself. "He won't be home tonight," she reiterated. She turned back to the main room, her features schooled. He hoped for her sake that Granny let it drop after this.

"But will he be home tomorrow?"

"Granny, did you say there was dinner left? I'm starving." Violet spun suddenly and started rummaging through a cabinet, pulling out a plate and spoon.

"Oh! Of course, dear! It's in the box on the counter." Granny's voice was light and vibrant again, without the questioning tone.

Obed could almost feel Violet's sigh of relief as she turned to get herself supper.

He wondered what on earth she had been so frazzled about when she arrived earlier. It must have been important. She had been white as a sheet, and her demand that they stay inside made him nervous. She had told him enough about the Kingsmen that his own heart beat a little faster in fear when they were mentioned. Hopefully, they weren't in trouble.

Darkness had fallen over the land, and he could see she was still on edge. She kept going to the window, cracking one of the shutters that closed on the inside and peeking out for a few moments before she shut it again, sighing and turning back to her spinning wheel by the fire. She winced as she gently touched the arm that was bandaged. It didn't look comfortable for her to be working at the spinning wheel with that injury to her arm.

He wound another skein of yarn around his hands and held them up again while Granny wound the thread into a ball. He winced himself as he stretched out his injured leg on the floor in front of him, straightening his back as he settled on the stool in front of Granny. There was something soothing in her motions as she wound round and round, pivoting her hand every so often as the ball grew under her fingers.

"What happened to your arm? You never said." He suddenly felt uncomfortable with his own voice breaking the stillness that had only been accentuated by the crackling of the fire and the whirring of the wheel. Violet's foot slowed on the pedal, and the whirring came to a stop. Her green eyes were wide with surprise, as if he had startled her out of her own private thoughts.

She cleared her throat. "It's nothing." The wheel started

again.

"It doesn't look like nothing." He knew he was pressing her, but he was desperately tired of the silence. He needed something to occupy his mind; it felt so useless otherwise. And it wasn't like they could really hide much from each other. They shared the same place and amenities. Or rather, she shared with him.

"I scraped it on a wall, all right?" She huffed, then stopped suddenly, holding her hand to her wheel and straining to listen, her eyes fixed on the fire past him and fear swallowing her features.

"What?"

"Shhh." It was harsh, cutting through the room with its forceful sound. Even Granny stopped wrapping the yarn. "Do you hear that?"

He strained to hear what she did. Nothing but quiet met his ears.

She stood abruptly, her chair making a racket as the legs scraped across the plank floor. She darted to a window and cracked the shutter again. Her face lost all color, and she swayed, catching herself against the windowsill. Slamming the shutter closed, she dashed over to the door where she bolted it shut with the heavy bar across the middle.

Her chest was heaving when she turned back toward them, and the look of utter terror on her face. She closed her eyes, her back against the door, and took a deep, trembling breath, letting it out slowly through pursed lips. She opened her eyes, and there was a flinty resolve there, deepening the green to the color of the forest at dusk. She strode over to Granny, took the yarn from her hands, and knelt in front of her, wrapping the old woman's hands in her own. "Granny, I need you to be strong. There are kingsmen who are coming, and we need to be brave."

Granny started to tremble.

"Lord, I just ask for your peace to surround our home right now, in Jesus' name." Violet stood again, and only now could Obed hear the thunder of horses' hooves.

How she had heard that a few moments ago with how faint they had been, he had no idea.

But it was the fear on Violet's face...it was so raw; his throat closed up around the realization that Violet, the one who seemingly had everything together, who always had a plan and a way to make everything work, was terrified beyond reason. He watched her close her eyes again as she took another deep breath. Her lips moved without any sound. Outside, there was the tumult of soldiers reining in their horses, creaking tack, and the clatter of stomping hooves.

A pounding on the door startled Violet out of her silent prayer, and she jumped as if the knocks had pulled on a string tied to her very soul.

"Open, by order of the king! You have three seconds before we break the door down!"

The voice on the other side of the door held a menace and impatience to it that sent chills down Obed's spine. He couldn't tear his gaze away from the door, but he felt Granny shift behind him, as if seeking shelter from the monsters outside.

Violet hurried to pull the latch, her fingers fumbling with the board, and it fell from her clumsy grip back into place. Too late. The door gave way with a crash that tore through the house, and Violet was thrown violently across the room by its motion. On instinct, he jolted forward in an effort to lend a helping hand to Violet. She kept her feet at first but was shoved to the floor by the first kingsman who came through the doorway.

The kingsman's emerald green cape fluttered back from the leather pauldron encasing his shoulder with the crest of a lion and a crown impressed upon it. He was tall and broad shouldered, his face stern, with hard, dark eyes that held no light or life behind their sharp depths. A captain's insignia was marked upon his leather breastplate. He stalked to the middle of the room, his all-seeing gaze taking in every aspect of their little home before he turned to Violet, who by now had stood on her own.

Obed was torn between her and Granny. He could tell Violet was trembling, but she lifted her chin and set her face like flint.

"What is the cause of this invasion into my home?" Her words almost didn't sound like a question in their flatness.

A slight, smug smile tilted the corners of the kingsman's mouth. "Not that you have any right to ask, but I'm feeling generous today. Every house is to be searched by order of the regent. His Majesty, the Royal Highness, is missing, and we are to search every residence for anything pertaining to his whereabouts."

Violet's face paled.

Without taking his eyes off of her, the captain spoke to his soldiers. "Tear this place apart."

With barely half a second past this order, the two kingsmen directly behind him strode into the room. One turned over the spinning wheel as he pulled the chairs away from the fire, while the other tore the kitchen cabinet off the wall and dumped its contents with an ear-splitting crash to the floor.

"No!" Violet cried and lunged toward the kitchen, but the captain raised his arm and swept her to the floor with hardly any more effort than he would exert killing a fly.

Obed wrapped an arm around Granny, her shoulders quaking beneath his grip. If only he could protect them both. He felt his blood boiling and his pulse pounding in his head at the injustice of it all as the kingsmen tore the house apart around them. His chest heaved, and fire sparked through his veins, sweat starting to drip into his eyes, every muscle wound tight as if ready to spring.

Violet cowered on the floor, fire flashing from her eyes as tears simultaneously fell from them, glittering in the firelight.

The two lower ranked kingsmen shoved Obed and Granny out of the way as they approached the fireplace. Obed slyly led Granny across the wooden floor toward Violet. Before they reached her, the captain grasped her by her bandaged arm. A yelp escaped her lips as he dragged her from the house.

Obed followed, his mind spewing anger that made his throat clench and his grip on Granny tighten. He would not release her to save his life. Somehow, he knew that Violet would have wanted him to guard the old woman before her. At the overwhelming odds against him, helplessness suddenly drowned him in ice. The feeling was so entirely new and overwhelming, it nearly choked him.

He sank to his knees beside Violet as she stared into the house, the sound of more crashing and splintering reaching his ears. He touched her shoulder, and she winced beneath his touch. Her jaw was clenched so hard he saw the muscles strung taught beneath the sun-roughened skin of her face. The freckles across her nose seemed stretched thin.

The kingsmen filed from the house in stomping fashion, their boots heavy on the ground. One swung a money pouch from his gloved hand.

Violet lunged to her feet, taking after the kingsman. She grabbed his arm and reached for the money pouch. "You can't take that! That's mine! I need it to pay the taxes!"

The kingsman shook her off with a laugh. "Taxes are due now then, I'd say. Wouldn't you, Warde?"

She reached again for the burgundy leather pouch, the outline of coins visible through the soft skin.

The captain took her by the collar of her dress and slung her to the ground, giving her a swift kick to her side. He laughed. "You are a glutton for punishment. I can think of a few things to do with you, my pretty maid." He sneered as he leaned over her sprawled out form as she tried to right herself and disentangle from her skirts.

Obed felt the boiling in his blood reach a fever pitch and something snapped inside of him, anger welling up beneath the surface. Fire burned in his throat. "You there! Leave her alone!" He dashed toward the captain, his full weight lunging toward the man who would dare harm a helpless maid and her grandmother.

The quiet, stealthy shriek of a sword being drawn from its sheath registered in his brain a moment before a throbbing pain crashed through his head, and the world went dark.

# Ten

## BITS AND PIECES

VIOLET SOBBED AND pressed the back of her hand to her mouth to muffle the sound as she saw Obed hit the ground, his body limp as a pile of laundry fresh from the wash.

"It's always a little more fun when you peasants put up a fight." The captain sneered, re-sheathing his sword and stepping back toward Violet. "Your husband doesn't seem to understand the futility as you do, does he? Or is he your brother?"

Violet didn't answer and didn't dare look the man in his evil eyes. Everything within her froze at the very thought of what he was about to attempt. She was well aware that any move on her part could be a possible trigger that would set him to upending her world in the most unsavory of ways.

With a sudden movement, he gripped her under the chin with his massive hand, pulling her up by her head. Her neck strained, and she struggled to get her feet under her to relieve the pressure. "Speak, maid." He spat in her face.

"He's a cousin." She rasped out, the odd angle of her throat making the words a struggle to release, the lie flying from her tongue faster than she had time to comprehend, but fear clouded all thoughts of regret or remorse from her decision.

"Ah." His voice was softer, and a glint of something more menacing glittered in the dark brown orbs of his eyes.

An odd thought came to mind, humanizing him in a way that made her heart feel disgust all the more readily. His mother must have thought these eyes beautiful in her child. But somehow, the idea of this man, a cherished babe on his mother's lap, seemed utterly impossible in this moment.

"Perhaps you will be a pretty plaything, eh?" the sneer made her gag. The new glint in his eyes was lust. She thought she might pass out. *Lord, help.*

"Captain! We found a horse. It looks to be a king's horse!" The shout from the barn distracted the captain, and he dropped Violet as if she were a rag doll, striding toward the other kingsman who held the beautiful black steed by his halter.

The captain perused the horse a moment, then turned his steely eyes to Violet. "A king's horse, eh? And how did you come upon such a possession, wench?"

Violet stared at the dirt between her hands that rested on the ground, trying not to quiver and forcing herself to breathe evenly. She expected a kick or a punch at any second.

Instead, a laugh met her ears. "You may be a bit more enterprising than I thought. Ah, well, the fun is over for tonight, but I won't forget you. Make no mistake. Mount up, lads!"

Within seconds, the sound of tack creaking and stomping

hooves turned into a thundering that soon disappeared down the road, Obed's horse in tow.

The pounding in her head didn't stop as Violet continued to stare at the dirt in front of her, her heart beating wildly, willing herself to return to reality. Her surroundings felt hazy, and her mind knew that she should move and check on Granny. Make sure Obed was okay. She could sense his unconscious body still lying where he fell off to her right. But for some reason, her limbs refused to cooperate. Her body stood in direct rebellion to her mental commands. She hadn't realized that she had been holding her breath and drew in a deep one, choking on the oxygen that threatened to burst her lungs. Breath coming quick and fast, her vision blurring around the edges, the pain that she had been in too much turmoil to feel suddenly fell upon her with a heavy weight that sought to drown her.

A trembling hand on her shoulder was just enough to bring her mind to some semblance of order, and she looked up to see Granny, perfectly unharmed. A sob escaped Violet's tight throat as she gripped the shaking, elderly hand. *Thank you, Lord.* The fact that He had spared Granny from any pain or harm made her heart turn over with gratefulness for His mercy.

Violet wracked her blank brain for something that she knew would bring comfort and ease to Granny's anxiety. The dear old soul was under far too much fear to even speak, her body trembling all over, and her cloudy blue eyes wide in her pale face. Violet stood, her knees knocking as she did so. She grasped both of Granny's withered hands in her own. The old woman needed something to do.

"Granny, could you go inside and make us some tea? I know I would be so grateful for a cup, and Obed will need some as soon as he wakes." She daren't look just yet at the man sprawled not far from her feet. She might lose the rest of her composure completely.

Granny only nodded, but a certain level of normalcy returned to her eyes as she nodded once more, as if convincing herself of her new task before she made her way into the house. Violet heard some dishes clattering and some mumbling as she collapsed on her knees beside Obed.

"Don't you dare die on me now, after all I've gone through for you," she scolded, gripping his shoulder and straightening his awkwardly collapsed form. She lifted his head and saw a small cut above his eyebrow. Blood trickled from the small gash down his face, and it was slowly bruising, but nothing more. She knew that head wounds could be nasty things and the recovery time was far from exact. His previous bout of mental trauma could be exacerbated, unaffected, or possibly reversed. Gulping at the thought, she prayed that the internal damage was as minimal as what was visible to her eye. She pressed her sleeve to his eyebrow and hesitated before she took her fist to his chest and rubbed up and down with as much pressure as she could muster.

He groaned and squeezed his eyes shut harder. Then slowly blinked them open. She released a sigh of relief, her shoulders rounding forward.

"What happened?" He groaned, teeth gritted, and brought a hand up to where hers stemmed the bleeding.

"You did something very foolish and were hit on the head." She couldn't keep the scold from her tone. As stupid as he had been, he didn't really deserve the harshness. But it seemed to jump out of her mouth before she could do anything about it. The anxiety, anger, and fear all converging at once was wreaking havoc on her emotions.

He closed his eyes again with another groan, but she shook him by the shoulder. "Don't go to sleep. We need to get you inside and to bed."

"My head is killing me."

"Well, I'll really kill you if you don't get up. You can do it. I can't drag you, not again. Not tonight." Her last words turned into a moan that she tried to stifle. Obed thankfully didn't seem to hear it.

As Violet helped him up, he wavered on his feet, leaning heavily on her uninjured shoulder. Between the two of them and their four clumsy feet, they made it inside the house. Violet almost cried with despair when she saw the state of the room. Granny had salvaged a few dishes and was humming softly over the tea kettle, simmering atop the kitchen fire.

Sometimes Violet envied her grandmother's empty mind, her quickness to forget, and the ease with which she returned to a peaceful state. It was almost as if the disease didn't allow anything but good thoughts to remain in her mind. Any trauma and evil seemed to vanish as soon as it could.

Ignoring the disaster that currently was her home, she settled Obed into a seated position in the rocker near the bed while she remade the tossed over tick mattress that had been pulled to the floor, the blankets in haphazard bundles nearby. What they thought they would find buried in her mattress was beyond her.

Within moments, she had Obed onto the mattress, and he

103

curled on his side, gripping his forehead with one hand while she pressed a clean cloth she'd retrieved from the drawer in the bedside table to his cut. She lifted his hand and placed it atop the cloth to hold it in place, then turned to survey the room.

First order of business, she stuffed everything that had been vacated from the bedside table back inside the drawer and shut it. She would refold its contents at a later date. She needed to get Obed some of the powder that Fendrel had given her for his headaches.

As she took a step away from the bed, a sharp pain seized her side, causing her knees to collapse, and she hit the floor with a moan, gripping the muscle that was cramping. The full weight of her injuries finally caught up with her, and completely devoid of any energy, she curled on her side on the floor, silent tears falling down the side of her face and dripping onto the floorboards. The misery of it all struck her anew and her mind, spirit, and emotions seemed at war with each other in an attempt to sabotage her very sanity. She was so overwhelmed. Her thoughts flew everywhere.

"Jesus, please, I need peace," she begged around broken sobs.

A soft, cool hand stroked back the disheveled curls from her forehead, and a wavery voice started singing. The gentle hymn flowed over her tattered mind and body, and a deep breath left her, drawing the tension out with it.

*Your peace you gave us*
*Your heart divine,*
*Your blood was spilled*
*What a mighty prize.*

*Grant us now Thy tender mercy,*
*Your peace surrounds us now.*
*Let every heart, tongue and nation,*
*Before you Jesus, bow.*
*Peace peace,*
*You brought us peace*
*Let us dwell at Your table,*
*On what You provide we feast*
*Take our hand in this brokenness*
*Hold us gently oh Lord*
*We pray and ask you for Your presence*
*Lead us through this wilderness.*

The next day was a difficult one for Violet and her household. Violet herself was incredibly sore and broken physically. The mess of her house almost felt like more than she could handle. Keeping her head high, however, she plowed on, picking up the disaster that the kingsmen had made in her home, sweeping, mopping, and tidying until near day's end when it finally resembled its usual organized self. She had trundled her splintered spinning wheel into the corner, and now as she sat at the table, hunched over a bowl of cabbage soup that Granny had made, she felt the tears come to her eyes and flow down her cheeks as she stared at the shattered wheel.

The wheel was a pitiful sight, and the loss of income that it represented to Violet and Granny, as well as the time it would take to repair the mechanism, made her heart ache.

"The Lord has a plan." Granny said as she sliced a generous portion of the steaming bread, fresh from the oven, for Violet and set the chunk in front of her granddaughter.

Violet choked and swallowed hard, willing the lump in her throat to dissipate, and clenched her jaw so as not to bite off Granny's head in a retort that surely was of no one's benefit.

A moan from the bed caught her attention, and she looked over her shoulder to check on Obed. He tossed on the mattress, mumbling in his sleep. The cut on his head was small, but even from the table she could see the bruise that had blossomed across that part of his face, and the wrinkles in his brow betrayed the pain he was in. She rested a hand on her side where her own discomfort nagged with every movement. The kick from the kingsman last night had given her fits all night as the muscles didn't seem to want to relax in the least.

"When is Richard coming home? He'll be able to fix your wheel quite nicely. He always was handy when it came to mechanics and them wheels and things. I never could get the hang of it. It's getting late; I wish he'd come in and wash for supper."

Violet bit her lip. Maybe if she didn't say anything, Granny would forget. But somehow these bouts of broken memories were becoming more frequent of late. Her old mind was stuck in a loop of the past, reliving the moments before her son had been taken from them. She seemed unusually fragile today, even in comparison to her recent decline, and Violet's blood boiled. Trauma or stressful situations always seemed to make Granny a bit worse. Just one more thing to deepen Violet's bitterness against the Kingsmen. Hopelessness tried to take hold of her, and she stood abruptly, hiding the rest of her portion of bread in her apron pocket.

"I need to feed the stock." Before she was too tired and stiff to even think about moving. She whisked her shawl from the peg by the door, and her breath caught as she wrapped it around her shoulders, the movement pulling at her bruise.

"Tell your father to hurry up out there. His soup is getting cold."

Violet felt her shoulders buckle and give way under the emotions. She took a deep, trembling breath. "I will." Pulling the latch, she slipped outside and leaned her back against the door, the tears that had burned at her eyes spilling over and a small sob escaping before she pressed a fist to her mouth. "Lord, it hurts." She whimpered softly. "When will it end?"

The despair weighed heavily as she swallowed back the tears, straightened, and whisked the back of her hand over her cheeks. She needed to get the chores done. Striding toward the barn, she ticked off a mental checklist: Feed the cow and the hens. Lock the hens in for the night. Bring in a bucket of water from the well. Feed and medicate Obed. Get Granny settled for the night. Collapse in sleep.

The sooner she could get to the last thing on her list, the better. Her side ached almost unbearably, but she knew there was no way that she could leave anything undone. The consequences of such were far greater than her pushing through a little bit of pain or exhaustion. She needed to stick to the plan. She was the only way this family could stay together, and now that their funds for the summer taxes had been taken from her, she would have to work extra hard to not only recoup those funds but earn more toward their winter store. Winter wasn't kind to anyone, but least of all those who couldn't afford to remain warm or fed for the five months of freezing wind, sleet, snow, and ice.

Her mind was busy as she went about the chores, putting out salt for the sheep that roamed the hillside and the forest but would return to sleep on the hay she laid out for them in the farmyard. They would need to harvest as much wool as possible in order to make the items that sold best right before winter. Her spinning wheel was just the beginning of an enterprising business that Violet and Granny had been able to manage for the last few years. Granny had taught her to knit at the tender age of five, and making woolen sweaters, scarves, mittens, and hats was one of the ways they could earn enough to set aside, keeping the farm going, as well as providing for the seasonal taxes that only seemed to grow higher and higher with each passing quarter of a year.

Firewood would need to be chopped, enough to last all winter. And none of that work helped in keeping up with the fields. It was only late spring yet, but she needed to be ahead enough now that when harvest time came, she would be ready to help the other farmers as they rotated harvesting crops.

Not everyone could bring in their own harvests, so the farms and hands gathered in each field, helping each other and working through the crops that were ripe till they were all laid away. Because they all pitched in for each other, there was no need to pay wages, and it ensured that everything got done that was needed. After each field was brought in, there used to be celebrations. Large feasts and dances that would go on into the night.

The whole idea of the communal harvest season had been

108

something Violet had concocted, waking her father up in the middle of the night once to tell him her grand idea. He had been so proud of his little girl, and she felt the tears fill her eyes at the memory. His beaming smile and soft, but squared, features tilted upward in a look that still warmed her heart to this day. She had lived for harvest season, her papa having quite the time of keeping his lively Blue Violet from running herself ragged, dancing with everyone she could whisk away and eating more sweets than she ought. A small smile touched Violet's face at the bright, warm memories but was promptly swept away by the remembrance that those dances and feasts were in the past, just as surely as her father, a good life, and any hope for one were.

She shook her head, steeling herself against the pit of despair. All one had now was hope. She couldn't let herself lose that. No matter how bleak things got, she would hold fast.

Kingsmen. Marching. The horse beneath him shifting over the rocky pathway as he balanced back and forth. Deep voices, nagging, speaking, too many all at once. The feeling of anger, searing hot, that fell into a low-lying smolder. Rejection. Tree branches flashing overhead, intense pain.

The taste of alcohol, the sound of music, bright lights flashing, and loud laughter. A party. Many parties. A feeling of dullness amidst the gaiety. As if something were amiss. Broken. Lost. Numb.

The stamping of many feet, twirling, a girl upon his arm, then another. Their faces blurred in his sight. Combining, and then morphing back into individuals. Swirling, spinning, dancing the night away. Laughing, falling into a chair, and pulling a woman onto his lap. The feel of her hair tangled in his fingertips, but the room continued to spin as he leaned in for a kiss. She laughed and tilted her face, and he found that the angry feeling returned, muddled emotions of anguish and wrath. He slammed his fist down on the table.

Obed startled awake, mid-toss upon the bed. It was dark. The soft, orange glow and the sound of the gentle fire crackling on the hearth and a quiet snore from across the room were the only things that met his senses. He shook his aching head and raised a trembling hand to his brow. He felt so beastly hot. He swallowed against his dry, scratchy throat, confusion swirling in his brain like a melting pot, washing away the vague sights and feelings that had tormented him in his sleep. He gripped his temples, trying to hold onto the visions, willing them to make sense. Willing them to stay.

But his desperation was for naught. Nothing made sense.

# Eleven

## SPARKS ALIGHT

*TWO WEEKS LATER.*

Obed wiped the sweat from his brow and shook back the brownish blond locks that had fallen over his forehead. He blinked hard to remove the sting from the perspiration that had dripped into his eye.

He didn't know how Violet managed to work harder and faster than he did, dressed in as many layers as she was. How could she look nothing but attractive as the dampness on her face glowed beneath the afternoon sun? Her straw hat hung from a string around her neck and bobbed against her back with the movements of her scythe as she cut swaths of sweet grass ahead and to the left of him. Her curly locks had frizzed with the labor, and tendrils of it had loosened from her braid, tickling her neck and fluffing around her face and ears.

She was sweaty, and red faced, and glowing, and…beautiful.

She stood, pressing a hand to her low back and leaned backward, stretching out what he knew to be sore muscles. His own were on fire. The realization that she did this for hours on end, day after day, gave him a greater respect for her strength. He wondered if he had done this in his past life. Based on the pain level he was currently experiencing, he would guess not.

Violet turned and caught his gaze, and they stared awkwardly at each other for a moment.

"What?" She asked, bringing a hand to her forehead and smoothing back a few tendrils of hair.

"Nothing."

Her brow pinched for a moment before her eyes traveled to his sweat-soaked shirt, then back to his face. A half smile tugged at the corner of her mouth. "Tired already? You've become rather decrepit in your old age."

The teasing tone to her voice had equal effect, surprising him and intriguing him at the same time. Violet was always so dedicated to her work and the plans she had for each day. He had yet to see her loosen up a little and speak in a way that was more familiar. She had held him at arm's length ever since he had known her. It wasn't until the last week or so, since he was now willing and able, that she had finally given him tasks to do. He had practically begged her to allow him to help, delighted to be able to lighten her workload. If there was one thing that he had noticed over the weeks that he had been living in her home, it was that she carried much upon shoulders that were still so young, but somehow experienced and capable.

"Here now, as an invalid, I believe I have a bit of a right to be a bit derelict when it comes to such heavy labor."

She shook her head as she stretched one more time and turned back to her row, raising her scythe. "Laying in bed so long must have made you soft. No one should be as soft as you are. Especially not—" Her words cut off at the same moment that her back stiffened. He could sense her tension and waited for her to finish her sentence, but she bent again, swinging her scythe expertly in a chopping motion in front of her as the grass fell in lovely layers upon itself.

A lump was in his throat. He ached to know what she had been about to say. She still hadn't said anything about his identity, and while part of him was filled with an unutterable desire to know what she held back, the other part of him respected and trusted her too much to pry. She had never lied to him, and her blunt honesty had often been more of a comfort than a pain. When one's brain was so empty, having someone to share the facts and build up the caverns of reality within his mind was not only beneficial, but necessary. And he was grateful.

Bending forward, the muscles in his back screaming, he swung the scythe to and fro while his brain worked double time to put his suspicion to rest. Perhaps she didn't know anything. Perhaps she just assumed he had been a farmhand or an apprentice like any of the other men around here. It was odd for a man of his age to be so inexperienced in the way of the farming tools she had been trying ever so patiently to teach him.

But he was terrible at everything. He tried not to be discouraged and wondered if his attempts to help were more of a hindrance than a blessing, but he couldn't give up. He needed to take his place in society. It was the most troubling and infuriating feeling in the world to have nothing to do, nothing to call his own, and to watch two people slave away, day in and day out for the crumbs that they could afford at their table and which they so generously shared with a total stranger.

He had to remind himself often that he was a stranger. At times, he almost felt it easy to believe the lie they had conceived of him being a distant cousin. Granny especially treated him with such kindness that he often wished he were one of the family. But no. He must stay firmly rooted in reality. That was all that was left to him now.

Besides, a cousin stood no chance of winning Violet Frell's heart…or hand.

He knew he had nothing to offer, but he hoped it would not remain that way. It couldn't be forever that he would live in oblivion of who he was. A man had to discover his purpose in life sooner rather than later. And while his journey might be a bit harder than most, and he had been set back by the unfortunate accident that had wiped his memory, he would work twice as hard to achieve a place in this world. Without that, he had nothing to offer her. And nothing was not something any man should bring to the table.

Violet's back ached terribly from wielding the heavy scythe, and though her ribs were better, they still felt tender from the attack from the kingsmen. She felt her breath hitch at a stitch in her side, and she dropped the scythe, leaning backward, resting her fists on her hips to stretch out the painfully tight muscles.

The sun shone bright, and she squinted against it as she turned around. Sweat soaked Obed's once white shirt that hung limply from his shoulders. His eyes were narrowed in concentration at the row of long grass in front of him. As if sheer determination alone would make up for his lack of experience or skill. She stifled a small grin. He really was helpless; he didn't have the faintest idea what he was doing. She would wager that he had never done this work before a day in his life, which begged the question: what exactly had he done?

Letting her strained and sore legs release, she sat hard in the freshly cut grass, soon to be hay, dust and chaff rising into the air around her and filtering the sun with its cloudy haze. Flopping down on her back, she threw a hand over her eyes to protect them from the blinding midday light. She needed a moment to rest...and think.

Every task she had given Obed in a hope that something would jog his memory and give him a glimpse of his past had been to no avail. Not one memory had surfaced; no familiarity of muscle or movement returned. But she heard his moans in the middle of the night, the strangling gasps, as if his memory, lost to him in life, somehow came back to haunt his sleep, like a vicious ghost clinging to a life it could no longer have. She half wondered if she dared put a sword in his hand, but the thought chilled her, even in the blinding heat. She had taken great care to keep any weapon from his grasp. She couldn't risk it.

"Are you all right?"

Violet started and tried to sit up, failing and bringing a hand to her heart to still it's exploding rhythm.

Obed stood over her, his head, cocked to the side, blocking the blazing sun. A remorseful look crossed his face, and he twisted the straw hat Granny had made for him between his fingers. "Sorry, I didn't mean to startle you."

Taking a deep breath, she shook her head in reassurance but still scanned the area, as if a kingsman might be lurking, ready to pounce at any second. "It's no matter." She flopped back down again, patting the rough ground beside her with an open hand. "Sit a spell. We've earned it today, I'll wager."

The smell of the sweet grass and the tickle of the chaff hitting her nose filled her with memories. She had done this every year as a child with her father. He had made her first scythe himself, teaching her to wield the small child's tool, less than half the size of his own. She sensed Obed collapse onto the ground beside her and drew another deep breath. Without opening her eyes, she knew that she could touch him just by moving her hand an inch. She stiffened. Why did the idea of brushing hands with him suddenly make her uncomfortable? She lay there, stiff, trying not to think about it and simultaneously feeling it swallow her conscience without her permission.

Then his hand did brush hers, and she felt the hair on the back of her neck stand up. She shivered, even in the heat, covered in sweat as she was, and sat up so fast, Obed himself jumped.

"Enough rest for me. Back to work." Her voice broke, and she stood swiftly, grabbing her scythe and stomping back to her row, swinging with all of her might, completely ignoring the look of confusion Obed sent her way.

"Violet!" The new voice, deeper and throaty, calling to her caused her to tighten her grip on the scythe and wheel fast, her skirt flying with the movement, its hem whipping against her legs. Relieved, she lowered the scythe and drew a breath. It was Everard. Beside him, like some gift from heaven above, majestically strode the black stallion that she had sheltered in her barn before the kingsmen had taken him. His mane and tail flowed in the breeze, burrs and grass matting them down and a fine layer of dust coating his hide. His height was a better match for a man like Everard, who towered beside him.

She dropped her farm tool and rushed to the horse's side. She petted both sides of his face, looking deep into his dark, soft eyes. He did nothing but flare his nostrils, his quiet demeanor and peaceful calm soothing her soul. Animals were highly sensitive, and when they were at peace, it took all of the panic from her soul and settled her into the same rhythm. If he had nothing to fear, neither did she.

Leaning her face against his, she drew in a breath, feeling tears burn in her eyes, though for what reason she didn't know. It was just a horse, and not even hers at that, but somehow, it felt like a benevolent gift from above. When people who supported her were scarce, it was the animals that comforted her, soothed her, and joined in her prayers as she mucked out the stalls.

"What? But how?" She turned to Everard. She knew she wouldn't get much of a story from his quiet, stalwart personality, but she needed to try.

"Found him standing in the forest next to your property line."

She shook her head. The horse certainly looked as if he had walked the thirty miles from the garrison, and no mistake. "You poor dear."

"Keep him hidden, Miss Frell." The solemn warning in Everard's voice, scratchy and deep from its seldom being used, had a warning note than she dared try to interpret. She looked into his eyes. Something was wrong. She couldn't tell what it was, but she could discern the storm behind his gaze.

Obed was now standing next to her, his hands running over the horse, pulling burs from his mane.

"Everard...what is it?" she asked.

He didn't respond at first, and she could sense his hesitancy, almost feel him start to pull away.

Grasping his massive, work-rough hand, she tugged. "Something *is* wrong. What is it?"

His Adam's apple bobbed in his muscular neck.

Dread filled her spirit.

"It's the prince. He's been declared dead."

The Regent's reign would be prolonged. Horror filled her soul. What hope was there for them now?

# Twelve

## AWAKENING THE DRAGON

VIOLET STRAPPED THE large basket onto her back while Obed did the same with his. He hunched his shoulders to right the basket's position and raise it higher to a more comfortable place. It was full of the early produce that her garden had given them. Leafy greens, which were thankfully on the lighter side, but wheels of cheese from their cow and sheep rested beneath them. She would get a fair trade for the cheeses and the butter that Granny had churned and shaped with the hand carved molds her father had made in the shape of forest leaves

Granny bustled out of the house, two small bundles in her hands. "Here, dearling. Don't forget your dinner. You'll be tired and hungry before you are done at the market. Will you tell Fendrel that I send my greetings and tell him to send us more of those herbs? We are almost out."

Violet nodded, taking the bundle that was handed to her and

119

stuffing it into the pocket through the slit in the skirt of her dress. Obed stooped to let Granny tuck his into the top of his basket. Violet watched the two of them together. For a kingsman, she was surprised at how gentle he was with the old woman. The two had spent more time together, getting to know each other, than she and Obed. She was often busy out of doors, tilling the garden, working with the animals, and when she finally came inside, she was too exhausted to function. His recovery had been long, and he had been alone with Granny in the cabin for many weeks, first lying in bed, then helping her with little tasks about the house here and there, mending garments as he mended his body. The work had been petty, small for a man like him, tasks that most grown men would disdain to touch, but he did it with a willing heart, anxious to show his gratitude, though he was clumsy at the work.

The only explanation for the man's good heart, his kindness toward Granny, and his willingness to help with the work was that he had no memory of his previous life. Though she felt guilty for the gratitude she felt for his lack of returned memories, she still prayed every night that they would never return.

Living life as though waiting any moment for a slumbering dragon to be awakened was one of the most terrifying and frightening things she had ever lived through. Day by day, her worry lessened, and every week that passed with no improvement in his mental faculties eased the constant tension in her muscles.

She felt the frown deepen on her face. His nightmares were troubling. She could hear him tossing and turning every night, moaning at something he saw in his dreams.

Their walk into town was not as long as she had thought it would be, though it was silent. Obed wasn't one to run at the mouth with too many words; nevertheless, she was grateful for the companionship. Traveling the roads alone was a temptation for evil, as her father had always said. And in those days, things had been a little easier with less unrest as there was now, if that were to be believed.

Though silence often suited her, the question growing in her mind made her uncomfortable with it. She so desperately wanted to voice it but didn't know how.

"Obed." Her voice broke, stuttering on his name. This was not starting off well.

He turned to her for a moment, his amber eyes quizzical.

"I hear you at night. You seem to be dreaming. Do you...remember?"

His eyes grew stormy now, his face clouding with confusion. Shaking his head, he turned his attention back to the road. She could see his jaw clench and the muscles in his neck tighten. "Nothing."

She turned back to the road as well, biting her lip. She felt bad for the rush of relief that coursed through her veins, but what else was she to feel? Should she wish that the memory of a killer would return? She swallowed back the fear. It was best not to live with that. Hearing him sigh, she looked back over at his face. It had grown darker in just those few seconds.

"I don't know what to do. I just get pictures, strange happenings. I see them as if they are someone else's life, even though I am the one within the dream. I don't know if they are memories of my past life or if they are random imaginings. I can't say that I hope for either. Neither of the options makes any sense. I think it would be better that I didn't dream at all."

She lengthened her strides to catch up with his unconscious intensity of pace. She didn't know what to say in response, so she said nothing, hoping that her companionship would be sufficient. *I pray you don't remember.* It was the only thing she could think to pray. While it was the truth, it was a terrible truth she would keep to herself.

Entering town this time felt even worse than last time. There was a heaviness to the air. A subdued panic, as if the people within its walls were holding down fear so heavily, it could explode at any second. It choked her throat, and she felt the anxiety creeping up at her back, ready to pounce. She swallowed hard, her stomach tossing and turning like a leaf blowing on a tempest's wind.

"Let's trade these goods in the market as quickly as possible. I don't like the feeling here. Something isn't right."

She hurried through the gathering of people to get to the market, Obed following close behind her quick footsteps. It would be busy by now, the sun high in the sky, nearing mid-day. She hoped they could sell their wares and leave the village before any kingsmen showed up this time. She winced at the remembrance of her last encounter in the village. She didn't need to tempt fate, nor did she relish the thought of feeling any sort of pain.

Specifically of meeting the kingsman who had threatened to return to her homestead. He would surely recognize Obed and herself. His words had not sounded like an empty threat, and now with the prince dead, who was to say what their actions would be? If they felt the nauseating fear that pervaded the village and acted upon it, their actions might just be devastating. And she didn't want to be on the receiving end of them.

Swallowing hard at the memory of the captain's threat, she clutched the straps of her basket close. She didn't think for one second that she would be safe from his clutches should he choose to live out his base thoughts and words.

"Peter." Violet greeted the merchant as she approached. "I have cheese today." He turned toward her as they approached. She almost stopped walking. His face had a suppressed look of terror. "What is it?" she asked under her breath as she came up to him, glancing around as if she could ascertain the reason for his fear and simultaneously motioning for Obed to remove his basket from his back.

Peter looked between her and Obed, searching their faces, shifting back and forth in an effort to establish trust. He shook his head and ducked down to dig through the basket Obed had set down in front of him. He rose with a few wheels of cheese in his arms, their yellow-colored rinds protecting them from the dust of the day.

Violet grasped Peter's arm with her slender fingers, staying his movement and forcing him to look her in the face. She dropped her voice low, barely above a whisper. "Everard said the prince was dead."

He nodded, as if hoping that all she needed was a confirmation.

She didn't let go and squeezed harder. "Peter, you know we get no news in the country. What's going on? Why is everyone walking on eggshells?"

He shook his head, then looked both ways up and down the

bazaar's pathway. It was a busy, bustling event, the noise and chaos having a more urgent feel than normal. Peter suddenly grasped her by the arm and jerked her behind the booth and between two of the shops that lined the street. He pulled her along until they were hidden in the shadows. The panicked look in his eyes when he turned to her nearly pinned her against the mud walls, his breath heavy and near her face in the small, crushed alley.

"You heard the prince died. His successor for the time is the Regent Enguerrand. He will continue to rule as chancellor."

She drew a breath. That name alone carried a darkness and deadly implication that made her heart stop. Enguerrand was said to be the most ruthless, ill-willed, and power-hungry of the prince's advisors. He commanded the Kingsmen and had been the one to issue orders again and again that had affected the lives of the kingdom in countless, devastating ways over the last year or so. Before the king's death seven years prior, Enguerrand had been behind a move that had threatened to crumble the border towns of their neighboring country Pavlin. His heavy taxation attempt and the added military presence and alliance with Rusalka, which he had personally funded, had been the start of every political mess and signaled the end of a freedom-focused rule. With Enguerrand's rise to power, the Kingsmen would have full sway over the country. Their lawless, violent acts would be free to run unchecked, and who knew what this development would mean for the future of the kingdom. Many citizens secretly hated and opposed Enguerrand, but none stood up to the power of the government's far-reaching fingers. None that lived to tell the tale, that is.

"He issued a statement that an heir to the throne would be debated on should any deserving family member be found, but we all know those words mean nothing from a man like Enguerrand. His words are but lip service to buy him time to win the allegiance of the other lords and rulers. He will not let anything get between him and the throne if he can help it." Peter shook his head ruefully. "His hands were already at the helm ere the king died, sorely troubled in body as he was, and now there is nothing to stand in the way of his evil plans. The prince had been our only hope, as he was to come of age this year and assume the throne. While little was known of him aside from his wild and self-centered life, at least he was King Indulf's flesh and blood. Indulf was the last ruler to reign with a strong hand for the freedom of Elira. The people now worry if our country will survive the year."

Violet felt the weight of the news press on her chest, and she lifted a trembling hand to it, staring past Peter's shoulder as she assimilated the information. The prince, the last tie to the kindly and wise Indulf line was dead...and that announcement left political terror in its wake.

But Peter did not wait for any acquiescence before he continued. Much as though a river, once dammed, could not help but to spill over until all of the reservoir had been emptied. And Violet had little will and strength to make him stop. "There has already been talk of war with Rusalka, but now they raid us via Pavlin and their own borders, yet the Kingsmen have put up no fight. It is said Enguerrand, and the royal counsel, covets the mountain pass to the east. We have always been at peace with Rusalka, keeping their lawless ways at bay outside of our borders, but now..." Peter stumbled over his words and rubbed his upper arms as if he were cold.

"Now, who is to know if Enguerrand will quench Rusalka's bloodthirsty goals or allow the Kingsmen to run wild."

Peter nodded. "Everyone is in an uproar. They are buying what they can afford, hoping to stock up on anything they might need should all hell break loose. You'd best do the same. Better safe than sorry."

Violet nodded, a headache forming at the front of her temples. *Lord, help me focus on what I need to do.*

"But, Violet." Peter gripped her arm as she started to turn away. "They just took Wilhelm."

She froze at the mention of one of the regular merchants and dwellers of Padsley. "What?"

His eyes were strange, wide, and his right one twitched, his fingers biting into her arm with more force than she was sure he meant to inflict. "He didn't have sufficient funds to pay the taxes, and they sent him to the mines."

*The mines.* Few returned from there. Whether it be from ill health or who knew what other treatment...those that were sent to the mines as corporate punishment were seldom heard from again.

She swallowed the bitter taste at the back of her throat. A silent look passed between her and Peter. Wilhelm's poor family. She would pray for them and get Granny to make them a meal. They might as well have been widowed and orphaned.

Obed's ears burned with the wealth of information he had just obtained from overhearing Violet's conversation with Peter. Her intense fear of the Kingsmen—truly, every one's fear—had started to affect his own mind. He was in the same boat as they were, and he had accepted Violet's way of life as if it had always been his. Perhaps it had.

He knew nothing of the names the two spoke of, but he could sense by their tone and body language as well as their words that the new person in charge of the country was a poor choice. At least, as far as the people were concerned. Nobility and the soldiers would do just fine with him, no doubt.

Violet strode out of the alley and grabbed his arm. There was an intensity to her grip as her long fingers encircled his forearm, their tips biting into his skin in a way that sent shivers of trepidation up his back. "We need to get as many necessities as we can. There's no telling what could happen. Worst case, we are stocked up for longer than we need, but I would rather be safe. Take the money that Peter gives us and go to the butchers. Get three times the smoked meat that I brought home last time. I need to run around to look in on Fendrel. Granny needs more of her herbs."

He merely nodded in response. Once Peter had paid them for the quantity of cheese that he had purchased, Violet pointed Obed down the street to the butcher's shop and took off in the other direction. He watched Violet's light brown hair sashay against her waist, the tail of her braid mixing with her apron strings, her near-empty basket swinging from one shoulder. Her form disappeared in the crowd with a swiftness that set his teeth on edge. He was on his own.

The loneliness felt strange. He realized that since the

moment he had come to, laying in bed at the Frell house, bandaged, bruised and broken, he had not spent one moment alone without either Violet or her grandmother at his side, teaching him, ministering to him, or guiding him along the way. The independence felt natural, as if he should be used to it, but he missed the calming comfort of their presence nonetheless.

He took a deep breath. He could do this on his own. The fear that threatened him was ridiculous.

Hiking up his empty basket, he took off down the cobblestone street toward the butcher. The bazaar was crowded, and he had to be careful, weaving in and around the mass of people. Their frantic, hurried steps reminded him of rabbits as they skittered from one side of the road to the other, their business scattered about the market. There was no air of relaxation or neighborly fun. There was a hush, but a buzz at the same time. Not one person was smiling, and their eyes hid shadows of fear, dulling the light that should have been in them on this delightfully warm early summer day. The sun was shining, the birds singing, but their songs seemed out of place here, the joy of it clashing with the busy and focused intent of every single person at the market.

Everard hadn't said much when he had brought back the horse, but he had sensed it in him as well, the same feeling of fear and concern. Everard was massive, larger in person than he had expected. Violet's description had not done the man justice, though Obed doubted that any description could ever really do so. Obed was taller than Violet by at least a head, but the top of his own head barely came to the middle of Everard's massive chest. If the giant of a man with hands the size of

128

shovels was worried about the current political climate...Obed didn't know what else to think than that there was definitely something to worry about indeed.

His throat scratched as it tightened, his hands starting to burn at the remembrance of the visit from the kingsmen at the cabin. He could still see the leer in the captain's face as he had towered over Violet, prone on the ground, her expression a helpless mix of sadness and terror. But it had been the anger and the fire that flashed in her eyes that had astounded him. To be in the dirt, helpless against the forces of evil, and still carry a torch within you...that was a capacity for courage which he desperately wished for. What was it that could have a person on the brink of the most terrible moment of their life, but they still stood, unwavering in the face of such evil?

He imagined that was what every citizen felt in their hearts. The panic of oppression. Not knowing what on earth to expect to protect yourself and your family from, and the fear of losing it all.

This anger roiling inside of him felt ready to boil over. Seeing people in this much fear, panic, and anguish, all because of one selfish ruler, made him want to hurl the basket on his back across the market and then kick it for good measure. It was sudden, the realization that this wasn't right. That what was actually going on behind the scenes was ugly, vile, and should not be occurring. He hadn't felt so driven by purpose and desire for as long as he could remember. Which, granted, wasn't very long.

It was the most uncomfortable feeling to have the knowledge, the muscle memory, the reactions ingrained into him, but to have absolutely no idea why or what from. He

129

didn't know where all of these ideas or thoughts, even the emotions, came from. But here he was, experiencing things he had no basis for in real life. It had been long enough that he was starting to realize what his scope was for handling these things, but it was still new, challenging and confusing, every time something came up. Now was one of those times.

All because of a ruthless monster.

When he arrived at the butcher's, he put in Violet's order.

The poor man was sweating, his round face and bald head red with exertion. He shook his head and used his apron to dab the sweat away from his eyes. "I don't think I'll be able to do that. You will have to tell Violet that everyone is buying more than I have stock for. I can give you twice, but not three times, your monthly order. That's the best I can do or I will be completely divest of stock by the end of the day."

Obed nodded, raising a hand to brush back a lock of hair that had fallen from the tail tied at the back of his head. His hair had grown over the last few months, and this in-between stage was irritating. It was barely long enough to tie back, and it sometimes slipped free. Compassion rose in his heart for the man. "That's fine. I will let her know. Let me help load it so you can focus on other things. Here is the pay." Obed handed the man the silver coins Violet had given him and swung the basket from his shoulders to fill it with the meat that the butcher threw over the counter to him.

The wooden walls of the shop were darkened by the smoke used to cure the meat. The chimney worked just fine, but with the amount of volume the shop produced, there was a thick haze in the room that touched his nose with the smell of spices, smoke, and a sweet, woody scent.

Once his basket was full, he swung it onto his shoulders, grunting under the weight of it. He had grown weak after the weeks on bedrest, and his muscles complained at the intense use he had been putting them through of late.

Stepping out onto the street, he was walking toward Fendrel's house as Violet had directed when a commotion at the end of the street drew his attention. The chaos grew louder, and it arrested his steps, forcing him against his will to follow the shouting. He could hear a child crying, and the sound rent his heart. His head grew so hot he thought it might explode. That sound sent chills down his spine and quickened his steps.

He drew near the gathering crowd that shrunk away from him as he pressed through, parting the way and giving him a clear view. A kingsman stood next to his mounted fellows. He held a mess of fur covered in what looked like blood in one hand, and a little tow-headed boy by the scruff of the neck in the other.

The child whimpered, his disheveled hair falling in front of his sharp blue eyes that were not only brimming with tears but crackling with terror. His shirt was mussed and had a rent at the shoulder seam, his little trousers frayed at the edges, and his feet bare.

The kingsman laughed and thrust the ball of fur into the child's face. "Want to turn out like your pet?" He sneered, his leather helmet hiding most of his face, but Obed didn't need to see it to sense the utter disregard for human emotions that emanated from the kingsman.

The little boy cringed, whimpering and curling away from the bundle of fur, which Obed now realized was a dead, orange-striped kitten, blood caked to its fur.

Fire shook him to his bones, and Obed lunged forward without a second thought. He grabbed the kingsman's arm, shook it loose from the child's neck, and swept the little boy behind him for protection. He could feel the rage emanating from himself like heat from a furnace, and there was red around his blurry image of the kingsman. A sword to the back of his knees sent him to the ground.

# Thirteen

MERCY

VIOLET SENSED THE panic before she saw anything.

A tumult shivered along the ground and wound its way up her ankle. And she knew instantly. Something was wrong.

"I have to go find Obed." She shook Marcus's hand from her arm when he tried to stay her quickness. "You don't understand. Something's wrong." She was suddenly frantic, the feeling in her stomach all too familiar. She didn't know why she felt the way she did, but she needed to listen to the promptings, regardless of their meaning.

His gaze held hers. "How do you know?"

"I just do. Let me go. I need to find him."

"Your cousin?" Marcus's face fell a bit at her reaction, and there was a disappointment in his eyes that she didn't have time to decipher.

The pressure gathered around her neck and shoulders, compelling her to move quickly. Gasping for breath as her feet took to the cobbles outside, her hands mechanically stuffed the medicine she had retrieved from Fendrel into the leather bag slung from one shoulder and thumping against her opposite hip.

She couldn't shake the realization that she had felt this feeling once before...and the outcome had been devastating.

She started to hear the murmurs of the crowd and the raised voices at the end of the square. Her steps quickened even more, if at all possible, and she dashed toward the commotion, slowing only when she reached the outskirts of the crowd, pushing her way through, desperate to find out what was at the center, yet afraid of what she might find there. Of what she *knew* she would probably find there if her premonition was correct.

And to her dismay, it was.

"How much power do you truly feel lording your great strength and prowess over a tiny child, too small to fight back?" The words and tone didn't match the calm, broken farmer she had grown to know. They were sharp daggers, thrust into the gut of the vile kingsman with the precision of a hunter, flaying his quarry without qualm or hesitation.

The stunned silence that met Obed's accusation confused and terrified Violet. She needed to get him out of there. Before he died for his cause.

"How dare you." The kingsman spat, his comrades for some reason entertained and therefore ready to let him fight his own battle with the peasant.

"How dare I? How dare you use your position to torture a child for doing nothing, while you have everything that could be desired. I daresay the prince would be sorely disappointed in you." The authority that rippled from Obed was not only a contradiction of his usual confused and hesitant character, but also a threat to their entire way of life. She had to make him stop antagonizing the kingsman. This would not end well.

Bitterness scratched at her throat, and her limbs trembled, but she drew a deep breath before she made a move. *Lord, help me extract him from this situation...without casualties.*

Obed took a shudderingly deep breath to quell the fire in his veins, to no avail. The heat coursing through him was almost painful, and entirely out of control. He felt as though someone else had inhabited his body, someone that somehow felt familiar, but entirely antithesis to his current life. He had no idea what to make of it, but his head suddenly hurt.

"That's enough out of you, cur," growled the kingsman, and the blow Obed had been expecting long before now descended on his shoulders as he ducked his head out of the way just in time.

He might have counted the consequences before he placed himself in a position that would put his head at risk again for injury. The quivering child at his side caught his attention, and that thought disappeared for good. Protecting this innocent mite was worth the whole of the punishment which he did not doubt would descend upon him any second now.

"Sir! Please, if I may beg you mercy, he is quite ill and does not know what he says. He has fits and doesn't remember who he is. You can ask of the local medicinal, Fendrel. He has been treating him for some time for an injury to the head."

Violet's voice. What the devil was she doing here, and why was her hand suddenly on his shoulder?

He willed her away with his glare. He had gotten himself into this mess; the least he could do was get himself out or take the consequences. She had risked enough taking care of him. This woman who was brave enough to stare down a kingsman on his behalf. Who had taken a beating from them herself, yet still stood alongside him to defend the weak and lowly. The flame in him was suddenly kindled in a new way. And it wasn't anger.

She was whispering, and it didn't seem to be in English, but it was so quiet, he couldn't be sure. The words were fast, nearly silent, and breathless. He could feel the tremor of her hand that rested on his shoulder, the heat of it searing him through his shirt.

A sudden shift in the kingsmen confused him, but a roll of thunder in the distance pulled his gaze to the sky, and he noticed the gathering clouds and darkness rolling in from the north.

"Let it go, Gale. Don't bother with the peasant. We can always punish him later. You know we haven't met our quota of coin. And I don't want to get stuck in the wet of that storm."

The kingsman named Gale huffed. Shook out his leather armor, letting it settle more comfortably. He gave one quick nod, clearly reluctant to let it go. But the other two kingsmen were already turning their horses' heads and kicking them into a trot.

Before Obed could react, Gale grabbed a handful of his hair, pulling hard, the pain ripping across his scalp.

Gale's face turned ugly with hatred as he drew near, his hot

136

breath smothering Obed. "Don't think for one second that I'll forget you, forget this." His words hissed even quieter, deadly, poison lacing their every syllable. "You'll pay." With that parting word, he thrust Obed's head from him, leaving Obed to stumble back into Violet's legs, she in turn barely keeping her feet.

He watched, stunned, as Gale climbed upon his mount and galloped off to catch up with his fellow soldiers. The entire crowd let out a collective sigh, as if they had all been waiting with bated breath to see how it would end. Obed stood, still confused as to the outcome, and turned in time to catch Violet before her knees buckled.

With one hand, he held onto her elbow, and the other wrapped around her waist. She was pale, her green eyes glassy and welling with tears like a forest in the rain. She was close, her body fitting perfectly in his arm. Reflexively, he tightened his grip.

Violet felt Obed's grip tighten around her waist. How could one feel comfortable and uncomfortable all at the same time? One feeling followed close after the other. With a hand she loosened his grip, stepping out of his protection, her knees still weak but steady enough to hold her weight. Sudden anger boiled up within her. How dare he? The danger he had placed himself into—yea, the entire village—was not to be taken lightly. "We need to leave." She retrieved his basket that had fallen by the wayside and thrust it at him, a little too hard, feeling her anger abate just a bit at the satisfaction of seeing the confusion on his face. But then it steeled up even harder.

He could have died.

Swiftly, she returned the little boy, who looked up with worshipful, puppy dog eyes at Obed, to his mother, gathered her own things, and straightened her skirts before starting for the edge of the village and home.

Obed followed, brow still puckered.

If he didn't know what he had done wrong at this point, there was no help for him. She might as well throw him to the wolves now, or she and Granny might pay the price. All she wanted was to live her life in quiet peace. Tending her farm was hard work, but it was work worth doing and something that she took pride in. If this peasant thought he could show up at her house, be taken care of with the utmost sympathy, and then parade around in town as if he owned the world, antagonizing the kingsmen and bringing the wrath of the ruler upon their heads...then he could take his chivalry, reform, and good looks somewhere else.

Her steps faltered. Did she just think *good looks*? She cast a sidelong glance at Obed, who was almost trotting to keep up with her angry, torrid stride. He was studying her as best he could while avoiding potholes in the dirt road, and she looked away quickly. She was too mad to even think about responding to those looks and pleas for explanation.

"What's wrong?"

What's wrong, he wondered? *How dare he...* The anger was suddenly filtered through sadness, and she felt tears well up and start choking her throat. "You really have no idea, do you?" She scoffed, her words coming out squeaky as if they didn't know how to behave themselves.

138

"Idea about what?"

She spun, the hem of her skirt whipping around her ankles in her aggression. "You nearly got us killed!" Her voice broke on the last syllable, and she trembled in every limb. Her vision blurred around the edges, and she suddenly felt as though she couldn't take a breath. All she could see in her mind was the image of her father, being dragged away behind the kingsmen's horses. His eyes desperate for her to keep still and not say a word lest she be taken next. She saw him fall, his face getting buried in the dirt, his hands tied behind his back, keeping him from catching himself. She saw the bruises, and in a flash, she saw his body hanging, limp.

A touch on her shoulder jerked a cry from her lips, and she blinked away the memory, flinching and pulling away from the hand, suddenly brought to reality and feeling her face drenched with tears.

Obed's face was full of concern, questioning.

She shook her head, stepping back. She didn't want to be near him, didn't want him to see her pain. He didn't deserve to know her like that. She dashed a hand over her face, trying to remove the traces of the tears. "You can't blaspheme the ruler. Men have been killed for less." She turned hard and strode toward home, her feet taking longer steps, her chest heaving. The pain and weight there made her feel heavy, unable to drag in enough oxygen. Her vision blacked around the edges and next thing she knew, she was on her knees, gasping for breath, a hand at her chest, trying to pull the collar of her shirt loose to let in some fresh air. Why couldn't she breathe?

Obed's hand touched her shoulder again, and she

involuntarily jerked away. He had set his basket down, and he crouched in front of her, now holding out his hands, palms forward in a pacifying gesture to give her the room that she needed. "Hey, take a deep breath. Look at me. Breathe. In and out."

She followed along with his coaching, desperate enough to follow his directions despite the fact that she felt like clobbering him if she only had the strength. She hadn't had an attack like this in over a year. The events of the day struck too close to home…to close to reality, for her to walk away completely unscathed.

She broke away from Obed's gaze, gripping her head in her hands and focusing on her breathing. She knew what to do. Granny had been far too ill to actually help her granddaughter fight off this new enemy since the death of her son. Violet had been forced to cope on her own. After fainting several times in the fields, she had learned that she needed to master her own attention and force the breaths until she was able to clear her vision. She didn't need Obed, but for some reason, as mad as she was, his company was exactly what she desperately wanted.

Once her breathing was under control, she looked back up at him, hoping that with the earnestness of her gaze, the import of her words would strike home. His brown eyes studied her, their depths more vibrant and alive than she had ever seen them. He had taken a long journey to get to the level of health that he now carried, and while she was glad to see it, with it brought new dangers. Today had only been a taste of what could be their punishment for the lengths she had gone to in order to protect him.

"You need to understand. One does not have any interaction with a kingsman that ends well. Many of us have suffered tremendously at their hands. I know you meant well, and I don't know that it wasn't the right thing to do...but who's to say that they wouldn't have let the little boy go after a few more minutes? Sometimes you have to let lie."

Disappointment flashed across his face. "You don't mean that."

"I mean it more than you might realize. They wreak nothing but havoc; the better choice is always to let them be and pray that the consequences don't bring harm to anyone."

He stood and shook his head, taking a step back. "I wouldn't have thought it of you."

"I beg your pardon?" She stood too, her legs still shaky, but able to stand on her own.

"You of all people. I would have thought you would have been the one willing to stand, no matter the cost. I don't think you really know what you are saying."

She stared at him blankly, genuinely shocked that he had not only spoken so frankly but also effectively thrown her under the turnip cart. But no. He couldn't understand. He wouldn't. He had no knowledge of a world before his injury, and that world was a dark place, where girls' fathers were dragged away and hung for standing up for justice. Just like Obed had done. "You can't understand." She said it more dismissively than she had meant to.

The disappointed look on his face deepened. He shook his head. "I'd have thought better of you." He turned without another word and walked away, picking up his basket again and heading for home.

She stared after him, dumbfounded. While she tried to brush off the words as if they were of no account, they stuck with her, trapping her beneath the weight of their import. He truly didn't understand what he was saying. How could he?

But somehow his words dug a hole in her heart and made her feel ill. What had she become?

# Fourteen

## BORDERLAND

**VOICES PLAGUED HIM.**

He knew he must be sleeping, but perhaps not.

A lush garden with the heavy scent of roses, lily of the valley, and lilacs clashed together to make a sickeningly sweet smell that stuck in the back of his throat and made him choke on their sweetness. A woman lounged at his feet, her laugh loud, fetching, harsh. Another sat in his lap, playing with his hair, toying it around her fingers. Her large eyes, rimmed with black to make their depths appear larger, were close to his face, her breath hot against his cheek, tickling his eyelashes and filling him with pleasure. He felt the enjoyment of the moment but also felt repulsed. As if he were watching himself from a distance and inhabiting himself at the same time. Darkness within and without.

The marble and stone structures throughout the garden spoke of opulence, class, richness. He felt comfortable in

143

these settings. Familiar. As if they had once been his home.

The sultry woman on his lap leaned in for a kiss, which he indulged, deepening it, enclosing his arms around her. Seeking solace, a knowing...some sort of acknowledgement of his true self. To be loved.

Flashes of light brought to mind the stained-glass windows of a stately hall, an ornate rug spanning the distance, brightly-colored and woven, adding chaos to the room floating in a sea of fragmented color from the cut glass. His boots echoed off the walls of the hall, their tapestry hangings not enough to dampen their sound.

A man, still fuzzy to his eyes, sat in a chair at the end of the hall, others standing to his right and to his left. The eyes that watched him from all sides were full of...something. Distance, darkness, envy, and something else...something evil.

He felt dizzy and sick beneath the spell of the glittering lights. He strained to make out the man on the throne, for that was what it must be. Who was he? Even fuzzy, there was a vague familiarity to it, but then it was swallowed by the blackness.

Running. Heavy breathing. Horses' hooves and cracking branches. Searing pain and heat for days.

Obed gasped and sat up from his cot beneath the window in Violet's cabin. He was drenched in sweat, his shirt damp and suddenly cold against his burning skin, his eyes hot and watering.

He raised a hand to his temple where his head pounded, and phantom pain gripped his chest between its gnarly fingers. He clutched at the sheet and used it to dab away the sweat from his face. Gasping for a deep breath to fill his lungs, dispelling the unsettling feeling that crept like a snake in his belly, filling him with an uncomfortable and unknown feeling. He held his breath, praying he hadn't woken Violet or Granny, but he heard their soft breathing from across the room and let out the air he had been holding. He hadn't woken them. He had been told that while he was ill, he had often cried out in his sleep. But his awakening seemed to have been silent this time. Thankfully.

He lay back gingerly, hoping that the straw the tick mattress was made from didn't rustle too much while he settled. He couldn't bear to close his eyes. To experience something in a dream that felt so like reality, but have no memory in the mind to cling to, was an unsettling feeling. One he did not relish.

Morning dawned, and though her body went through the same revolutions she completed every day, Violet's mind was turned elsewhere. She didn't know what to make of Obed. She felt hurt, her heart heavy beneath the double burden that she had somehow done something wrong and also hurt Obed in the process. He seemed restless, his work more dedicated than usual, almost as if he were attacking the chores to separate his mind from his surroundings.

Obed had become a hard worker since taking on some chores around the farm, and while his hands had once been less than calloused, they showed the roughness of a farmer now and had grown supple and strong, used to wielding the farm implements that had been a part of her daily life since childhood. For the most part. There were moments where he was so awkward with a new tool that she wondered what on earth he had been prone to do as a young man. Perhaps he had only ever known a sword.

She shuddered. The sound of ringing steel was one she remembered from the training yards on the far side of the village and from which her father had always steered her clear from. The sound of metal slicing flesh sprung to her memories, sickening her.

Something about Obed made her wish they could live this quiet, tucked-away lifestyle forever. She felt a prickle of remorse in the back of her mind, and she swung the hoe extra hard into the dirt, nearly uprooting a tomato plant. Tossing the tool from her, she knelt to replace the roots and install a bit more dirt around their base to solidify their placement.

There was something in her that perhaps felt…just maybe, she had done wrong deceiving Obed and making him think he was different than he was. She had never been one to lie, but it surprised even her how naturally this omission of the truth had come to her. To hide behind a falsehood, the whole truth lost to the wind and burned from existence by her own actions. Falsehood was not something a Frell was known for. Her father had certainly never abided by such rules…but then, he had not lost his family to the monsters that ruled this country.

Drawing a breath, she stood again, dusting the dirt from her hands and using her apron to mop the sweat from her face. The hem in the front of her dress was gathered and tucked into the belt that wrapped around her waist, a pocket hanging from the other side. Her hair was braided and piled on top of her head in a crown to get it out of the way, but tendrils tickled her face and the back of her neck and she swiped at them with

146

irritation.

The niggle of doubt that bothered her mind made her want to swat at the thought like a fly. She felt the distance from Obed today harshly. Violet carried a world on her shoulders. Her world. The one within the four corners of this little farm plot. They were hers to manage and hers alone. Sharing the responsibilities with a strong character like Obed had been...refreshing. She felt the weight even heavier with this sudden distance from him. Her attempts at conversation had fallen flat. He had been distant, aloof...even, dare she say it, sullen.

She glanced at him again. His brow was so deeply furrowed, she worried it would stay that way. Darkness and pain etched in the lines across his forehead, his eyebrows shading his eyes, their depths swirling with a melted brown that made her heart ache to see and her knees soft. They were eyes that she knew could burn with fire, and they terrified her just as much as they drew her in.

He glanced up, and they locked eyes. Her heart stopped. Seconds froze, and she barely saw his Adam's apple rise and fall in her peripheral vision, for her eyes did not leave his until he blinked, set his shoulders, and turned away.

Her soul felt emptied.

Nary once did they speak throughout the day, and her heart ached by the end of it. She wished to hear his voice again, but it was not within her to break the silence. They walked the cow and sheep in, the stick in her hand rough against her skin, which was hot and sore from wielding the hoe and then a hammer that day. Her skirt was still tucked up into her waistband, her apron mussed and cockeyed on her waist. She had no strength to right herself. She was exhausted, physically and emotionally. She hadn't realized how much she had come to rely on the companionship of this young man.

And it scared her.

Their hands reached for the same milking bucket at the same time, and they brushed. She recoiled as if bitten by a snake, her face suddenly hot like fire. She turned away and grabbed the feed bucket without a word, her movements stiff and jerky.

This could not last. Violet was stalwart and strong in heart, but this was a new feeling for her, and it was not one she relished. Being pulled in so many different directions, between the truth and the shadows of lies and falsehood. Between relationship and loneliness, strength and weakness. She longed to show the soft side of herself, the inner most hidden secret…the one that wished to be held, nurtured, and carried. The part that couldn't hold it all together, that felt broken beneath the weight of the pain, the responsibility, the world pressing in against the four corners of her little plot of land.

The fear and panic of the current culture poured in from every side. She worked hard to keep her borders set, her heart firm and stern….every single wall up and reinforced. She had sensed the darkness for some time, creeping into her favorite place, the woods. It's murkiness, the green turning gray with each passing day, other's fear pressing against the land she called hers. She fought it back. Pushed hard against the darkness that sought to swallow her up, devour her land and take what little spirit she clung to. It had snatched her most prized possession once before, and it would not get so close

148

again.

Her hands worked vigorously, spilling the seed for the hens that clucked at her feet. She glanced at Obed. His back was to her, his movements mirroring her own as he pulled the milk from the udder, his back stiff and the muscles of his neck tight beneath the skin, pulling his shoulders up with their tension. Armed with a brush to clean the horse's coat, she felt the tension filling her own body, and she fought it, willing herself to relax her shoulders when the steed shuffled uncomfortably in the hay when her strokes grew faster and harder with the tension. She had worked hard to stay at peace, to create an atmosphere of her own choosing around her: this had become the only place where that was the case most of the time.

Her quiet happy place, the forest, had become a spot that reflected the fears that gripped her spirit. It was filled with shadows, the pain cowering behind every trunk, the moss creeping, suffocating the plants, sucking the life from them bit by bit. The leaves blocked out more sunlight day by day, and she no longer found solace within those shadows. Instead, it was a darkness, roiling, billowing around her, choking the life from her with every breath that she drew. The woods were no longer a safe space, but a place where her deepest fears felt more real than anywhere else. Where, if she turned fast enough, she might just catch them jumping from behind a tree to catch her with their claws.

Suddenly, a dark feeling shivering up her spine, she sensed the borders of her land were being threatened. Lifting the brush, the horse shifted his feet and tossed his head at her frightened movements. Straining her ears, she took a step toward the open barn door. She could feel Obed's eyes on her, even though every one of her senses strained toward the end of her property where a cloud of dust was now appearing in the gathering dusk. The blood left her head, and her knees threatened to give.

She turned. Words caught in her throat on their way out, and when they were released from the blockage, they came out of order and confused. "Kingsmen. Quick." Her mind drowned beneath the onslaught of thoughts, fears, panic, and direction that flooded through her.

"They're coming. Again."

# Fifteen

## A PROMISED RETURN

OBED LUNGED for the horse as Violet had directed, and he grasped the halter, pulling the black beast from his comfortable stall and propelling him with swift feet to Violet's side. Quicker than he thought possible, she drew him out of the barn and around back. He was startled when, before he knew what she was doing, her hand came down hard on the horse's flank, and the stallion jumped, throwing his head back to look at her with what seemed like reproach before he took flight into the nearby forest.

Heart thrumming in his ears, he felt his throat grow tight. The headache that always seemed to lie undercover descended and caused him to blink hard. Not now. The last thing he needed was a headache. He shook away the pain and followed Violet as she hurried to the front of the cabin. He knew her destination and determination. She needed to warn Granny. He feared for what the state of the woman's mind would be if

151

she was surprised by kingsmen.

Violet was grateful her skirt dress was tucked out of the way in the front. The hem was heavy with mud from working in the garden all day and hauling water from the lake up to the field to hydrate the plants. It hadn't rained in some time, and the foliage had desperately needed the water.

He saw the horsemen and knew instantly that her attempt at rushing to the house would be too late. Anger rose in his chest when the galloping kingsmen dashed up to the house, their horses stamping and snorting, their breath making little puffs of dust with the dirt that was trapped in their hair.

Violet pulled herself to a hard stop when the lead Kingsman reined in his large black horse directly in front of her, the hooves pawing the ground mere inches in front of her bare feet. She jerked back, her nose now close to the horse's withers. The gleam of the kingsman's filthy smile beneath the leather of his hood and the cowl that he wore made Obed's blood run hot. If Violet couldn't make it to the house, perhaps he could sneak by and warn Granny. He moved as if to do so.

"You there! Stop by order of the king."

Obed halted at the harshly barked order that had been issued from one of the kingsmen.

The leader just sat atop his horse, his eyes never leaving Violet. There was something strong and dark within his gaze. He had next to no expression, but Obed knew his intent was evil. He had yet to say anything, but somehow Obed could feel it.

"There is no king."

Obed choked at the soft sound of Violet's nearly imperceptible words. He barely heard them at his distance from her.

"Well played, wench," was the subtle rejoinder from the leader. "The current ruler will be proclaimed king within these three days. Semantics, really. We all know whoever rules the kingdom is, by rights, the king."

"So it is said."

What was she doing? Obed felt his breath come thick and hot. This was not the same Violet that had been terrified when he had spoken similarly to the kingsmen just yesterday. It was as if something else was inhabiting her body. Something brave, courageous, and perhaps a little foolish. Something like the person she was always reading about in that book of hers and Granny's. He sensed the fire in her soul. The woman who had endured much that she had yet to share with him, but bore it silently, until the fire could not be contained and burst forth, its flames slowly but surely rising against the dryness of the men who carried out the ruler's impervious commands.

The commander's hands jerked on the reins, and the horse stamped sideways, the whites of its eyes showing as its head came up, the reins gripped tighter than they ought to be. Obed cringed. The animal's mouth was red around the corners where the bit had been chafed. His nostrils flared, and he pulled against the bit as his head was pulled in and under in an uncomfortable position. Even the animals beneath the rule of this current reign seemed to wthither under the roughness and injustice of his reign. The man upon the animal's back did not react aside from the subtle twitch of his hands that tightened the reins still further.

"You had better accept his rule should you want to remain in control of your life." The words were spoken softly,

153

offhandedly, as if they weren't laced with a threat.

"What are you here for?" Violet's voice was still soft, her question not giving a bit of ground to the commander who seemed to be fighting a silent battle of control over the young woman. Her shoulders were taught; he could see it even from this distance. If anyone touched her, he thought she might fly like a toy wound tight on a spring.

The commander never broke eye contact with Violet. "We are here to collect the taxes for the year."

For the first time, Violet moved, her feet shifting underneath her, and her fingers tightening in fists at her side. "They aren't collected until the fall, once the crop has come in." Her words were tight, and she spoke as few as possible, as if the rein she held over her tongue was tighter than the commander's over his horse.

"The King has commanded that they be collected early this year." He broke eye contact for the first time to glance at Obed, his steely eyes giving one look from his head to his feet that made Obed feel undressed. As if the commander had analyzed every inch of his being and read everything that he needed to see there. Then his gaze flicked back to Violet. "This house was only listed as having two occupants; taxes will have increased now that there are three. You owe the kingdom one thousand, nine hundred ninety six bits."

Obed saw Violet tremble a little from behind. He couldn't seem to breathe, everything suspended in mid-air. He was a burden.

"He is merely a guest."

"Albeit one that has lived here for some months. You don't think I know of the goings on in this town?"

Violet shook perceptibly now.

"Nothing escapes my notice, and your 'guest' seems to have found himself quite comfortable here, Miss Frell. Perhaps a little too comfortable." The not-so-subtle meaning behind the commander's voice froze the blood in Obed's veins, and his heart leapt into his throat.

She was ready with a rejoinder. "Despite that fact, we will need time. I don't have the funds. Name whatever price you will, but we cannot pay until the harvest is in. It has always been this way, and I cannot make something exist that does not."

The words left her lips and hovered before her, as if the commander would not receive the explanation. They sat in the open air, hanging between them. Darkness pressed in on every side as the last rays of the sun cast a dusky, orange glow over the land, throwing menacing shadows upon the faces of those present.

The stand-off was palpable. Silence deafening as the commander drilled Violet with his eyes. His gaze broke when he deliberately scrutinized every inch of her with one long look from the top of her head to the bottom of her bare feet, his purpose obvious and intentional.

The man had not done or said a thing, and yet Obed felt anger rise hot in him. His muscles grew tight against the strain it took to stay still and resist the urge to pummel the man into the very dust that he had crawled out of. He realized that his fists were clenched, and the bitter taste at the back of his mouth hinted at trouble.

"There are other forms of payment we are willing to accept." His words didn't need to say what they so obviously meant, and Obed felt as though he were a firebrand that had suddenly been plunged into ice water. Violet didn't say anything, and turned away from him as she was, he had no idea what she must be thinking. He wanted to see her face, understand what thoughts were running through her mind. He desperately wanted to take this entire situation in hand and destroy each and every inch of the beast that sat atop his horse in the form of a mortal man.

Violet reached to her waist and snatched the hem of her skirt, frantically pulling it from her belt and tossing it to the ground to cover her leg that had been visible to the knee. In her haste she didn't see the vulture-like movement as the commander leant down from his perch and wound one of her soft curls around his index finger, the look in his eyes growing deeper as he did so.

Obed lunged forward, every control over his body lost in that moment as fire raged to his very bones. "Don't touch her."

"Restrain him."

Two men dismounted in a flash, and before his last step could bring him within reach of Violet and her taunter, he was grabbed from behind by two kingsmen. He fought like hell, straining with everything in him to protect the suddenly vulnerable woman in front of him. Her eyes were as big as plums, and her face paler than the death she would wish upon herself if the commander had his way with her.

He broke from their hold and fell when one of them threw a kick to the back of his leg, sending him crashing into the dirt upon his knees, his long hair flicking in front of his eyes and sticking to his sweaty face. A third man joined them, putting a knee against his back as the others twisted his arms behind him, popping one of his shoulders and pulling hard against the muscles that strained with everything in him to get away, to swoop in, to rescue Violet and bring down hell upon those who dared to treat her in this manner.

Violet jerked away, her eyes filling with tears. "Don't touch me." Her voice trembled this time, and the fear in her eyes was so palpable, it made even Obed choke up.

The commander dismounted slowly, somehow never taking his gaze from the woman in front of him. It was abundantly clear that he held her life in the balance and knew exactly which way to twist the verbal knife to exact the most pain. He ran a hand down her jaw and leaned in close now that he was standing in front of her, no horse between them, nothing to separate them. "You sure you won't share?" His finger paused on her chin and lifted her face to look directly into his, towering over her. His voice was a mere whisper, and his resemblance to a snake so uncanny, Obed thought he might have a forked tongue. "It might ease a lot of your—how shall we say?—hardships if you were to give me the most valuable thing you own. The taxes are worth little in comparison to what I ask. Just one time, and all your debts will be eliminated, the slate washed clean."

Obed wished death upon the man with everything that was in him. If a man he truly was and not some dastardly being from the dark world, a demon from the pit of burning fire.

Violet tried to step away, but the commander caught her chin forcefully between his fingers, the skin pressed tight beneath them as he gripped her. A whimper escaped her lips as she grasped his wrist in an attempt to release his grip which only caused him to strengthen it, lifting her slightly so she had to stand on her toes to remain in a position of the least pain.

The menace in his tone was deeper now, and anger flickered in his gaze. "You have one more chance."

Violet didn't even take one second before she was shaking her head in what little manner she could with it so tightly in his grasp.

Obed's world stopped, and he knew in that instant nothing he could do could stop this man from exacting whatever punishment he wanted upon Violet, Granny, himself, or any other human, beast, or item that he wanted to.

"God, please," escaped him in an imperceptible whisper, the lack of sound coming from his lips made up for by the despair and cry from his heart. He hadn't known if he believed in the God that Violet spoke of, prayed to, and worshiped, but if there was an all-seeing Being in the world, then now would be the perfect time for Him to show up.

"Let go of me." Violet's words were muffled, laced with pain, and strained against the constrictions of her throat. But they were unalterable and shattered the level of control the commander had over her at that moment.

A pause. Then the commander let her chin go with a shake of his hand that was but a flick of the wrist for him, but sent Violet to her hands and knees, trembling at his feet. "Fine. Have it your way. I may yet get what I seek. But for now, I'll let you live your fantasy of purity and uprightness. But mark my words, everyone will be brought to a point of begging. If not now, then in the future. I'm a man willing to wait for what I want. Hent! With me. We'll search the cabin for any valuables. The rest of you, stay with the horses and guard these peasants."

"No! Wait, my…" Violet clutched at the commander's dark cloak as he moved to stride away. But with one sound kick, as if she were a mongrel at his heels, she fell back to the dirt, her hair tumbling from atop her head, the braids partially unraveling and mixing with the dust of the path, a moan escaping her lips.

Obed trembled beneath the weight of the intense rage that coursed through his body, pulsating against his bonds and the men that held him back from what he knew to be the only thing on earth he wished that he could do: avenge the acts of terror that this man was exacting upon the woman that he…loved.

Time seemed to stand still as crashing came from within the house, and he heard Granny's cry and a heavy thud. Obed strained anew against the men holding him back. Holding him back from the terrors he knew existed within the cabin that had held such comfort for him and was now a room of chaos. More crashes and a bright glow ensued, growing in the window nearest to the kitchen fire. Obed thought he might vomit, his mind unable to comprehend what was happening within the cabin.

The commander and his kingsman cohort exited the building, the leader swinging the meager money pouch and his henchman carrying an armful of other valuables from within the house. While the kingsmen mounted their horses, aside from the two restraining Obed and the one who held Violet on her knees, restraining one arm behind her back, the commander swung the pouch in front of Violet's face. Her hair was falling over her eyes and blowing in the wind, sticking to the tears that chased their way down her dirt smeared face. Red marks from his hand were already evident upon her delicate, freckled skin. With his other hand, he reached and grabbed her throat, and she gasped for a breath, terror exuding from every pore of her body.

He grinned wickedly. "This won't cover what you owe, and since you refuse to give me the only thing that will absolve you from your debt, I'll give you one week. When that time is up, and the money is still not in my hands...I'll take what I want. With or without your permission, princess."

The poison of his words sunk into Obed's bones, willing him to break free from his captors and this hellish moment he was living.

The commander released Violet, sending her sprawling and gasping for breath, and mounted his horse, whistled through his teeth in a piercing cry that rent the night air in two, and galloped down the path. Following in the wake of the rest of the kingsmen, Obed's captors were the last to move after shoving a boot into his gut that caused him to see stars and double over with the explosion of pain across his middle.

With gray edging his vision, he scrambled across the ground to Violet who sat sobbing in the dirt, not having moved from where the commander had thrown her in his controlled fury. He touched her shoulder, and she jerked away, pulling at the peasant top that had torn from her shoulder in the tousle. "Don't touch me," she rasped out, begging between her sobs.

A crackling sound filled the air, and he didn't know what it was until smoke caught his nose and he turned, horror filling every inch of his body. The cabin was alight. "Oh, dear God," he cried under his breath, unable to move and frozen in a trance as flames licked at the window panes.

"Granny!" A harsh cry flew from Violet's lips, and before he could move, she was scrambling across the path and running into the cabin.

"Violet! No!" he bellowed, running after her.

The onslaught of smoke at the door and the burst of heat singed the hair around his face and burned his eyes with its intensity. The cabin, old and dry in this rainless weather, was lighting up as if it were kindling dried especially for this purpose. He coughed as the smoke hit his lungs, searing him from the inside and out. "Violet!" His scream for her was raspy and almost difficult for himself to hear above the roaring of the flames. As his eyes adjusted and he fought his way into the room, he caught shadows of the furniture amidst the flame, and he nearly tripped over a pot lying on its side in the middle of the room.

Then he saw them. Violet was bent over, dragging the prone and limp form of Granny across the floor from the direction of the bed, the tick mattress was an absolute inferno. The dry straw had been just the thing to launch the flickering flames into a holocaust of their living quarters.

Coughing, his lungs positively on fire within him, he stumbled forward, reaching out to take Granny's arms from Violet's grip. She instantly fell to the floor in a coughing fit, her face covered in soot, and the hair around her face singed with sparks and embers alight in her clothes. One side of her skirt burst into flame when one ember caught the fresh air from the door. He dropped Granny's limp and blackened hand to stamp out the burning fabric as Violet coughed and slapped at it with her bare hands.

161

"Out! Get out! I'll get her!" he commanded, grabbing Granny's hands and pulling hard as he coughed. Violet disobeyed and grabbed Granny's arm, renewing her strenuous tug of war and made for the door with him. They were faster together and would soon be out. The large dark rectangle of the open door offered solace in the fresh breeze of the evening. He pulled even harder, the light leaving his vision as he felt the strain of every single effort within him to get air into his lungs.

Air, there was no air. He gasped, but all that filled his lungs was smoke, blackness, inch by inch devouring his throat and squeezing the very life from him. The coughing was to no avail as his vision narrowed, little left in him to fight, but fight he must. One heavy foot in front of the other, tightening his grip so he didn't drop Granny, he plowed forward. One more plunge, and they would be free of certain death.

One.

More.

Step.

A thundering crack filled his ears. Violet's raspy scream threatened his existence as everything went black.

# Sixteen

## REDEEMING GRACE

VIOLET COLLAPSED on the threshold of the house.

Everything in her fighting the urge to die on the spot. One more thing. She needed to get Obed out. Granny lay on the ground beside her with a small burn on her face and her clothes completely covered in soot.

*God, don't let him die.* The words didn't escape her lips because her throat was far too raw, but instead fled her mind in prayer. She dove into the orange flames once more, everything around her threatening to give her a taste of the hell she had been promised to avoid with the death of her Savior. *Give me one more breath. One more step. Jesus, don't let him die now. Not after everything else.* Her thoughts were prayers she knew her Savior heard. This was not how they would die. Of that she was certain.

With a cough and a groan that felt like it came from her very toes, she grabbed his arms and pulled with all her might.

163

His lifeless form budged ever so slowly from beneath the rubble from the beam that had fallen, clipping him on it's way down.

"Don't. You. Die!" she screamed, pulling with all her might.

Suddenly, they were out on the dirt in front of her house, the heat no longer devouring her every fiber. With what little strength was left to her, she weakly slapped at the lazy flame licking at her arm. She didn't even feel the pain of the burns that covered her hands. The flame died beneath her efforts, and she stumbled backwards, falling to the ground, the stars her only view. Their lights were bright, twinkling in the black sky, every one she knew had a name. Had been formed by the hand of her Creator. It had been a long time since she had looked at the stars. Admired them. Praised their Maker.

But then, they too were gone.

Violet felt the sensation of pain before anything else, then the remembrance of it all exploded in her mind as if she were living through it all over again. *Obed.*

She gasped at the pain in her ribs as she struggled to a sitting position, or at least tried to. Hands were on her shoulders, forcing her back against the sheets. Every square inch of her body was on fire. So hot. Her skin was burning. Her lungs were on fire. She still heard the massive roar of the flames in her ears. Taking her breath away.

Obed. Granny. Where were they? Were they okay? Her eyes were on fire, just like everything else, and she tried to open them, but the pain was too great. A moan escaped her lips and reverberated through her chest.

The roaring in her ears started to settle. She felt coolness touch her face. It stung a little, but it also soothed the burning. Softness dabbed at her eyes, and she was able to wrestle them open. Not much was visible, and what she could see was incredibly blurry and out of focus.

"Marcus?" She may have tried to say his name, but it came out sounding nothing like it. A cough brought on by the use of her voice set her throat to scratching and sent pain exploding across her chest. A cool glass was pressed to her lips, and she tried to swallow the soothing drink between her wheezing. She blinked some more, swallowing hard against the soreness of her throat and finally getting the hacking cough under control.

"You need to rest." Marcus's voice was worried, his green eyes even more so. They shimmered in the light from the candle, and she shook her head and tried to fend off his hands on her shoulders, forcing herself into a sitting position and looking around the room.

"Gran," was all she eked out before another cough wracked her frame.

His brows furrowed. "She is fine, but you need to rest. Master Fendrel said to make sure you stayed supine till he gave his express permission."

A slight twinge of relief was instantly replaced by the memory of dragging Obed from the ruins. Her house. She couldn't think of the cabin now. Where was Obed? Was he even alive? The panicked feeling attacked her chest again, crushing her beneath its weight. She frantically looked around, suddenly feeling confined beneath the sheets. She tried to throw them off of her, gasping for breath, but her bandaged hands made the process impossible as she fumbled with the length of fabric. "Obed," she croaked, fighting through the pain and feeling panic rise at the intensity of it. She felt trapped by these blankets, and her throat started to swell shut, the wheezing intense in her own ears.

Fendrel came into the room and took one look at her before rushing across the floor, nearly stumbling at the foot of the bed.

Why was no one helping her out of these blankets? If she didn't get out soon, she thought she just might fly to pieces. The room started to grow even more fuzzy and dim around the edges, and the hand on her shoulder caused her to flinch. It was removed, and a glass held to her lips. She attempted to swallow, choked, and swallowed again at the liquid being forced down her swollen throat. She tried to listen to Fendrel's voice beside her; Marcus's worried face blurred near her own. His lips moved, though no sound came out, and she knew he was praying.

"Listen to me, Violet. You need to take a deep breath. Try to reach your stomach with the air you take in. Good. Look at my eyes. Don't look away. Keep your focus here. Good. Breathe. Try to reach your toes with the next breath. Good. Good girl." A hand was on her back, one of the only parts of her that didn't burn with hell fire.

She gulped and gasped in another breath, trying to force it to her toes. It ended up only somewhere around her knees, but she was trying. "Obed," she choked out again.

The hand on her back rubbed in soft circles. It soothed her, bringing with it the memories of gentler times. When a deep voice had spoken over her and comforted her. It was easier then. Easier when she could release all of the worries in her heart to her father. She knew he would carry them. Every day, he had taught her to empty her "worry pocket." As a little child each night before prayers and bed, she would take out her invisible worries from the tiny pocket of her shift, laying them one by one into her father's large, calloused hand. He would gather them. Thank her for giving them to him, kiss her forehead with his whiskers tickling her soft skin, then pray with her. Each evening was the same. If only it were that easy now.

*You can still give them to your Father. I'm ready to take them. Empty your pocket, dear one.*

Tears flowed down her cheeks. The words sounded deep in her spirit, but they were heard. She tried to release the worries, and the tight feeling of a hand gripping her throat abated a little.

A hand touched the top of her head, and the fatherly gesture helped her relax even further. The medicine that Fendrel had given her was starting to help as well, slowing her mind and giving her the rest that her body denied her. "Obed is still unconscious. I don't know what damage was done internally. He took a nasty hit to the head and has suffered as many burns as you. It will take some time to mend, and I hope that he will...but, Violet, I don't know how severe his head injury is...after the trauma he has received..." Fendrel's voice was soft and peaceful, quieting and not increasing her anxiety. Fendrel had mastered the art of delivering bad news gently. He shook his head, and Violet felt her gaze grow even hazier.

167

"I don't know if he will still recover. I hold hope that he will, but I wanted to be honest with you. We need to pray."

Tears from the smoke damage, the burns, and the pain welled out of Violet's eyes and trailed down the side of her face. One pooled in her ear, and she sniffed.

*God, please, don't let this be the end. I can't lose someone. Not again.*

Darkness and pressure. Distant sounds. So distant.

Rock walls surrounded him; tapestries hung. This place again. He had dreamed of it before. But perhaps it was more than a dream. He tried to touch the tapestry. Maybe then he could know it was real. It burned like fire, and he dropped it from his scorched fingers and stepped back. He tripped and fell. Green engulfed him. The clang of a sword rang in his ears, and pain exploded around him, his foot twisting in agony. It was spasming, and the muscles that wound their way up his leg were tightening, twisting, like a knife stabbing through skin and muscle. Bone cracked. Heat exploded around him. There was a weight on his neck. He reached up a hand to touch it, and suddenly flashes of scenes poured through his mind. Memories. Dreams. Dreams within a dream. Ballrooms full of strangers, oppressive weight pressing in around him, jostling him on every side. A sword in his hand, sparring with a man in leather armor. A garden full of laughing women, their dresses revealing and lewd. Masks hovered over their faces, concealing their identity. A sick feeling settled in his stomach.

Whispers in his ears. Now on the right, now the left. Words, woven trails of hurt, resentment, bitterness.

Stone halls again. Shouting, his throat raw. An old man, bent with age, a sad look in his eye. A crown on his head. Obed stepped toward him, reaching out a hand. The old man's shoulder was within his grip, and he shook, throwing the old man against the stone wall. Hurt welled in his own heart. Pain and fear. He was overwhelmed. Too much. It was all too much.

A pound in his head as if someone had struck him, his ears ringing. Horses hooves pounding, pounding, the rhythmic triple thud of their canter. Again and again...

Something clanged hard, and he startled awake, his eyes jolting open when the loud noise assaulted his ears. It reverberated through his entire body, setting his teeth on edge, and one long ache slammed through his being.

The bright light aggravated his eyes. He felt as though suddenly he was living two lives, both at war within his being.

He knew. Without a shadow of a doubt, he knew who he was. Elgon. The memories of palace life, his father the king, and many others filled his mind from before. But he was also Obed. Images of the farm, blistered hands that had grown calloused, and the tilling of dirt. His eyes were shot through with the light, blinded and blurry. He couldn't see. He tried to catch a breath and couldn't breathe. Everything, it all slammed into him at once, painful, overwhelming, swallowing him whole from within and without. Water trickled down his face, and he gasped, a small bit of air greeting his lungs and only increasing his need for more.

Air. If only he could get air. The pain and darkness clutched

169

at his chest, and hands were touching him. He burned at their touch. He didn't want anyone touching him, and yet he desperately craved the feeling, the comfort.

If he couldn't get air soon…yet he felt as though he didn't deserve the air. For with a sickening horror, he knew who he was. More so than ever in his life, he knew. He saw it all. The darkness, the sin. Yes, sin. He couldn't breathe. *Take it away. Take it away, or I must die.*

*I already did so that you don't have to.*

Obed. Elgon. He shuddered. The pain was too great. The shame, the grief. He thought he might just give in, succumb to the darkness and never live again.

But the fire lapped before him. Red. Hot. Evil. Overcoming him and licking at the very edges of his soul.

*Come to Me. I can make you whole. I can rescue you from the fire. I gave My life to save yours. My blood for yours. An atonement for your sin.*

He tried to gasp. Nothing met his lungs, and the darkness pressed closer, the pain shutting him off from the world. From anything and everything. He knew the voice that whispered to him. He had never heard it before, but he knew. He couldn't speak.

*Jesus.* It was only a thought. But that one name broke the hold over his body, and a blessed breath of air met his lungs. They filled, the air bringing light to his body.

*I carry too much shame. This world. It is of my doing. The pain and fear. I made this. How can you take all of that? I've been the one wreaking the havoc in this world.*

*You were a vessel for the wrong thing. The devil's purpose is great, but Mine is greater. My blood speaks louder. My light shines bright enough to purge the darkness. Do you believe that My blood is strong enough? Sacrificed for you. Do you believe?*

Hope filled his restless and broken heart. He lifted his battered, shameful soul and offered it. *Take me, Jesus. Cleanse me. I believe.*

Blessed relief. Not just relief. But...wholeness. Light collided with the darkness and won in an instant. The war within him ended, and he sank back on the pillow, fresh air and life flowing through every single fiber of his being. He felt so alive, yet at rest. So full of purpose, yet at peace. He closed his eyes, taking in huge lungfuls of air, a sweet taste to them. The battle had been fought and won. His victory was here, felt, though not yet seen. Soft gray clouded his vision. Not the darkness of before, but a quiet, soft gray that covered him like a mist, the comfort palpable, and sleep gathered him in its arms.

# Seventeen

## IDENTITY

VIOLET'S HANDS shook as she fiddled with the ties of her dress. Her hands were still bandaged, and only a few of her fingertips were exposed to grip the strings that tied the front of her bodice shut. She groaned in frustration and felt tears form. The pain was dulled thanks to a draught that Fendrel had forced down her throat, but it still thudded in the background, like an ache that wouldn't go away.

She hadn't been there when it had happened, but Fendrel had said Obed had awakened, fighting, gasping, barely breathing, but awake in a frightening mix of living and dead. Fendrel thought he would die. But something happened. After a struggle, he fell into a deep sleep. Peaceful, resting. His breathing came easy, and his face was unmarked with pain. Violet had stolen away to his bedside more than once to bring her cheek close to his face to feel the air softly entering and leaving his lungs, ensuring that he lived on. Every time she

173

held her breath, waiting to feel his.

She sighed. It had been two days, and he had hardly stirred, let alone opened his eyes. Fendrel had finally eased the sedatives he had given her, but she had walled off a part of her mind. There were too many things she needed to think about, but so much that she couldn't even fathom. The cabin, the encounter...she shuddered. She hadn't even told Marcus and Fendrel of the encounter with the commander. Nausea reared its ugly hand and clenched at her throat. She swallowed hard, threw down the ends of the strings she could not tie, and stepped from the room at the back of the house.

Marcus stood on his good leg, the lame one resting slack next to it as he pounded out herbs in a large mortar with a pestle. They smelled good, but heavy, and as she drew closer, she turned to catch a sneeze in her elbow. A spasm ripped across her chest, and she grimaced, moaning. No amount of pain-relieving draught would stay the pain of her cracked ribs.

Marcus turned too suddenly, losing his balance, and caught himself against the table since his lame leg could not do it. He steadied himself, then gripped her elbow, drawing her to the table. She shook her head when he tried to get her to sit.

"I've been sitting for days." Her voice was hoarse as she pressed a hand to her side to still the throbbing. The kingsman's kick had done more harm than she had realized at first, and thankfully adrenaline had allowed her to pull Granny and then Obed from the fire. "Can you tie this?" Violet gestured to the front of her bodice that still remained un-fastened.

He worked at the laces, glancing up at her face. "Are you

174

doing all right?"

He had caught her staring vacantly across the room. She blinked and drew in a breath as he stepped away. "Thanks." She smoothed a hand over the tied bodice and glanced longingly at the chair he had offered to her before. Sitting sounded mighty tempting, and she had only been standing for several minutes. Long enough to get dressed and then wish she had stayed in bed. She leaned against the table. "As well as can be expected, I suppose. Where's Granny?"

Marcus resumed grinding the herbs but kept his eyes on her face. "There's bread there; you should try to eat some." He nodded his head toward a wooden board with a loaf from that morning, half missing already.

She was in a strange mood. Food sounded good and repulsive all at the same time. She shook her head and finally gave in, sitting down on the chair and leaning her head in a hand, elbow resting on the table.

"She went with Fendrel to visit a sick woman across the village. He thought getting her out of the confines of the house might liven her up a bit."

"The animals?" Even in her own pain and fear, she still worried for everything that had been under her care.

"Everard partitioned them out to the neighboring farms. They will be taken care of till you have need or ability to care for them again. The barn is all but useless for them at the moment."

Violet felt the hair on the back of her neck stand on end, and she shuddered, wincing at the pain it caused. Fire flashed across her memory in a vision. She tried her hardest not to remember that night, the horror of it. But it intruded once in a

175

while, images flashing across her mind's eye with intensity, as if even unbidden, they would haunt her every waking hour. Granny had been a mere shadow of herself since the incident. Her mind, already frail and broken, had been wandering, fluttering about like a lost bird inside a house, unable to free itself and running into the windows in desperate hope of escape.

"Lord, please, heal her mind and bring her back. It hurts too much to see her like this."

"Amen." Marcus added, shaking his head slightly. She hadn't realized she had spoken out loud.

"Do you ever wonder what it's all for? Why are we still here? Wouldn't it just be easier to end it all?" The words tumbled out of her mouth like grain from a broken jar, nothing able to stop the pouring, and it all lay out on the floor for all to see the mess.

Marcus set the pestle down with a clink, but he didn't answer right away. Finally, he said, "You can't think like that, Vi."

"But why doesn't He come rescue us? Why doesn't He unleash His judgment? He could end all of this with a snap of His fingers, yet we suffer." A tear leaked out of her eye, but she vehemently brushed it away.

Silence met her questions. *Of course.* No one had good answers anymore. They knew it was wrong to think that you should end life, but no one knew the right thing to think.

"He knows our time. He knows our weakness and where our breaking point is. Jesus never said it would be easy. He did say we would have trials and tribulations and that the pain we bore would be great."

"Is that supposed to be helping me right now?" Her stomach rolled over, and she pushed the bread farther from her.

"You didn't let me finish. Are you truly asking Him right now? You should be asking Him, not me. His strength is made perfect in our weakness. He knows we can't carry everything the world has to throw at us, but that's why He asks us to enter into rest with Him. Because that's the only way to truly have peace." He gripped his hands together, absentmindedly rubbing a knuckle on the right one. "We need to remember, that He does have it all in control. He knows when the breaking point is, not us. We have to realize that, while we are weak and want all of this to be over, He knows every single piece of the puzzle and the perfect timing for it all to fit together.

"There is good left in this world, Violet. We can't expect Him to destroy every last inch of it just to rescue us. This isn't the first time in history that His people have been cut down and destroyed. Remember Shadrach, Meshach, and Abednego? They were thrown into a fiery furnace. He rescued them. Will He not do the same for us?"

The mention of fire made her wince. "The furnace feels mighty hot right now." More tears gathered, one slipping down her cheek.

Marcus limped to her side and crouched in front of her, taking her hand in his. "But He's right here with us in the fire. Don't you see Him?"

A sob ripped from her throat. *Give me eyes to see.* She saw Him hovering over her as she rescued Obed. While it had been a great sacrifice at first, and she had been scared to death to do so, she saw now that God had brought her Obed at just the

177

right time. There were so many things that He had lifted from her shoulders. Burdens she never thought she would be free from, released and shouldered together. She had not carried it all on her own. The Lord had sent Obed to be her go-between. To represent Himself in her life. She knew that Obed didn't know the Lord. Not really. But He had mirrored Christ to her. The care he took of her, the willingness to ease her burdens. She had carried it all herself before, never once thinking she would ever be able to share them with another. The weight of the responsibility that was hers, that of Granny's care, the tending of the garden and fields, earning an income to keep them both alive...she knew it had worn on her. More than she had even realized until that weight had been shared.

She saw the Lord in the narrow escape they had experienced in the village. In the protection from the certain violation that had almost occurred. She shook. The kingsman could have taken from her what he asked, but for some reason, he did not. He had left her nearly unscathed in the midst of such evil. She had looked into the very eyes of the devil and had walked away intact. A little worse for wear, with a few bruises, but what was that compared to the potential outcome? She could almost see Him standing there, staying the hand of the man who had threatened to take everything from her.

She saw Him in the way Granny had walked away without even a burn upon her person. She had been unconscious in that fire. Violet and Obed had dragged her from the cabin, and yet not a scratch marked her frail form. She shook her head. He was even now healing Obed. Or so she hoped. What else could such a peaceful sleep after so much turmoil mean?

"Violet." Marcus's voice caught, and she looked up to see

his face; it was a mixture of fear and hope, as if he were about to ask her something but was too timid to try. The hesitation and pause in his voice confused her. He was about to speak, seemed to think better of it, then shook his head. "Nevermind."

He turned back to the pestle and mortar and attacked it with a vengeance. She wanted to ask him what he had been about to say, but a noise came from the other room, and they both started. She shot to her feet. Perhaps Obed was waking up. Her too-quick movement nearly sent her to her knees in spasms of pain from her ribs. Marcus wasn't much faster with his lame leg, but he gave her the support of an elbow as they limped together across the floor. *We are quite the pair.*

Obed was blinking his eyes at the light from the window, the thin, muslin curtains doing little to shade the afternoon sun from his eyes. He was attempting to sit up, but she rushed to his side, wincing at the pain it caused but hardly caring.

"Obed!" Even she caught the joy in her own voice. He seemed to be all right. The bandage on his head did him no favors in the looks department, and there was little skin showing from beneath the bandages that was not slightly marred with burns, though none as bad as the blistered and flayed skin on her own palms. She settled on the bed at his side, laying a hand on his shoulder and pressing him back into the bed. "Shhh, rest."

He leaned back, his eyes on her face. Feeling flashed across them. He swallowed visibly, but confusion and fear trembled in his expression. "Water," he rasped, then exploded into a cough. The smoke had done its damage to all of them.

She filled the glass from the bedside table and held it to his

179

lips. He swallowed gratefully, but then he drew back. The look on his face confused her. Why was he acting standoffish? What was going on? "Obed? Are you all right? How are you feeling?"

He hesitated, his brown eyes begging. Begging her for what, she knew not. "I—I remember."

She felt her eyebrows dip as she tried to understand what he was telling her. Then her heart stopped.

Panic rose within her, and her heart nearly exploded out of her chest. She, too, swallowed hard, willing herself not to recoil and flee from the room. In her heart, she knew what he meant. But perhaps she was wrong. "You remember what?"

His steely gaze burrowed deep into her own. "Everything."

Elgon knew he had said the words she had most dreaded to hear. She didn't recoil, but he felt the tension growing like a canyon between them, pushing them apart instead of together. Sadness filled his heart. He desperately wanted her to know that Elgon and Obed were one and the same. He hadn't suddenly become a monster, simply because he remembered his old life. He felt the bile rise up in his already raw throat. What he had been disgusted him. He had a little knowledge of how she must feel about his former character.

He saw emotions darting across her face, one after the other—shock, confusion, pain, but the last one smote him like an arrow to the heart. Fear. She stood from the bed and backed toward Marcus, seeming not to realize that she had gone so far until she bumped into the hand he placed protectively on her shoulder.

His heart sank. She had every right to be afraid of him based on her last interaction with a kingsman. Every right in the world. He sat up slowly, testing out his muscles as he did so. Nothing was incredibly sore except his head, but everything ached dully, deep in his bones.

"Violet, what is it?" Marcus's voice was firm, his eyes sharp as he darted a look Elgon's way, then back at Violet's white face. Her chest was heaving as she grappled for breath, and he wished with all his heart that he could make the panic on her face go away.

"I won't hurt you. I promise. It's still Obed."

She shook her head, but she seemed to calm a bit at his raspy voice. He stifled a cough in his elbow.

"What. Is. Going. On." Marcus hissed between his teeth, his eyes shooting daggers at this point and his hand tightening on her shoulder. She winced away, and he placed his hand at his side, instant regret cascading across his face.

Best not to leave the young man in the dark any longer. "My memory has returned."

Marcus glanced back at him. "What memory?"

Violet turned suddenly and darted from the room with a limp even Elgon noticed, despite the quickness of it.

"Violet?" Marcus turned sharply, and he would have fallen if he hadn't caught himself on the doorframe. He looked after her and shook his head, as if realizing he could not chase her. He turned back to Elgon with furrowed brows. "Explain," was all that he forced from his lips. He pulled over the chair by the door with the edge of his cane and sat down, extending his bad leg in front of him.

181

Elgon felt the blood leave his head. This was not going to be enjoyable.

# Eighteen

## ALL OF YOU

VIOLET PRESSED a hand to her side, half limping, half running down the dirt road outside of the village, her dress catching the dirt and spinning it in swirls around her feet. She tripped on a hole in the road and pitched forward, catching herself on her good arm, cradling her bad side with the other. A cry spilled from her throat, and she bit hard on her lip, tears streaming down her face.

She had hoped…

She didn't know what she had hoped. How stupid was it to hope that a man who had lost his memory would lose it forever and stay with her for the rest of her days? She hadn't thought that far intentionally, but now that the opposite had come true, she desperately wanted to rewind the clock and claim the slight happiness that was hers in the moments where she thought it might be true. She struggled to her feet, holding her arm tight to her side and straining for breath.

She took a slower pace this time, breaking to let the sharp pain in her side ebb. The sun was well-nigh into the afternoon when she finally stopped short. There was still smoke rising from the ashes. It had been three days, and yet the remains of everything she once held dear still smoldered in a pile of black coal and gray ash.

The green of the forest was tainted by the blackness that had shriveled the leaves, their edges crinkled and torn with the heat. It was dulled, its usual vibrancy masked by the blackness of soot that had drifted atop the leaves' silky surfaces.

The pile of rubble was so...small. All of her belongings, her home, reduced to a pitiful heap of rubble. She gulped back the sob that caught in her throat and headed at a slower pace toward what had once been her home. Her haven, her one safe place, made safe no longer by the Kingsmen. She kicked viciously at a piece of coal that had snapped from the fire, probably from the intense heat, and now sat a long distance from the center of the conflagration.

The same kingsman who now lay in a bed at Fendrel's with his past to reckon with and his previous self to morph back into had once shared her home and her life. She had no doubt that the persona of Obed would slip away forever and the farce that she had lived these last few months would disappear. It would leave her with just another loss in the wake of a long life tortured and destroyed piece by piece by the Kingsmen he was once a part of, and no doubt would be again.

She glanced at the fields, half of the crop burned to a crisp, gone with nothing to show for the heavy labor she and Obed had devoted to it. Tears smarted in her eyes. So much devastation from one wicked act. An entire livelihood, destroyed in the matter of an hour. The other half of the field of wheat would need to be tended properly, or it too would not survive. Even now she winced. It needed water to even try to become green again. The barn was nearly gone, half a wall still standing, the interior just as dry as the house had been. She stumbled toward the back of the house where the well had stood, now a pile of stones, the roof gone.

She stopped short, her eyes running along the length of the forest. Shadows crept at the edges, their blackness encroaching but being forced back by the smattering of light that shone through the sparser leaves on the edge of the forest. Its denseness made it dark, ominous...overpowering. She longed for the happy forest whose greenness had beckoned to her as a child, its playful light, color, and patterns soothing her soul, encouraging her imagination, and filling her with life.

But now, it taunted. Her imagination was a place to fear, and she desperately avoided going there at all costs. Something that had once held so much life and joy for her had become dark, mirroring the world around her, its presence growing more ominous as her thoughts had. She couldn't remember the last time she had been in the forest, aside from rescuing Obed. She had lived her life staying on its edge and avoiding the place that had once been her safe haven. She worried that if she entered, the place that had once held so much charm for her would swallow her whole, devouring her in her thoughts and bringing to mind the memories of a time long by, when she had once been happy, protected, and loved.

Tripping over a stone, she caught herself, wincing at the pain. She needed to get to it. She couldn't leave it out here. As much as she wished it had burned in the fire, or been destroyed, she had made the choice months ago, and she felt compelled to give it back, despite the fact that she wished to do nothing but melt into the earth or perhaps bury herself instead. But when God asked her to do something, she would do it. No matter how much she wanted the contrary.

Sweat beaded on her forehead, and trembling, she fell to her knees at the edge of the forest, pressing a hand against the tree trunk with the soft 'X' etched into the bark of an exposed root. Shuddering at the closeness of the woods, she stared deep into the forest, the creaking of the branches, once a soothing sound to her fanciful ears, now mocked her in nightmares and chased her thoughts about with shadows. Nothing out of place met her eyes, but her wariness made the skin at the back of her neck prickle.

She pulled at the weeds at the base of the tree, then started digging with her hands. She gasped when a splinter lodged itself beneath her fingernail, but she stole herself against the pain and pushed on. She caught her breath and cradled her bruised side with one hand, digging furiously with the other. She would not change her mind.

*You can still burn them. Rid yourself of them.*

No. She must do the right thing. Even if it meant losing everything. She stopped as a sob ripped through her. Her father had once done that. He had done the right thing and lost it all. Her fingers closed around the leather, and she used her hands to hollow out the ground around the small parcel, struggling to free it of the dirt. Even the ground seemed hesitant to let it see the light of day. Wresting it from the earth's grasp, the leather fell away from the oblong bundle and the clank of metal hitting the ground echoed in her ears.

The bright and ominous mark of the king seared her eyes from the medallion that now lay in the grass beside the sword with a crown marking its hilt.

Fear clenched her throat. For this, she might die. Just like her father.

Elgon sat up in bed, his throat still raw, but for some reason, nothing bothered him too much. He was sore, to be sure. He had learned that a beam had come down in the fast-burning house and had knocked him clear out with a blow to his head and shoulders. His muscles were sore with the healing bruises, but he had experienced enough headaches over the last few months to notice he wasn't experiencing those side effects this time.

Marcus had brought him water with a soothing herbal draught that had coated his throat and left a taste of bitter herbs laced with the sweetness of honey hugging his tongue.

Marcus had been unbelievably understanding. His light green eyes had gazed deeply into Elgon's, as if he looked beyond the pain, the worry, the fear and frustration, to see something beyond Elgon himself. As if he looked so deep, that he seemed to see past all of the chaos that Elgon still carried and came back with something he either resonated with, approved of, or somehow, trusted.

"So, you mean to tell me that you aren't Violet's distant cousin?" This was the second time he had asked the question, but his dark blonde eyebrows, darker than the hair that fell at the base of his neck and around his forehead, quirked quizzically as if the first time he hadn't quite believe him.

Elgon felt a small sense of panic rise in his throat. "No! I am not her cousin." It came out a bit faster than he had intended. He wanted it to be known that he was the farthest thing from a relative or cousin of Violet. Claiming to be a family member made things too messy and she had…she had become dear to him.

"You love her, don't you?" It wasn't said as a question, but Elgon reacted as if it were a slap to the face.

He started. "No!" he stuttered. "Of course not!"

Marcus raised an eyebrow again, his arms assuming the folded position, a slight smile on his face, but almost negated by the pain in his eyes, carefully concealed, but still visible to Elgon, who knew that look…because he had experienced the feelings himself. "So, you don't love her then?"

Elgon felt anger rise in him. Marcus knew full well what he was doing, and he was quite smug about it, and Elgon, like a helpless idiot, was falling right into the trap. "I mean, I don't *not* love her. I mean, that is, I do love her. Well, just not…"

Marcus laughed. A gentle laugh that ended on a slightly harsh note. "To know Violet is to love her." His tone was serious, a stark contrast to the laugh of before. He picked up Elgon's empty cup and headed for the door, his limp pronounced. He turned back to Elgon just as he reached the doorway. His face was intense, his eyes more so. Resolve and strength straightened his back, and he stood tall. "If you dare to hurt her, harm those she loves, or even so much as think about ruining her…I don't care who you are, prince, pauper, or kingsman—I'll give my dying breath to see her avenged."

He didn't ask for understanding, but Elgon knew beyond a

shadow of a doubt that Marcus would die a thousand deaths to save Violet from any pain. It was evident in the steely resolve in his eyes, the tight-knuckled grip on the handle of his cane, and the straight posture that must be painful for Marcus to maintain. Elgon knew he had nothing to fear physically from Marcus; it wouldn't take much to beat the fellow in a fair fight. But his throat tightened. Hurting Violet would never once be anything he wished to do. In fact, quite the opposite.

After a respectful nod of agreement, he followed Marcus, who had seemed to accept the exchange as a matter of course, from the room. The evening shadows lengthened from the window, and Marcus looked through the panes, his brows furrowed with worry. "She shouldn't have gone far. And if she's not back before curfew…"

Elgon shuddered. Even knowing who he was still left him helpless to protect her. The Kingsmen would not respect who he was, would probably even disbelieve him if his identity was to come up. The helpless feeling filled his gut again. Even knowing who he was did not give him the power and strength he had hoped for. He had hoped for confidence, the ability to change things, the strength to know what he ought to do. Instead, he felt completely lost.

"Marcus, how do you pray?"

Marcus turned, giving Elgon a long stare before picking up a bundle of herbs and shoving it deep into a pot boiling on the stove, his cane handle looped over his wrist as he leaned a hip against the table next to the woodstove.

"Pray, eh?" Marcus smiled. "All you have to do is talk."

Elgon was confused. The churches he had been to had

189

included…ceremony. Pomp, scripts, and elaborate folding of hands. "Don't I have to…" He raised his hands and mimicked a prayerful pose.

Marcus' smile widened, and he shook his head. "You can if you want, but the act of prayer is simply communicating with your Heavenly Father. The One Who created you. All you have to do is talk. And listen. It's a two-way street."

"Like, a conversation?"

Marcus nodded, stirring the pot with a long wooden spoon. "That's all it is. He's just like any father; He wants a relationship with us, His children."

Flashes of time spent shoved away with nannies, trainers, and anyone other than his own father filled his mind. "Not mine."

Marcus stopped what he was doing and shot a glance over his shoulder. "But your father was well loved by all, surely…"

"Surely nothing. When a man has a job to do, it takes away from the relationship that he should be cherishing most." The bitterness in his own voice was just as raw as the rasp of his burned and scathed throat.

Marcus stared at him, his eyes pools of compassion, knowing, and understanding. "God's not like that."

"How do you know?" Elgon didn't mean for his voice to be so forceful. It was as if the words coming out of him were not under his control. They were raw, and real, and utterly broken. Hurt and desperation laced each word.

"What manner of love has the Father bestowed upon us that we should be called sons of God?"

*Son.* The word stung when it came from Marcus's lips with such reverent, loving tones. It felt like a barb. Anytime he had heard that word in relation to himself it had come with judgment and disappointment dripping from the single syllable. Daggers forcing their way into a heart that just longed to please but could not succeed in doing it well enough.

"And love consists in this: not that we loved God, but that He loved us and sent His Son as the atoning sacrifice for our sins."

An arrow to the heart. God loved him enough to sacrifice His son, then let Him take the punishment of his sins…of which there were many. Seated at the table, he laid his warm and scuffed face into his bandaged hands. He was overwhelmed with the depth of what he had done. "God, I didn't know. I…I want to feel your love. Let me know what it's like to be loved by you. I've never received that from anyone before. I just want to know."

A wall of emotion slammed into the front of him, nearly knocking him from his seat. Everything within him suddenly felt…whole. As if every last place of brokenness was flayed raw, and the scabs scratched away, then the soothing coolness, the healing, the fulfillment of what love truly was. He was shaking, his face wet with the tears that flowed down his cheeks; he hadn't known he was weeping, and there was no way he could even open his eyes. There had always been a part of him missing. As if he wasn't whole, wasn't complete. He had thought he was just not like what he was supposed to be. That he had messed up and could never be who he was meant to be. As if he had failed to become the man that was expected of him. But now it wasn't missing. It was there. Complete. Unbroken. The way he knew he was meant to be. And it overwhelmed him.

Every sense took a back seat to the realization that he was loved as he was, that Someone had taken his place in punishment. In the very depths of his heart, he knew that every ugly piece had been exposed, but it didn't fill him with fear. It was as if the Lord had seen through every little detail, every wall, every facade and desperate searching for fulfillment. He had seen the pain, the evil, and the sin within him, had lifted his face in gentle hands, caressed it as a father does a child with a nightmare whose tears streak their cheeks, looked him in the eye and said:

"I love you. All of you."

The door burst open, and Elgon's heart jumped into his throat. The tears had dried, but he still felt shaky inside as if his heart had been turned to jelly. All of the pain inside him was gone, but his middle quivered with anticipation, and a firm resolve echoed in his soul. He knew what he needed to do. Because he knew who he was. He was Elgon.

Violet stood at the door, a dirty bundle clutched in her hands and her face as white as death. Her dress front was stained with dirt and grass, her soft, sun-kissed brown hair escaping from the knot in which it had been tossed that morning. Her green eyes were large, standing out in her pale face, a terror in them that he hadn't seen since the night the kingsman had abused her.

Marcus limped to her side and drew her into the room, looking out down the cobblestone alley before he shut the door. There was still reason to fear. Reason to batten down the hatches and keep windows and doors shut.

But Elgon suddenly felt the fire of passion burn within him. Had she been...perhaps kingsmen had found her on the road and...his imaginings were too cruel for words, and his breath caught as he stood, every feeling within him on fire at the thought. He didn't know what he would do in this state, but everything within him rose up at the injustice against the innocence of Violet, a young girl, her youth stolen by trial and her fear written on her face.

"What happened?" He finally got out through ground teeth.

She stumbled forward, her expression not changing, but the lines around her mouth grew deeper with the pain she must've been in. She dropped the bundle on the kitchen table between them. Soil and leaves fell from the package that appeared to be her apron, within it a leather bundle. Something shiny protruded from the worn and dirty leather.

"I hid it. I know that there is something within it. I wanted to destroy it. I almost did." Her lip quivered, and her eyes filled with moisture. "I had a feeling that I shouldn't. That this would be needed one day even though I hoped it would never be so."

Her hands gripped the back of the chair in front of her as if it would fend off the world from attacking her, and her knuckles grew white through the dirt staining them.

"Are you—"

"I'm fine. Open it. You should have it back. Whether you deserve it or not."

The fire and trembling within her voice struck a chord within him. She was distant, terrified, placing a wall between him and her as if the table and chairs between them would be enough to shield her from whatever she feared of him. He gulped. He hated that wall. He was tired of walls. He wanted nothing more than to tear it down, brick by brick, and remind her of how much he...he cared for her.

He looked down at the bundle. He knew he should know what was inside, and part of him did. The length of it gave away its contents, but it was a fuzzy memory, one that he wasn't sure he wanted to relive. He opened the pack, unfolding the soft and supple leather from around the items. Sheafs of parchment tied together with strips of leather, an amulet hanging from thinner, braided leather cord. And a sword. His sword. The long silver blade and the handle tipped with a crown.

He touched the amulet, light enough to wear around the neck, but large enough to be seen at a distance and make people aware of his status. It was the king's seal. A lion on his hind legs, rearing and roaring in the midst of the Eliran royal crown, a circlet of thorns around the edge. How had he never realized the significance of the seal until now?

Something in him rose with staunch resolve. He needed to go back. He needed to put this to rights. Not another day would go by on his watch where the serpent would interlock the lion within its grasp, squeezing the life out of this nation, bringing pain and terror, bondage to its people. This country needed to be free. That could only happen from the inside out. Hope stirred in his chest. A tree with strong roots could overcome having its entirety chopped free and could begin again.

"Is that the king's amulet?" Marcus peered over Elgon's shoulder and shivered, his face a mix of awe and resignation.

194

"Yes. Mine now, I suppose." The words formed a lump in his throat, and he turned it over in his hand, then clenched it in his fist. He wouldn't let this go. The last thing he wanted was the responsibility, the need to return to the capital, to put a stop to the treason that had been committed. It unnerved him, and he felt far from equipped. But something had to be done. He knew that he had a job to do. He could not look God in the face, not having at least tried to do his duty and right the wrongs that had been wrought in his wayward days.

A small sound escaped Violet's lips, and both the men looked up. She swayed at the chair, her white-knuckled grip barely holding her upright.

"Who...are...you?" The question came out broken, her eyes begging for an answer, but fear swallowing them whole, the edges of her irises turning dark green like the forest in a fog.

"Prince Elgon, the crown prince of Elira." The words felt false on his tongue, as if that was no longer who he was. A burden he bore that had been placed on his shoulders. A responsibility, like the weight of a cloak, heavy and right at the same time.

Her face lost any remaining color, and she sank to the floor, her eyes rolling back in her head. He rushed to her side, he and Marcus both at the wrong side of the table to catch her. How had she not known? All this time, he thought she knew.

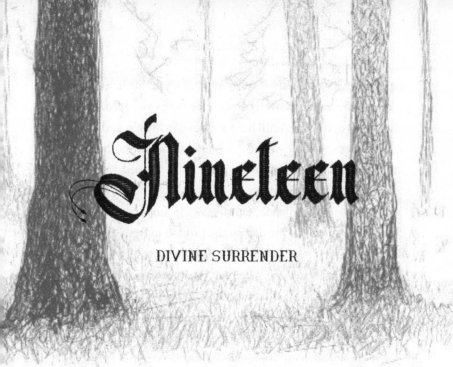

# Nineteen

## DIVINE SURRENDER

VIOLET FELT BLACKNESS envelope her as she sank into a sea of pain and exhaustion. The vision before her eyes brought agony to her soul, and a scream clenched her insides, but it didn't leave her lips as she descended into darkness. She saw him, her father, the rope around his neck. The pain on his face when he caught sight of her in the crowd. He had expressly forbidden her to be there. To watch this. But she had traveled miles, and to the very last minute she had held out hope, her heart swelling with it. Waiting for the moment when God Himself would reach down a hand and pluck them from this misery, this agony.

But no hand appeared. They didn't even give him the dignity of a bag over the head. Just the raw, ugly contortion on his face that lack of air created. She wasn't supposed to be there. The last look on his face was one of terror, disappointment, and pain. He had looked deep into her eyes, begging her wordlessly to turn away, but she hadn't obeyed, glued to the scene in front of her. Her limbs were frozen, and she didn't even blink until he was raised in the air, and she fell to her knees, her legs devoid of any strength. She heard the struggle, the noise loud in her ears as he gasped for breath. She couldn't breathe either.

Then there was silence, and the world stopped around her. She saw nothing but the dirt on the ground in front of her. Her hands spread apart in the dust, supporting her trembling shoulders until those too gave way and the only thing she saw was a dizzying array of feet moving and shuffling around her. Breath didn't seem to enter her lungs, and she wondered if she would ever be able to move again. Every muscle and bone in her body ached with longing. She hardly noticed and didn't move when hands scooped her up, sheltering her in large, muscular arms that encircled her, holding her close to a broad, strong chest.

She floated above the crowd, unseeing. Her head fell against the large shoulder, and she was shifted in the arms to give her neck less of an intense angle. Soft and scratchy straw was then her cushion, and a warm, soft, equine nose snuffed her cheek. A wet cloth touched her face and washed away the dust and dirt from where it had stuck to her tears. Blinking, her eyes focused. Everard, the giant of a man crouched down in front of her, his body so bulky it looked like he was trying to fit inside a box to be even close to her height. She was curled up in a stable atop a pile of straw, her body leaning against the wooden wall that vibrated with the sound of the traffic in the streets of Niran.

The rush back to reality overtook the numbness, and she

198

heaved. He held her hair in his hands as she retched into a bucket. His horse snuffled and stamped a foot uneasily. She trembled, every muscle on fire with the agony of it, the incomprehensible pain she had witnessed. She writhed, but a massive, gentle hand was placed on her head, whispered words coating her soul, taking away the sting, and it was then that the tears flowed. Emotions high, she threw out a fist that hit the solid torso in front of her. But then she was enveloped in the hug of a giant.

Violet started awake. Three sets of eyes stared at her. She felt empty, hollowed out. As if there was nothing left in her to give. Her spirit was flayed raw. Her eyes focused on Obed. *No. Elgon.* The crown prince. As good as king. The man whom everyone thought dead. She hadn't just provided shelter for a kingsman. She had thought she harbored a lowly guard, but instead it had been the mastermind himself. The man who was supposed to be running the country. The man who was heir to the throne when her father had been killed, strung up like an animal for protecting a young boy. For protecting Marcus.

Her gaze cut to her best friend. There was gentleness and caring behind the deep blue of his eyes, but there was also a storm. Their lightness was clouded with gray and navy, swirling in their depths. He was upset. She had upset him. He hadn't known she had been there at her father's death. He would never know, and Everard was the only one who would. But she knew he had dealt with the weight of being the cause.

Marcus's salvation had resulted in the demise of the one they both looked up to and loved with their whole hearts.

She choked, suddenly feeling smothered. She needed to get out of here. She was resting on a bed after her faint, but she had no idea how she had arrived there, nor did she care. Everything that she had long held in control was spinning endlessly out of it. Her grip on her life, her reality, her emotions, her will, her body, and her future had disappeared without warning, and the void felt a lot like that after her father's death. The swirl swallowing her whole in its darkness. She gripped the one lifeline she knew.

"I have to go." With a groan, she resisted the three sets of hands that strove to keep her confined to the bed. Fendrel was with them, and his deep voice was the only one that she really cared to listen to. But she wasn't about to stay here one moment longer with Obed, Elgon, or whatever monster or animal that he now was. She needed to retreat. Find the one rock that knew, that had been there and seen it all. She heaved herself up off the bed and limped across the room, pain blazing across her side with her fractured rib. She almost didn't care. Broken bones be hanged, she needed this. And everyone in this room was only serving to make her feel even more uncomfortable by the moment.

"Violet, you shouldn't be moving. You need rest." Fendrel's voice could barely be heard above the roaring in her ears. He didn't know, and she didn't care.

Out of the room, her gaze was confronted with the pain all over again. Granny stood there, her eyes longing, worry crossing her face and panic starting to creep in from the edges. "Richard? Where is Richard? He said he would be home by dinner. Violet, do go call him in; the kingsmen oughtn't to catch him out this late."

Something in Violet exploded, the pieces of her heart shattering into a million pieces. She burst from the cabin, not even caring that dusk was gathering and a kingsman might find her. She shivered in the air, her thin white chemise barely covering her arms, and her chilled body begged for her sweater knitted from the yarn Granny had spun to layer over the bodice that covered her torso. Half blind with tears, she stumbled down the cobblestone street, ignoring the voices calling out behind her.

The livery. She needed to get to the livery.

She stumbled on the door jamb and fell into the door, crying out at the impact. Gasping for air, she knocked faintly, her whole weight leaning into it, praying the wood could support her in a way that her legs could not.

A small slat above her head opened, the peephole for the occupant. Almost instantaneously, the heavy wood gave way and swung inward, causing her to fall through the doorway and into a large set of arms. Gasping for breath, she grabbed one of his sleeves in her hand and tried to straighten her legs. To no avail.

Her eyes met his, and the understanding within them calmed her soul. He knew. The compassion in his eyes made her insides knot, and with one last gasp for air, she let herself collapse into his arms.

"There, there, little one." Whispered words breathed into her hair. Then unintelligible ones of prayer stirred the room around her; peace like a weighted blanket wanted to settle on her shoulders, but it lingered inches away, as if waiting for her to accept it.

"You need to let go, little one. This is not yours to carry. You can't lift the load. But He can."

Where had she gone wrong? Where had she come to believe that she was the only one who could handle the pain, could carry the responsibility on her own? It had been a relief when Obed was there, taking some of the weight from her shoulders. A slight reprieve from the heaviness of it all that had descended back again upon her shoulders now that she realized who he was. Who he needed to be. Who he had been. It rocked her and she had no ability to even handle the realization.

She was alone under the weight. Again.

A sob caught in her throat, and she gasped, begging air to reach her lungs. Everard's hands lifted her off his chest and held her upper arms, keeping her upright. "Let go." The gentle, loving whisper wrapped her in its tendrils.

*I surrender.*

Air filled her lungs. She collapsed again. And this time, the peace descended, wrapping her in its comforting arms.

Marcus had come to walk her home. He had traversed the streets, bad leg and all, to make sure that she was all right. They moved as quickly as they could, staying in the back alleys to avoid the kingsmen's patrol. Her heart felt lighter, still broken and sore, but lighter, as if some of the burdens of the world had been released and she had less to carry.

A sound skittered down the street, and they both pressed

into the shadows, their breath barely hissing past their lips until they knew it was clear. She reached over and gripped his hand. He squeezed back. A mutual understanding between them.

They had been close as children, and their friendship had always been one of the sweetest things in her life. Their free time between chores had been spent playing knights and princesses in the woods. They had been together the day he received his injury and their lives changed forever. It was a day when many catastrophes collided to create a cacophony of suffering. She shuddered. Another memory she didn't need to relive now, as thin and stretched as she was, as if she were the yarn that she spun, pulled tighter and tighter until it was taut and narrow. At least the yarn could be used to create something beautiful in the end. All she felt she had created was a mess that required cleaning. If only this mess was as simple as picking up her broom and beating the dust from the floors.

Marcus continued to hold her hand as they wound their way back to Fendrel's. The dear man had offered them a place to stay until they had another, and she was grateful that he had extra beds for tending patients; of which they had all three been such over the last few days.

Marcus's cane made clicking sounds as it hit the cobblestones between steps. She shuddered. What it must be like to live with an infirmity that kept you hobbled. Tied down to certain tasks, prohibiting you from fleeing. She couldn't imagine.

She thought of Granny and Elgon. She shuddered again. That name felt so out of place in her mind, on her tongue...in her home. The man who had been living under her roof this whole time hadn't been a kingsman after all. He had been Elgon, the crown prince, the man who should be ruling a nation, but instead had let his rulers take over. He was the man who was crown prince at the time of her father's death, and yet he did nothing. He would have been fifteen at the time. Old enough, surely, to put a stop to such insanity.

*No.* She couldn't blame him for that. Evil men may have ruled that day, but it had not been Elgon. Her hatred for the ruler had been so misplaced; she had misjudged him. If Elgon was capable of being Obed, even while under the effect of memory loss, certainly he was capable of being a strong, caring, dependable, gracious, and just ruler. Surely the man who had stood between certain death and a young, innocent boy's life would be able to harness that same strength and dignity to rule a kingdom. She shook her head. Did a man stay the same even after their memory returned? Or with a returned memory, did one become the person they were before? How did someone have two lives and remember each one?

"Are you all right?" Marcus's whisper was so soft it barely reached her.

"I don't know." Her own whisper sounded as empty as she felt.

He nodded, willing to leave it at that. They shouldn't be talking in the street anyway. She was grateful he hadn't asked her why she had lied to him about who Obed was. He had seemed quizzical, but it was one of those things they understood of each other. She had done it to protect him; he knew that. And while he might not have agreed with her methods, he trusted her intentions.

She was on edge as they approached the door to Fendrel's and Marcus pulled the latch. What if he was up and about in the common area, and she was forced to see him? To look upon the face that should have belonged to Obed, the man who had tended her crops, fed her animals, rescued her grandmother from the fire, and wormed his way into her heart. To see the face that should have belonged to the man that she had grown to…love, but instead belonged to the prince, a man so far beyond her grasp that nothing within her even dreamed of trying to reach for him.

Another loss had darkened the door of her heart. At least it was not in death. She prayed that he would be a man worth a woman's heart. A man with the heart of Obed, but who wore Elgon's crown. A lowly farm boy with a heart of gold and a strength to match her father's, but with the power to turn the tide and the will to do so.

The tension in her shoulders dropped the minute her eyes swept the common room and saw that he was not in it. Relief and then panic. Had he gone already? She hadn't wanted to say goodbye, but her heart would be rent in two without it.

"Where's…?" She shrugged. Marcus knew who she meant.

"He's sleeping. He was tired, and after I convinced him that walking the streets wasn't the best idea, he finally allowed me to fetch you instead and took to his bed. His face was rather gray. I think he needed the rest. With what I imagine is ahead for him, I *know* he did." Marcus pulled a chair from near the kitchen table, sinking into it with a look of relief as he was able to relax his leg, but his forehead still held lines of worry across it. He winced as he rubbed at his knee. That had been a long walk for him. And he had done it for her.

She kissed the top of his sandy hair. "Thank you. You're a dear friend." She fetched him a mug of water and set some to boil for tea. Tea always did the heart good when one had endured a day as trying as she had, and it gave her hands something to do.

"Violet." Marcus's voice was low. Full of import and a slight bit of pain. "Do you love him?"

She froze, her hand hovering over the stove with a piece of wood she had been prepared to put on the fire. A spark floated up, and its red light flickered out slowly as the ash rose in the air before her face. She dropped the wood in and replaced the hot plate. Straight to the point, that one. "I—I thought I loved Obed." Her voice trailed off.

"Do you love him still?"

She turned. "How do you mean? He is a completely different person than I thought he was. How can one love a man she never actually knew?" She wrapped her hands around her middle. The fact that Marcus was getting this out of her was a big step for her. She loved Marcus, trusted him; the boy who was her best friend had grown into a man who she trusted to keep her secrets safe.

He shifted in the chair, resting an elbow on the back as he looked at her with his hopeful silvery blue eyes. "Is he, though?"

She stared into his face. Tears started to her eyes, the breaking of her heart rising to the surface. The pain on his face deepened, compassion filling his gaze even though he didn't move. It was as if he knew that she would shatter if he tried to touch her.

206

"I—I don't know." The words came out as a broken whisper, and she squeezed her middle, hoping to hold every broken piece inside so that it wouldn't fall shattered to the floor.

"Violet. Don't—" His own voice broke, and his face started to crumble until he righted it, steeling himself. "Don't wall yourself off this time. The pain will be greater than before, and I want you to be happy. You need him. And I think he needs you. Vi, don't give up on him. Don't give up on yourself. Not this time."

Two tears trailed down her face, but not once did she blink. Their eyes locked, knowing hovering between them, and it was as if all the pain they had experienced together swirled and interlocked, drawing them closer together, but pushing them farther apart. "Marcus, I—" She stepped toward him and extended a hand to his face.

The hope in his eyes shattered, and he pulled away. Looking down. Breaking the ties woven between them. "Don't." His voice cracked. "I can't be the one that breaks you. Not again."

A sob crashed through her throat. "It wasn't your fault." She knew what he was referring to and the broken Marcus in front of her was not the strong, old, wise heart that had counseled her moments before. He was the boy, kicked and beaten, lying in the middle of the road with her father standing over him, protecting him from the fists and boots of the kingsmen.

He looked at the ceiling, drawing in a deep breath and then swallowing hard, wincing in pain. He squeezed his eyes shut and contorted his face, then composing himself again before he faced her. He shook his head. "Perhaps not. But I will live with it till the end of my days, and I pray that God gives you the gift of love that heals and restores every wound you have received. I love you, Violet. And because I do, I hope you will follow your heart. I think, perhaps, God brought you Obed to be the strong protector that you need. The one who will shoulder your burdens with you and carry them alongside you. You weren't meant to carry them alone. There is an equal yoke for you, and I pray and believe you have found it in him." He rose, reached a hand to her face, caressed her cheek with a warm finger and then turned, limping from the room.

She stood there, brokenness swirling around the empty kitchen lit from the warm light of candles and the fire burning in the hearth. But this time the pain was healing. A release. Another surrender. A heart yearning.

Yearning for hope.

Elgon downed the mug of water that had been left on his bedside table, setting it down harder than he had intended. He stepped away and straightened the shirt Marcus had lent him. It was a little snug in the shoulders, but a shirt was a shirt. And thankfully peasant clothes were cut large to allow the freedom of movement needed to tend crops and animals.

He glanced at the bed. Lying on top was the bundle of leather, wrapped around parchments full of execution orders that made him sick on one hand and his blood boil on the other. Then, there was the medallion. Fire burned in his soul, and he knew what he needed to do. Reaching out a hand, he gripped it between his fingers. He knew the man he had been

208

before had cared little for the needs of others.

He saw it all now, the way he had been coaxed and coddled to be a man who did not know what went on without the walls of his palace but who also did not care. The thought of his latter childhood, his rightful kingdom ruled over by another man, his life turned into an empty one of parties, women, debauchery, and other vices made him want to hurl. And while he wished he could blame it all on the evil man whose name he now remembered, he knew he had his own responsibility to take. He had walked on the path set before him, never questioning, never wandering, just plowing ahead in his own recklessness, not looking back to see whence or where his footsteps had led him.

Lord Enguerrand. The inky blackness of a raven coated his memories about him, and in his previously sedated state of living, he had thought that the man's intent had been good. Now, with all of its ghastliness and evil plotting laid before his unfettered eyes, he needed to be sure of the man's motivation. Would he stand on the side of the rightful king and freedom? Or would he reveal himself further to be a wolf in sheep's clothing?

Gripping the sheaf of papers, he saw the signet pressed into red wax at the base of each one. His signet, used for evil purposes and sealing the death of peasants whose taxes had been delinquent. He knew the game Enguerrand had been winning.

Fear equaled power. But Elgon now knew that kindness equaled loyalty, and he would fight with every fiery bone in his body to see justice done, the kingdom returned to its proper order, and the plans of the wicked set to flame.

He had hoped for a moment that, perhaps, he could leave things as they were, fight from a small place here, stay to protect Violet and Granny. He gripped the amulet hard in his hand. But this was his destiny, as much as his spirit shrank within him and his heart wanted to remain with the woman he loved, respected, and desperately wanted to keep safe. He knew that the only way to do so would be to take the crown that was rightfully his and wield the scepter for a noble, holy purpose.

With a deep breath, he lifted the leather cord and placed the amulet around his neck. It settled over his blazing heart. "Lord, give me strength. With all that is in me, I give to You my hopes and dreams and will sacrifice anything I have to set this to rights."

He stepped from the room and met the faces of the other four occupants. Granny, Fendrel, Marcus, and Violet, each set of eyes a varying mixture of pain and hope.

Resolve steeled his spine even as his throat constricted with tears that would not be shed. Not now. "I need to tell you something."

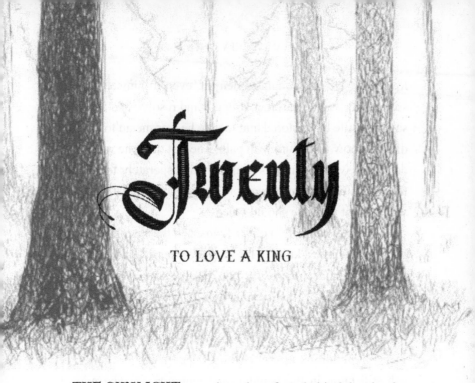

# Twenty

## TO LOVE A KING

**THE SUNLIGHT** came in and out from behind the clouds, throwing the world into a shadowed relief one moment, then brightness the next. The clouds chased each other across the sky, growing stormier in the distance. Elgon knew it might rain later. He had seen them gather like that many times earlier in the spring, but these summer months had been dry, with devastating results.

Violet walked next to him. Far enough away to be outside of arms reach, but still close enough that it was obvious they were walking together. The amulet hung beneath his shirt, and its cool smoothness bounced against his chest, chilling his skin. It reminded him with every movement of the purpose he carried, the responsibility he knew was his, and the destiny that he could run from no longer.

He so desperately wanted to reach across the divide, the wall that was between them, and grasp her hand. He knew he loved her. He had sought to deny it, even to himself, but in studying his own heart, her strength and resolve had not only saved his life but restored him to who he was meant to be. Her distance now filled him with pain. The last thing he wanted to do was leave her, and his heart ached desperately to ask her the one question that burned on his tongue, but that he knew was the last thing he should voice.

They reached their…no, *her* fields, and the sharp breath she drew in was like a knife to his gut. The wheat fields closest to the cabin had been burned away. All that remained was only there because of the neighbors who had come running, working together to dig a path against the fire. They had brought him, Violet, and Granny, all unconscious as they were, to Fendrel's house. He swallowed hard. The smell of ash still hung in the languid, dry, summer air. The pile of rubble that had been her home, her family's home for generations, lay in a ruin that he felt deep in his heart resembled the state of his country. The country that had been stolen from him and not only destroyed by the hand of another, but also through his own delinquency.

"Violet, I need to explain." He stepped toward her, reaching out a hand. "I have to go back."

She stared at him, her face white as a ghost. He so desperately wanted her to tell him what she was thinking.

"You…you want to go and…" She shook her head, her voice hollow. "You don't understand."

"Make me understand."

Her face contorted, and she sniffed, her eyes red-rimmed and brimming with tears. He felt the force of her pent-up words, feelings that had long been wrangled into their safe corner, away from the world, but with their wresting free brought a rawness and a devastation in their wake.

"My father...he did the same thing, and now my grandmother still waits for him to come home. Because of the regent, because of your advisor...he is dead."

His heart lodged in his throat, and he did his best not to keel over at the grief and shock of it. The confusion on Violet's face was only a tiny glimmer of what his own heart and mind were reeling from. He was a different man now. Had been for some time, yet he couldn't reconcile with all that had been done. All that he had allowed to happen. He knew her heart had been burdened with a pain beyond his understanding, but this? To know that his lack of control had allowed something this devastating to happen to the woman that he now loved...it nearly drove him to his knees. This all could have been avoided if he had known who to follow and what to do.

"What happened?" he rasped, his voice a betrayal of how raw his heart felt. He knew whatever was going to come out of her mouth was not going to be good, and he also knew that whatever she said was going to rock the very foundation of what he thought he knew about himself.

He saw her knees start to knock. He wanted so desperately to assist her, to gather her in his arms and offer comfort the way both of them must have longed for through their lonely, parentless years. But somehow, he knew that it was more than she would be able to handle at this given moment, so instead he ached as he saw her waver, then sink to a seat on a rock, right there in the middle of the field.

"He stood up. He never could leave well enough alone. And I was there to see it all." She shook her head and brought a shaking hand up, pressing it against the side of her face, her eyes staring ahead vacantly, but so full of the pain the memories brought. "They were beating Marcus. We heard the commotion from across the marketplace, and without hesitation, he took off running. He told me to stay where I was, but I couldn't. I had to follow him. Three kingsmen were beating Marcus; he was only twelve. He was curled up on the ground, trying to protect his head, but they just kept kicking him." Her face was full of so much pain and tears chased themselves down her cheeks, but she still stared, unaware of their wetness soaking her face. "I can still hear his moans." She shuddered and rubbed her arms. "My father stepped in between them, holding up his arms. They started beating him, but he fought back. Why did he have to fight back?" Her teeth were chattering as she shook.

"One of the kingsmen was injured. He broke his hand, I believe, when Papa used a piece of wood to defend himself from their kicks and punches. They took him to the lock up. I tried to run after him, his face was so bloody, I wanted to help him. But some of the others held me back. Fendrel was there. I wish I had gone to him. It was the last time I ever got to speak to him."

Elgon sank to his knees on the ground. He didn't have any recollection of what happened. This case had never reached his ears. He would have only been fifteen at the time, mourning the loss of his own father.

"They were going to have him tried. They took him all the way to Niran. I followed, catching rides with merchants along the way. The judge didn't even listen. He heard the guards' side of the tale. That my father assaulted several kingsmen and

214

attempted to kill them." A gut-wrenching sob broke from her lips. "He...he was sentenced to death by hanging."

On his hands and knees now, the weight of her sorrow pressed down upon his shoulders. His stomach heaved, and he swallowed hard, trying not to let the nausea overcome him. This monstrous evil had been allowed to go unchecked. Everything within him screamed at himself not to listen to any more, but this was a part of his story. Something that had been taken from both of them. This pain, this sorrow, this gut-wrenching agony...it was all because of him.

"I never got to see him again. He never came home. I hated him for trying. For standing up for Marcus. But I love him for it." She hugged herself and rocked back and forth. "If it weren't for him, Marcus would have never made it."

Marcus, the cripple. The young man who had the world in his heart, ready to offer comfort, wisdom, and healing to any who needed it. He shook his head, resolve like a rod of steel in his spine.

"Someone has to stand up. I have to stand up." He didn't hold it against her that she felt the way she did. His gut rocked with the guilt of it, that his carelessness had caused this. It was his weakness, his lack of responsibility and tendency toward fleshly pleasures that had blinded him to his duty. But it did not weaken the need he felt now to set it right.

She stood, her face broken with agony. "After all that...you can't go, don't you understand?" Her voice broke with the force of her words as she leaned into them, her shoulders hunched as if they took much from her as she said them.

He shook his head. "I have to."

Her face crumpled, her words barely above a whisper. "I

215

can't do it. Not again. You'll never make it back. I can't lose someone I—" She swallowed hard and hesitated, her next words almost inaudible. "I can't lose someone that I love. Not again."

His heart stopped at the confession. She…loved him?

He stepped closer. Reaching out a hand now, bridging the gap through the hole in the walls of her heart, the stone she had let fall, allowing him to see through the barricade and giving him a glimpse of the fragile garden behind it. He took her hand.

She didn't resist, and her gaze that had been resting on the ground raised to meet his, her eyes' green depths made brighter by the frame of the forest that skirted the field. They were full of tears, the water in them magnifying them and swallowing him whole. Hesitation lingered on her face, but her calloused fingers returned his grip. He could sense the longing that pressed into them both and bound them together.

He felt the stirring in his heart as the distance between them closed. Mere inches remained, buzzing with tension. She swayed, as if she might collide with him. But something stayed them both. Her purity giving him the courage to hold back, the control to stay still, and the willingness to protect her at all costs.

Something in her eyes changed as she looked deep into his soul. Emotions chasing each other across her face. Realization, sorrow, longing, then release. Her grip softened, and she drew back, lengthening the distance between them. There was a look on her face, almost otherworldly as she raised a timid hand to touch his cheek and brush a lock of his chin length hair back from over his eyes. She touched it briefly, like a breath skittering across his cheek. Then she drew her hand back, adding more distance between them, the longing still pulling them together, but her resistance strong, steady, in control.

"I see it in you." Her voice was husky, barely a sliver of a breath making it over her vocal cords. Her eyes held a world of hurt and hope, warring against each other in a fiery passion that remained contained but threatened to spill out from her eyes in the tears that gathered in the corners.

"What?"

Her lips trembled. "The leadership. That purpose was taken from you, but you were meant to be a leader. To carry this. To change this." Her eyes never left his, locked in a desperate clasp of passion, fire, and longing, but her hand gestured outward, toward the world sinking into decay and the people who dwelt in it, broken and misused. She took a breath, and it almost turned into a gasp as it entered her lungs. "You were meant to lead and restore." The words came from her lips, but it was almost as if they were spoken by another. The tone sounded familiar, even if it wasn't one he had heard out loud before.

His father. Not his earthly one who, God rest his soul, had little time for his son and while he loved him, had failed to teach him the ways of a king. But the voice of His heavenly Father. The true King. The Ruler over all.

She swallowed, and he watched her make a concerted effort. He saw the battle in her thoughts as they flashed across her face. "I know you must go." Her hand slipped from his grasp, and with one long look into his eyes, she turned to walk back toward the remains of the destroyed cabin.

Something rose up within him, and with one long stride, he took her shoulder in his gentle grasp, her hand in the other, turning her toward him. "Come with me." The words were forceful, as if the pent-up passion and desperate love had infused every syllable.

Her green eyes grew wide and deepened in color as his hand stole around her waist. She didn't pull away. Her eyes did not leave his. She stood strong on her own two feet, holding herself upright and not leaning into his embrace. But she didn't recoil.

Violet drew a breath, and it clung to her lungs from the tension that rose within her chest, her heart about to beat right out of its home. For one desperate moment she thought that she could make her home here, within his arms, sheltered under his protection.

But no.

She knew the destiny that he carried needed to be experienced and understood on his own before she could join him. If she ever did. The calling on his life was so much greater than she could imagine. It weighed on her soul. She would support him, lift him up, and carry the weight with him. But only in prayer. This was not her battle to fight. Not now. Not yet. She didn't, and couldn't, hold him to any promise. As much as she longed for it, she knew that the right thing was for him to go back and attempt to claim the throne. To fight with all his might for a justice that should be theirs by birthright. To change the world, fight the evil from the inside out. She knew his destiny could not include hers.

And she also knew that when he went away, he might not return. He would not be the same. Being a leader and a king required marrying a queen, a woman worthy of a throne. Worthy of the love of a king. No matter what Marcus had said about following her heart, sacrificing her desperate desire for Elgon, her Obed, would be what was required of her. She felt it deep in her spirit. Now was not the time.

"I cannot. You need to fight this battle. I will be here, with my responsibilities. I will pray for you every waking moment and never once forget you." The words came out of her in an impassioned expression of all of the walled-up love, longing, and sorrow, each feeling lacing every word. "But you must go. God will go with you. But I cannot."

Hesitating a moment, she reached forward, gripped his face softly between her hands and rose on her tiptoes to press a kiss on his forehead. It would be all that she could give, and instead of feeling like it was brought from the well of love within her, it came from something greater than her, like a blessing bestowed upon the only man who had ever won her heart.

The kiss felt like holy water on his forehead. Not one of passion, but born of purity, marking him forever with a calling greater and so far beyond himself. It baptized him for the path ahead. He knew his request had been made out of selfishness, and out of selfishness and love he had hoped she would say yes. But she was right. He needed this time to discover who he was meant to be. And he needed to do that before he could love this woman fully. He already loved her with every depth that was in him, longed to protect her with every breath of his being. But he knew he would discover new depths in the days and weeks to come, and it thrilled and terrified him in equal parts. And yet with those new depths, he knew he would be able to love her all the more. He watched her walk slowly toward her devastated home. He would set this right. Even if he died trying.

The journey must begin.

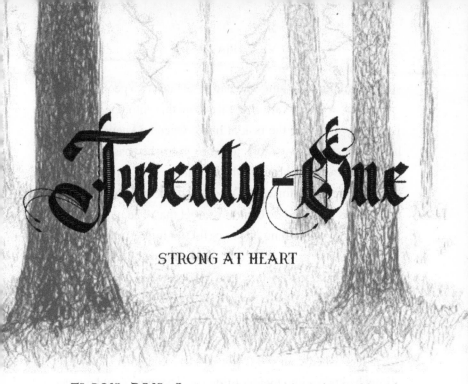

# Twenty-One

## STRONG AT HEART

ELGON RAN A hand through his hair, tucking it backwards and off his sweaty forehead. The summer air was heavy with the impending storm that had yet to drop its weighted load. He looked up at the gathering clouds. Still no rain and it had been over a day and a half since it had started stewing, like a person storing up grievances before they burst forth in a fury. He hiked up the pack on his shoulders. He was grateful Marcus had given him some leather twine to tie his hair back now that the military style had grown out. There was something wrong about returning to exactly the way he had been before.

He was a different man. Changed. A new creation. The Bible in his pack felt heavy and light at the same time. The weight of it made his soul sing. He was changed forever, and there was no going back. He felt he was more Obed than Elgon, but he would continue to use his given name. It was strange having two names; he had once been two people, lived two different lives. Marrying them together into one, who he was now, would be the task at hand. Once he knew the man he had been, he was able to learn from his past self and mistakes, growing through who he had become and into who he would be going forward. Obed had made him into the man that he was now, and he couldn't forget that. The name would always hold something meaningful to him. And perhaps, when he came back for Violet, the name would become a permanent fixture. To her, he was Obed. The man she had risked everything for to bring him healing and the man to whom she had offered her home, her heart, her prayers...and hopefully one day, her hand.

He had asked counsel of Everard, the big, silent man that Violet had taken into their confidence. That man could put the fear of God into anyone, and while Elgon was still somewhat afraid of the giant, he had grown to see some of the softness in him. The way he commanded a room, yet settled into the background at the same time. One couldn't miss the way that he hovered over Violet, as if he were a massive angel ready to safeguard a treasure. There was a knowing between the big man and his little woodland flower.

Between Everard's wisdom, Marcus's suggestions, and Violet's full eyes, the room had swiftly settled into a hierarchy, and while Elgon knew he was prince, and they treated him with respect, he was far from holding the final sway. And that was something he was perfectly comfortable with. He trusted these people, this ragtag group of freedom fighters. He trusted them with his life.

They had settled on a route that led through the forest. The stream he currently followed, its water shimmering in the scattered light that filtered through the jade canopy above, would be his guide through the dense woods of Raintamount Forest and onto the King's Highway. He would need to travel for nearly a day before he reached the capital city. Traveling on foot wasn't the best way to get there, but there were no horses to spare, and though he may be the prince, he had no money on him. He had earned his keep at Violet's, and nothing she had remained. Everard's words had been few and far between, but he had insinuated that if he had been in possession of a horse, he would have gladly given it to him.

The clouds overhead had grown darker over the last hour and Obed felt the oppressiveness of the weight of rain in the clouds. It was about to come down. He could feel it in the heavy, static air. Sweat was pouring off of him, and he gripped the straps of the leather pack, pulling them off his shoulders to give some relief. The darkness crept in from the edges of the forest, and unknowingly, his feet drifted toward the stream until he splashed into it with a stumble. Fear crept up at his throat.

Pounding hooves. The fall from the saddle. Those last moments had remained hazy in his memory as if they were protecting him from the pain and the devastation of the last time he had been in these woods. He had lost consciousness shortly after the fall. Tree leaves a kaleidoscope in his vision, crashing across the wooded floor, branches and rocks catching at his clothing, the intense pain in his leg that had been stuck in the stirrup of the saddle. He shuddered, his throat closing in, every snap of a twig setting his heart to clamoring in his chest.

Shadows lengthened, and he felt the muscles in his neck tighten. He tried to shake them out. He hadn't been alone since the accident. There had always been someone there, even if it was just Granny sitting across the room spinning her yarn or knitting something that Violet would take to market. His breath evened out at the remembrance of such a cozy scene. Company was a comfort, just having another's presence close by. The aloneness now crept in like the shadows lengthening across the emerald floor, the tree branches whispering, then clattering above his head with a gust of wind. A loose leaf on its flight to freedom brushed against his arm and another across his face, the wind at his back. Another twig snapped.

There was something other than wind at his back.

He spun, the stray hairs that had escaped from the bundle at the nape of his neck clinging to his face in sweaty tendrils. A snuffling sound made his heart stand still. And then he laughed, the joyous action feeling foreign on his tongue.

His horse, which had been lost the night of the fire, stood before him. Leaves were stuck in the corners of his mouth, and his flowing, dark mane was knotted with twigs, dirt, and other unidentifiable objects. Elgon stepped forward, running a hand over the front of the beast's face and down his muzzle, scratching in the spot just above his nose. "Seems you missed me after all." He chuckled when the horse nuzzled his chest. "I have nothing for you, you big oaf. Seem to have had your appetite satiated enough out in the wild. Useless nag." With a grin, he flung his pack across the horse's ample back and led him to a log. While not having ever been deemed short, Elgon still needed the assistance of a fallen tree to be able to spring to the stallion's back, clinging to the massive torso for dear

224

life with his legs.

Riding without stirrups, while not the easiest venture, did make for an easier fall, should that come about. He swallowed hard against the dizziness that crept around his vision. He couldn't help but remember what had happened the last time he had sat atop a horse. Even so, this animal was a godsend. Its arrival was no accident.

His horse's name came back to his memory, and he smiled. His mind was continually being repaired with sudden and random rushes of intelligence that returned bits of his lost memories. "Sigeric, am I glad to see you." Squeezing his legs and twisting his hands into the horse's mane, he urged him into a walk. Balancing himself felt somewhat foreign without the saddle, but it soon grew easier, though he knew he would be saddle-sore after a while.

The rains started with a gentle trickle that barely filtered its way through the leaves overhead, but then a crash of thunder sent the downpour upon them. Elgon barely had time to sweep his cloak from the roll attached to his pack. A gift from Everard and as large as the man himself, it covered his head with its waterproof hood and trailed around him in perfect protection against the rain. Bless the man. The sage color blended in with the scenery around him, and it not only protected him from the rain, but also surrounded him with the weight of comfort, nearly like a hug. Not that he had experienced many of those in his life, and none would compare to the motherliness and absolute perfection of Granny's embrace. Unless it was Violet's. He shook his head. No sense thinking about that now.

With the swiftness of Sigeric's easy lope, they had followed the stream nearly out of the forest within an hour. He saw the break in the trees in the distance. The rain that had pattered upon the canopy above had quickly become a driving rain. He had his head down against the wind, and Sigeric huffed as if to complain about the weather like a grumpy old man. He patted the horse's neck. The creek was rising, its water line starting to encroach above its banks and along the forest floor, taking small plants with it in its course toward the ocean, a long one though it may be. He sighed.

Sigeric's next huff made him smile sadly. "You're too young to be acting like an old man, friend. Quit complaining. We are here whether we like it or not."

He thought of the cozy fire with Violet in front of it. Her face lit, her hand busy as always, and her light brown hair, touched with the sunshine she spent so much of her time in, shimmering in the firelight. Trepidation filled him, and he shook the thoughts of comfort away from his mind. He was about to exit the forest into open country again, far enough away from the town to avoid any kingsmen who might know him, though none had yet. He assumed it was because of his new look and the months of his absence.

He remembered the picture of Violet and Granny in front of the fire, despite his best efforts.

His heart grew heavy with burden. He drew a deep breath. It was for them he would fight.

Elgon had only been gone for a day, and Violet felt bereft. She took a deep breath and gazed out the window, her knitting falling into her lap, almost forgotten as she watched the rain chatter against the foggy glass pane. She caught Marcus's gaze from his place at the kitchen table where he stood mixing herbs, and they exchanged sad smiles. Though there had been a slight shift in their relationship, and he was a bit more distant, she knew he would always be a close friend and one that she would hold tightly and close to her heart. She felt, deep in her soul, that there was something special ahead for Marcus. She hadn't the faintest idea what that was yet, but she knew it would come in the Lord's perfect timing, and she couldn't wait to watch it unfold. They had both experienced so much over the course of their friendship, it would be an absolute joy to watch something blossom in his life that would bring him happiness.

Thunder grumbled outside, and she started slightly in her chair, her hand flying to her ribs. She remembered Elgon's sheltering hand gently touching her waist. She shook her head, tucking a stray tendril of her hair behind her ear and picking up her knitting again.

Granny muttered from her place nearer the fire, and Violet's eyes filled with tears. Granny had grown worse, her memory sparser and her actions even more faltering than normal. It was as if the threads that were binding Granny to this earth were slowly snapping, one by one. A few words caught Violet's ears.

"A prince for my bonnie garden flower. My little Violet, nodding in the breeze. A queen." Granny shook her head and knitted a few more stitches, rocking back and forth.

Violet choked, her heart stilled. She wasn't one to believe in commonplace second-sight. But the Lord did sometimes open people's eyes to future events, their sight clearer into the ways of the Lord than those around them. She swallowed hard. Granny couldn't remember Elgon's name, let alone that he was a prince; furthermore, Violet had told her nothing of any feelings she had for Elgon, and she knew no one else had either.

She shook her head. Surely these were just the babblings of a woman whose mind had left her to handle life without the reasoning power of her faculties. Then again, Granny had always said, even when Violet was a child, that people for generations in their family had always grown clearer in spiritual sight the closer they were toward heaven.

Her knitting again abandoned in her lap, Violet pressed a hand to her mouth to silence a sob. There was something bittersweet about Granny going home to be with Jesus. She was the last living anchor Violet had to her home. To her father. The family that for generations had faithfully tended their little plot. "Please don't take her. Not yet," she whispered under her breath, dashing a hot tear away with the back of her hand before anyone else saw it.

"Violet." Granny's crooning filled the small room, and she reached out a hand as if she couldn't see in front of her. "Dear 'un, where are you?"

Violet heaved out of her chair and dropped to a knee beside Granny, gripping her wavering hand midair and running a gentle hand down her forearm in comfort. "I'm here, Granny. What is it?"

"You must tell Richard to come in from the rain. He'll catch a cold working in the mud and wet like this."

Violet bit her lip, running her hand up and down Granny's

228

upper arm, the frail muscles and protruding bone feeling sharper than usual. Had she been eating well enough? "It's all right, Granny."

Granny shook her head, her eyes gazing toward the window as a loud thunder blast rattled the glass panes and made all of them jump. Intense worry crossed her face, and she gripped Violet's hands in her soft, bony fingers. "Violet, you must fetch him. I worry for him. This thunderstorm isn't safe to be out in."

As if to back up her fears, the rain started falling heavier, and Violet herself shuddered. She was grateful that her father wasn't actually out in this storm. Worry worked its way into her own heart. Elgon was, and she desperately hoped and prayed that he was safe.

Elgon fought through the blinding rain on the open road. As much as the shadows of the forest filled him with worry, he had been sheltered under the massive boughs and green curtained ceiling. Sigeric huffed as if he were offended he was obliged to run in the rain. Elgon hunkered beneath his cloak, cradling his pack in his arms to keep what little he could dry.

"You've grown soft, old boy. You're a war horse. Quit complaining. Rain and mud are the least of your worries." Elgon patted the horse's neck appreciatively all the same. He was beyond grateful for the company and extra help on this journey.

Everyone thought the prince dead. Time was of the essence.

He drew a breath and swallowed hard as he neared the gate

of Valhaven, the last village between him and the capital. Taking the hike through the woods had not only helped him avoid any kingsmen who might recognize him as the farmer who had stood up to them that day in the village, but it had also saved him some time. Weaving through Raintamount Forest was rougher work, but even so, it had shaved off nearly a day of travel by the main route, which would have required him to go around. He needed to get through this one last checkpoint in order to make it to Niran. Everard had warned him that civilian travel had been limited, and unless one had a government pass, wares to sell that passed inspection, or you struck the fancy of the kingsmen on guard, there was little chance of getting through.

Upon the gate, he dismounted and gripped Sigeric's mane, leading him toward the entrance. He tucked his pack underneath his cloak with his free hand, while also trying to conceal the sword tied to his back beneath the heavy layers of waxen wool. If they found the execution orders in his pack, there would be a problem. He knew he needed them to prove his identity to those at the palace, but their presence on his person made him nervous. The amulet tucked snugly beneath his shirt did the same, but there was little chance of them finding that. They hadn't resorted to physical searches yet. Or had they? Swallowing hard, he realized that he genuinely had no idea how the lower classes were treated, which served to be an issue now that he was one of them.

His pulse beat harder in his ears as he neared the gate, but then a confidence that felt normal settled upon his shoulders, like the fur ruff of a royal's ceremonial dress. He straightened. He was the prince.

230

What felt like a whisper assuaged his ear, stopping him in his tracks. He pulled Sigric to a halt, causing the horse to stutter and shake his head in frustration at the mixed signals his master was giving him. Elgon gripped his hand in Sigeric's mane. Why was he feeling this halt in his gut? He hadn't felt it before.

*Don't tell them.* The words were like a clarion call in his mind, and he didn't know where they were coming from. His own thoughts moments before had been telling him exactly the opposite. He had been ready to burst into the guard house, remind them all who he was and take his birthright. *This needs to be covert. You won't make it to the palace if you don't stay hidden.*

He had heard that voice before, but it hadn't been so strong. It wasn't like the soft whisper of a breeze through leaves. It was loud and concussive like the crack of a tree finally breaking beneath a strain, its trunk snapping in two and thundering to the earth, taking anything in its path with it. He shook his head. Was this the Lord?

*Do not tell them.* What was the worst that could happen from following these internal orders? He would rather have listened to what he thought to be God's voice and have maybe made a mistake than completely ignore the direction and suffer the consequences. The words had been more than a gentle nudging—they had ramifications, and he felt them gather at his back. They had pressed in like a pack of wolves hunting their prey, ready to down their quarry within seconds if it made the wrong move. He took a deep breath. *Lord, give me wisdom. Help me accomplish what I have set out to do. I know you do not want your people to live in bondage. That*

231

*verse that Marcus read said as much. Help me to do and say the right things by your power. You saved me. It is the least I can do to try to save those you have entrusted to my care.*

He leaned over and whispered in the steed's ears, "Let's do this, Sigeric. For God and for country." The war cry of his forefathers slipped easily from his lips, and he drew his shoulders back under the heavy cloak. He would need to disguise the kingly bearing or else his chance would be lost, his directions incomplete, and his life mission without success. No peasant would meander into town with shoulders ramrod straight, astride a military horse with head held high. It was all in the disguise. He was grateful Sigeric was now covered from head to toe in a layer of mud. While the poor fellow would have a hard time of it when he was led for a bath, the dirt hid his majestic features. Having no saddle helped that image. They would be given away in a second if someone saw Sigeric in all of his gleaming black royal glory.

The gatehouse itself rose several stories above him, its brick edifices standing with intimidating height and girth making him feel watched. There was an uneasy feeling that clung to him like burrs sticking to the hem of his cloak as he passed beneath the cool, shadowed recess of the gateway. He swallowed. Finally within the town, he felt the air press down harder in his lungs, as if he couldn't get a deep breath. Why was he feeling this way? It was almost as if there was an oppression on the town, as if being inside of it created a heaviness that settled on him, weighing him down beyond the comfort of Everard's cloak. People hurried across muddy streets, some barefoot, others with shoes that could hardly be called as such. Their heads were down, their bony shoulders hunched against the rain.

Elgon's vision blurred with moisture. He saw them with new vision. He curled in on himself, hugging the leather bag close to his chest and feeling the amulet settle there.

He had been so blind before, unable to see the sorrow, pain, or the fear on any of their faces. All this time, they had fought alone, their heads and hearts bowed under an oppression that grew daily, a throne built on deception and manipulation, a rule that was domineering and cruel. Their pain led them, their fear guided them, and their desperation blinded them to any other way of life. They were trapped, like a deer in a snare, unable to free themselves and too afraid to try.

His compassion waxed hot for them. Little did they know of the life that should be theirs, if only someone was willing to stand up and fight. But there was such a one. And that person was him.

"You there! Halt by order of the king! Anyone entering these gates is subject to search."

Elgon stopped, pulling Sigeric to a halt beside him. *Lord, those hedges of protection would be quite spectacular right about now.* His memory was better than he had thought. Once he had gotten it back, all of the scriptures that Marcus had read to him, or that Granny had shared with him in his illness, or that he had heard Violet and Granny quote daily had clung to his willing mind like burrs to animal fur. The verses had all been helpful, edifying, and words that he knew he could cling to through the next few days as he sought to take up the throne and scepter from the illegal usurper. He swallowed hard. It was time for the show.

He turned and took a few steps toward the kingsman who

had raised his voice.

"Hold!" The command was stern.

Elgon felt the back of his mouth go dry as he slid the pack so it was hidden behind his back. He fought to keep his cloak wrapped around himself. His feet stumbled as they hit the cobbles, the ground uneven and slippery with the rain.

"State your business!"

Elgon drew a breath. This man was just doing his job, he reminded himself. If he cooperated, all would be well. He didn't need to tell an outright lie. "I am on my way to the capital city."

"What for?" Suspicion colored the kingsman's voice. "You know travel is limited between towns right now."

"Why is that?" Egon pressed. He didn't want to give away his nobility, so he changed his speech to have a bit more of the commonplace lilt that he had noticed in the villagers he had spent the last few months with.

The kingsman studied him quizzically. "Since the prince's death, the new king has ordered for restricted access to our cities. Specifically, the capital city."

Elgon's blood boiled. The new king? It seemed that Enguerrand was no longer a chancellor or regent but had officially claimed the title of king. Elgon might have knocked the man flat if he were any closer. "Do I look like a prince murderer to you?" Elgon added a waver into his voice and then coughed into his elbow. He was already hunched beneath the weight of the cloak and his sword, but he leaned into it to make himself appear smaller and weakly.

The kingsman chuckled under his breath. "I suppose not. You look about as sick as King Indulf did toward his last days." He laughed and waved off Elgon, ushering him on his way.

But Elgon stood frozen to the spot. His father. His memory flashed and a splitting headache started pounding between his ears. He rested his forehead against Sigeric's massive shoulder, no longer feigning his weakness. The memory was vivid, setting his head to spinning and his mind to racing. His thoughts flitted hither and yon as he cringed, and the muscles in his shoulders tightened against the pain.

His father had slowly grown ill over time. He hadn't just died suddenly, though that had been what it had felt like at the time. It had taken Elgon months to finally admit to himself that his father was growing weaker. But by then, Elgon had possessed little need or desire for a father's attention and had sought approval elsewhere. He had been old enough to realize that his father didn't seem to care for him, so why would he have tried to spend time with him? It would've meant more rejection, more disapproving looks and sharp words that struck at him like flint against tinder, setting ablaze the anger and rekindling the fodder of every previous wound.

Thoughtful, Elgon led Sigeric through the village and out the other side. His trouser legs were wet and muddy, his boots starting to take on water from walking through the dark puddles staining the cobblestone streets. His head started to ache with the effort.

There was something that kept coming to mind. It niggled at the back of his memory like a festering wound, something that caused pain and suffering but remained undetected. He had forgotten a lot of things about his past, and while many things had resurfaced right away, it was difficult to reconcile them all with old thoughts that stuttered to the surface like dead fish floating to the top of the water with its foul smell and rotting flesh.

He swiped the back of his hand at his nose as it started to run. The night air was taking a cold turn, and his cloak, while still keeping him mostly dry, was growing heavy with water. The cold moisture seeping through his boots was starting to cause his body temperature to drop. The headache pressed down between his temples, and he blinked hard against it.

Flashes of memories mixed with his blurry vision, and he almost wasn't sure what he was seeing with his mind's eye and what he truly saw with his physical ones. Gray walls, tapestries hung nearly floor to ceiling in the large hallway. The ceilings were so high that seven men would need to stand on each other's shoulders to reach the top, and a long red carpet woven with the beautiful, concentric designs of the Eliran royal line ran down the length of the hall.

Elgon drew Sigeric to the side of a road where a water trough sat, and he stood for a moment, letting his horse drink. Taking a leather canteen from the pack, he dumped part of the remaining contents into his mouth, letting it sit and settle on his tongue before he swallowed. The water left a stale taste in his mouth.

Next he led Sigeric to the first blacksmith shop he could find. He gave the man his boot knife, hand-made by Everard, in exchange for a bridle for Sigeric. A saddle would have to come later. He had no funds. It was strange how natural it felt to him to be at the mercy of his own wits in trade instead of having all of the coin in the world.

As prince, he had been so used to having everything he

needed or wanted right at his fingertips. It had been a completely foreign concept to work for a living, and not only that, but to toil desperately hard for the equivalent of the smallest crumb from the palace where he had once resided. Something in his heart ached at the idea of going back. His life working, eating, sleeping, and breathing the land and the toil had been an experience that, if the fate of a nation weren't hanging in the balance, would have tempted him enough to simply stay where he had ended up.

As he drew near the outskirts of the city, Elgon saw the walls of the capital city, Niran, its stone walls rising above the trees and settling against mountain crags on one side, the sea on the other. The wind whipping over the waves smote him in the face when he stepped from under cover of the trees along the road. The sea was a-toss from the storm, and Elgon felt static in the air, the bite from the salty wind stinging his nose. Emotions rolled through his chest, squeezing tight around his heart. The headache that had plagued him for the last few miles intensified, and he winced against the pain. An unnerving feeling crept up his spine and tickled the back of his neck.

Throwing his head around, he looked back up the trail behind him. Nothing hid in the trees except shadows that moved and lurked about the branches and leaves, now nearly inky black with the clouds overhead. He swallowed. The looming city ahead filled him with trepidation, the purpose within him feeling weak against the shadows that crowded in.

Sigeric turned and shifted uneasily underneath him. Elgon knew he needed to move forward, but the fear clamped down on his chest.

*Who am I to take this on? I was the worst of them.* Flashes of drunken parties, careless and foolish shouting matches with his father, offers of all sorts of substances that altered his mind and threw him into a temporary oblivion danced before him. He shook his head against the mental images and the overwhelming, crushing weight of the pain those memories caused. The people, *his* people, had been suffering. Day in and day out, the pressure had mounted as censure, abuse, and the hungry thirst for power overtook the palace. And he had done nothing.

The world had crumbled outside his walls, but he had not known. He had spent his days and nights drunk on oblivion and empty of any compassion or compunction for what should have been his duty. His responsibility. His calling.

Dusk trailed its hungry fingers across the moors and forests, dragging his spirit down into the depths of the darkness with it. Sigeric pranced uneasily down the trail at an angle and let out a nervous whinny, throwing his head back as if to check on his rider.

The weight of his cloak suddenly brought a pressure on his shoulders that hadn't been there before. He gasped and bent over under the heaviness that clutched at his shoulders. He had been responsible. He had been the one destined to protect and lead a nation, and instead he had let it go to ruin. Who was he to think that he could take it back and do any better of a job than he had done before?

*That burden was not for you at the time.*

The whispered words coated the burning, sinking shame in his heart with a cool breeze. Soothing for the moment until the next wave of pain overtook him, and he doubled over, his face tickled by the ends of Sigeric's damp mane that blew in the wind. He gripped the reins tight in his fingers, Sigeric hopping with the pull on his mouth.

*You were young. That burden was too heavy for a boy to carry. You cannot fix the past, and I already have done penance on your behalf. But the burden I have placed on your heart is for now. I waited until I knew you were ready to carry it.*

Elgon felt the darkness and shame within him shudder at the words that permeated his spirit. Whispers of accusation bounced upon the stormy wind, but they sounded farther off than they had a moment ago.

*My strength will be with you.* The words resonated stronger in his heart and the bitterness of the wound lifted a little.

A picture rose in his mind of a young Elgon, standing in the middle of the great hall of the palace, whispering voices on every side, tempting him one way then another, his father too far out of reach and his heart too young to care for anything other than sinful pursuits and pleasures.

But even farther into the vision he saw a little boy, the gold circlet on his forehead, his brown locks flowing around it and his amber eyes wide, large in his small face and full of tears and longing. Devoid of a mother and nearly without a father. A heart broken beneath the weight of his loneliness. Like a sapling bent underneath the weight of its leaves, having grown too fast for its roots to hold, he toppled over and fell from the calling and destiny that had been on his life.

*My forgiveness has covered you. My calling has marked you. My heart is strong within you. Fight now beside Me to master yourself and the voices that lie to you. Step forth into the destiny you were born into and the provision you will bring to this nation.*

It was like a battle cry in his spirit. Sigeric pranced, throwing his head back with grace and snorting with anticipation, pawing the ground as if ready to ride to battle. almost as if he had heard it too.

The last of the taunting voices fell away, and Elgon sat upright on his war horse's back, the hood slipping from his head and his long hair, having slipped from the tie, whipping with the wind. Water dripped down his back. He didn't even care. He would not be swayed.

With a squeeze of his legs and a "Ha!" to the wind that was as much of a battle cry as a call to action, Sigeric leapt forward into a run as darkness chased them across the moor.

No more time to waste.

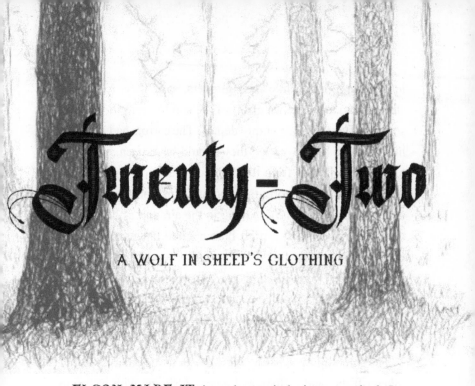

# Twenty-Two

## A WOLF IN SHEEP'S CLOTHING

ELGON MADE IT into the capital city unscathed. Its brick walls and edifices had been white washed with the salty sea wind, the layers of the city rising against the mountain scape behind it, barely visible through the mist and rain. Layer upon layer of buildings and streets led up to the highest point of the city where the castle stood, nestled with its back to the rock face of the Illias mountain pass. One side of the castle faced the sea, and two others faced out over the city like a dark, ominous throne with Elira's royal houses just below. The rest of the city streets gathered beneath it like a footstool, sprawled down and around to the main gate, where Elgon entered from off the moors.

He had replaced the hood on his head and snuck in behind a group of peasant merchants, their sickly-looking oxen pulling a cart laden far beyond their strength to carry with goods, weavings, fruits, and vegetables. The vegetation looked limp, much like their growers, as if they, too, were starved for care, one last effort of the soil to bring forth some sort of harvest from its empty depths. The carrots had a lighter hue than the bright orange they should have been, and their tops were yellowed from the dry spell that had only just now been broken by the storm that had met him along the way.

A dank, green mistiness hung in the air, and as he entered the outer rings of the city, it bore a smell that was far from enticing. Bitter and full of the scent of waste that had been long since left to rot filled his nostrils. He felt a gag rise in the back of his throat, and he tried to breathe through his mouth in order to keep the smell from coercing him to empty his innards.

The smell lightened as he drew closer to the palace. He had taken off the heavy cloak and covered Sigeric with it, trying to mask the massive haunches and warrior-like physique as much as the mud and the wool cloak could. Every other animal here looked like it had seen far better days.

But mud did wonders. Elgon almost didn't care that he was covered with it himself, caked as it was to his boots and coating as much of himself as he could see and probably some that he couldn't.

The removal of the cloak left his sword in its scabbard exposed. It at once felt very right and fitting, but as if it belonged to someone else. In actuality, it did. It belonged to the prince who had trained with it under the blossoms of the magnolia tree in the royal garden, not to the farmer who was more familiar with a scythe than a sword.

When he started to recognize the street corners, his heart beat faster, flying into his throat.

The streets grew whiter but were still coated with the thick mist that seemed to hover over the city like impending doom. Elgon felt the oppressiveness and anxiety of reaching his childhood home—so familiar, yet so distant. He swallowed. This was going to be harder than he thought. How on earth was he supposed to get inside, let alone seek an audience with the Chancellor Enguerrand?

*Enguerrand.* He muttered it under his breath. The man who had taken charge after his father had died had seemed like a godsend at the time but had turned out to be a wolf in sheep's clothing. Or so it seemed. He still held out hope that the advisor, who had once given the impression that he held Elgon's best interests at heart, still did.

He shivered at the things Enguerrand had suggested he do as consolation in his grief. Growing him old before his time, not with responsibility, but with frivolity. Jading any bright outlook he had on life, which had been nearly nonexistent as it was.

The intrusive, tempting thoughts that spoke of shame and guilt whispered in his ear as Sigeric's hooves clunked against the cobblestones. The sound echoed hollow and eerie in the nearly empty corridor. Not many wished to be out in the rain, and he was in the wealthier part of town now, the expensive brick houses creating a dark and narrow passageway between them.

For while white, whole, and beautiful without, the homes of the wealthy and the castle above them were dead, stinking, and rotten within. They had been ever since his father had died. Any last bit of warmth and integrity had oozed from these confines the minute the king's last breath had left his

243

body.

Grief overwhelmed him. His father had been the only block standing between integrity and evil, and he had been too embittered to see it.

"Halt there! Turn back, peasant. This is no place for you to come crawling."

Elgon's heart skipped a beat, and it felt like far too long before another breath entered his lungs. But then he felt some peace settle around his shoulders. "I have been on a mission. I am a kingsman, here to report to his eminence Enguerrand."

A snort from the passageway was his only reply for a moment. Then, "You don't look like you represent your station, soldier."

"Nor would you if you had traipsed through hill and dale for the last few days only to be soaked to the bone and drenched in mud." He whipped the cloak from Sigeric's back, revealing to the soldier's trained eye a horse with the stature worthy of a kingsman or a noble. "My steed has also sustained such treatment. Surely you won't let a kingsman of the mounted battalion stand without your gates when shelter, rest, and a bath is offered within?"

Skepticism moved across the guard's expression, now visible to Elgon as the man stepped from the alcove he had been stationed in, letting his face meet the dim, jaded light.

"What was your mission?" The question was timid, for even the guard knew that the question was not within his right to ask.

"I was a part of the search party for the prince." Elgon told the half-truth. The kingsmen who had been in his detail in the first place would have also been tasked with the job of hunting for him...or his corpse.

The guard seemed to find that mission one of import, for a look came over his face, and Elgon stuttered in his step when he saw it.

Confusion, relief, pain and...fear.

"Any luck?"

Elgon shook his head. "No such luck, I'm afraid. His Royal Highness was not found by the Kingsmen." Again, another mostly true statement. He hadn't been found by the Kingsmen, and when they had been in his presence, they hadn't known that the long-haired farmer with a protective streak and a tendency to headaches and rash decisions had been their prince.

But when Elgon released those words into the thick night air, the kingsman's shoulders fell with dejection. Almost as if he...regretted and mourned the loss. What did that speak of the one who ruled within? Or of the allegiance of the Kingsmen?

"Very well, soldier. You may pass." The kingsman had a sorrowful note to his voice, and Elgon questioned it in his mind as he crossed the threshold and was within the walls of his palatial home. Albeit in the stable grounds. A shiver went through his spine as the medallion thumped between his ribs.

Home.

He hoped.

He snuck into the stable and started cleaning and brushing down Sigeric. The other kingsmen were responsible for their horses, and the poor fellow needed a good bath. Elgon himself reeked of sweat, travel, mud and too much rain. His clothes were waterlogged, and his hair hadn't dried in days. Besides, he needed a moment to decide how to get an audience with the chancellor. Now that he was here, his mind seemed to have left him, all strategy blowing away with the damp, moorish wind that had tossed his hair. He started praying under his breath as he went about the mundane but soothing tasks of cleaning his mount.

No one seemed to mind him there. No one questioned him. There must have been a lot of kingsmen in and out. He wouldn't have known. He had never been down here in the stables before and had never known what went on within the military housing that made up the lower levels of the castle. He flexed his hand and shook out his arm, giving it a break from the stiff brush he was using to curry Sigeric's hair. He had, however, trained with the best of the warriors, and his skill with the sword, while still fuzzy, would be passable. That blade and the weight had felt right within his palm, and it comforted him now, hanging at his side. He was grateful for the hustle and bustle of the damp and steaming stable, the smell of horses, manure piled in the corner, the animal's warmth creating a foggy atmosphere mixed with the damp air. Everyone had a job to do, leaving him undisturbed in his appraisal of everything.

Sigeric had given him the cover he needed to enter within the walls. If only he could capitalize on that now.

He almost didn't want to leave Sigeric, his one friend and the only familiar face within these stone walls that now locked him into his destiny. Be it liberty or death.

Next step was the bath, which he was in desperate need of. The cold water turned a dark shade of gray when he finally removed himself from it, the mud and dirt washed thoroughly from his hair and even from behind his ears. The set of clean clothes from the pile left for the kingsmen fit him well, and he tossed the peasant clothes in the heap of other dirty laundry.

The long, bronze tunic brushed the tops of his thighs, and the soft, dark brown, leather breeches would be tucked into his boots that had desperately required the stiff cleaning he had given them. He used the leather cord to tie back his wet brown locks, and a few pieces fell in front of his face. He glanced at his reflection in the bronze half-wall that covered the lower portion of the stone walls as he knelt to pull on his second boot. The metal helped keep the heat and moisture in the room, and the distorted vision that met him was of a man that looked a lot closer to a prince than the mud-coated peasant that had entered the room. The leather vest he wore was for a kingsman's rank. As he ran his hand over the king's seal burned into the shoulder, he swallowed the feeling of fear that rose in his stomach. The same seal was on the medallion that swung from his neck again.

He had removed it for his bath and rolled it in his clothes until he had gotten out and slyly replaced it. He took a deep breath, his rib cage expanding beneath the concentric leather pieces that were buckled over his chest. Now to get to the courtroom without being recognized or stopped.

Or lost.

It was now or never. He guessed Enguerrand would get quite the shock when he showed up in the courtroom—the prince he thought was dead and would now take his place. The man would have to pay for his actions if he thought he was safe in holding onto the throne.

He marched through several halls, up a flight of stairs, and smiled softly when he recognized the halls around the kitchen. His throat felt choked. He remembered these halls fondly. The times he had spent sneaking down to the kitchen in the middle of the night as a boy to beg the cook, who seemingly never slept, for a glass of warm milk and a pastry of her making. It hadn't taken him long to learn that the pastries for the next morning were baked during the night, and if he arrived in time, he could enjoy them warm with his milk.

Another smile tugged at the corners of his mouth. His life had been a lonely one, full of few relationships with people who actually cared or loved, but it was little moments like those he was grateful to remember. To see the people he had forgotten about who had shown him love and care throughout the dark days of motherlessness that had plagued his childhood and sabotaged his youth.

He swallowed. "Lord, don't let me forget again." It was as if once he knew who he was, who he *truly* was—a son of God before he was the son of any earthly king—he saw the world around him through a new set of eyes. The people who had once just been faces, or a means to an end, were now truly people with souls and livelihoods that deserved respect, care, and love. Even from their king. *Especially* from their king.

His father had felt that. The weight of the crown was so heavy, Elgon had seen it drag on him day after day, his face growing gaunt before its time. He thought now of the counselors who had been his undoing. Enguerrand had led the charge, of that he was sure now.

While his thoughts had wandered, his feet had taken him down paths that his subconscious had remembered, and he glanced around a corner down a hallway to the next crossing, where a red carpet with ornate weavings led down the massive hall. Four kingsmen stood at the end, their hands on the hilts of the swords at their sides. Elgon instinctively reached for where his rested on his hip. He sucked in a breath. He needed to gain entry to that courtroom.

Back to the wall, he leaned over again to peer around the corner.

A hand gripped his shoulder in a massive, strong grasp, and an arm reached across his chest to grab his other shoulder, spinning him toward the stranger and into a closet along the hall. He fell backwards with the momentum when he was released, against shelves full of candles and sundry linens. He stumbled to his feet, bringing his fists up. He wasn't going down without a fight. The stranger in kingsman's clothing, with the scarlet ribbon of a commander fluttering from his shoulder, whirled after closing the door and held up his hands.

Elgon knew that face, though right now it was in an odd expression of wide-eyed surprise.

"Malcolm?"

"Elgon? Your highness. What—?"

Elgon grasped Malcolm's forearm and clapped him on the shoulder with his other hand. "It's so good to see you."

Malcolm's eyes grew wider and larger in his face. He shook his head, suspicion dawning. "You look like him, but…different."

Elgon held up his hands. "It's me."

"You are supposed to be dead." The flat tone in Malcolm's voice told Elgon that he had resigned to the realization after a long fight with himself. It wouldn't have been easy losing the man you had trained with and lived to protect as a part of the royal detail.

Elgon didn't speak for a moment. His eyes fell again to the ribbon fluttering from Malcolm's shoulder. He appeared to have risen to the rank of battalion chief while Elgon had been away. Their eyes locked, and Malcolm's grew wider with shock. The brown irises deepened in color.

"You are supposed to be dead." Malcolm repeated, a touch of panic in his voice, emphasizing the word "supposed."

Elgon grunted. "Clearly, I'm not."

"You don't understand." Malcolm leaned hard against the door, as if to bar out the world. "You aren't supposed to be here. Your death was not an accident."

Flashes of green, treetops flying by in his vision, horses hooves pounding deathly close to his eardrums, and the underbrush beating him on every side flashed through his memory. Elgon gripped his side, stumbling back a step from Malcolm. "What do you mean?" he rasped.

Malcolm stepped forward to grip his arm. "Do you not remember what occurred?" Solemness and urgency laced every syllable, his grip sharp against Elgon's skin, even through his shirt.

Elgon shook his head. "Just flashes of being dragged."

Malcolm spun away from him, pacing two steps in the small, confined space that they shared. His eyebrows were drawn, and his chiseled face was tight over his clenched jaw.

"What do you mean my death was no accident? What aren't you telling me, Malcolm?"

Malcolm whirled again and took a step closer, his head shaking and the internal battle within him evident in his every expression, every movement. The side of his face twitched.

"Your death was planned. The assassination was believed to be complete. I—" His eyes grew hazy. "I mourned for you. It was only after the attack that I found out. It was no accident that I was not in that detail. I had to work hard to convince them after the fact that I was one who could be trusted. A man on the king's detail who still remains with a close contact in the courtroom is far more valuable than a man beheaded for treason."

"What are you talking about?" The dread rising within Elgon was a black hand that gripped his throat and tightened the muscles around his neck, his shoulders rising beneath the strain and fear that drove into his very bones.

Malcolm gripped both of his shoulders, his shorter, military haircut in need of a trim as a few shorter pieces fell over his sweaty forehead, damp with his perspiration.

Elgon gasped for a breath. The air in this closet was getting close.

"You were assassinated," Malcom whispered hoarsely. "When your body was not found, a search commenced. They searched homes to determine if you had been taken in, but to no avail. When they did not find you nor your horse, it was believed that you were eaten by a wild animal and nothing remained of your body." His voice broke. "There was nothing that even remained to bury beside your father."

Elgon could hardly breathe. He had thought until this time that his accident had been a dreadful misfortune. But really, he had been living on the edge of a blade. Being found would have resulted in his death. Had Violet not taken him in, hid him from prying eyes, buried his identity…

He would have been hunted down and killed.

251

"It was made to appear as an accident to deflect suspicion. They lured you into the woods, convincing you that it was the correct path. Away from prying eyes, they were able to complete—or so they thought—the death of the crown prince. Do you find it a coincidence that you were just turning of age when this happened? How did His Lord the Chancellor phrase it—your 'defining mission'?"

Elgon just stared at him, all of the puzzle pieces clicking into place. He took a step back from Malcolm. Who was to say that he was telling him all of this, only to kill him?

The closet now felt extremely tight.

He gripped his fingers tight and they ached. "Why are you telling me this?"

Realization registered on Malcolm's face. "Why do you think? You are obviously here to claim back the throne. You can't just go barging in without a plan. And knowing you, you don't have much of one." A small smile changed Malcolm's face, and Elgon questioned whether his fears were true. This seemed like a small truce of friendship from the one man whom he had thought, of all others, that he could trust.

"And whose side are you on?"

Malcolm's fists clenched at his side, and then he raised his right across his chest in a salute. "My king." The voice was deep and husky, full of meaning, and Elgon thought he detected tears swimming in Malcolm's deep brown eyes as he slowly bent in a soldier's salute.

Elgon drew a breath.

*King*.

God help him.

252

# Twenty-Three

## FACING EVIL

NOW WAS THE time. There would be no more waiting to meet his destiny. After some discussion, they had decided it was best to show up in the king's court. Malcolm was sure there were more kingsmen who would be on Elgon's side, though Enguerrand would not go down without a fight.

He squared his shoulders beneath the armor that he wore. The leather felt right on him. He fingered the embossed detail around the buckles that protected his middle, and he felt the nausea swirl beneath. It had come full circle. To have started this journey by joining the kingsmen battalion, being rescued by a woman who thought that was all he was, then becoming another man in search of his former self...it was a mind-boggling turn of events, to say the least.

But he felt his Heavenly Father's presence even now. He was a new creation. A new man within the shell of the old. Living a life that was new and dedicated to a new Master, while moving through the halls and rooms of his former life. It was surreal. To be here, but be someone entirely different.

He straightened his shoulders. He belonged here. It was where his duty lay. He thought fondly of his father, King Indulf and saw him now for what he had been: a man overwhelmed and torn between the challenges of sheltering a kingdom and raising a son. A man who had made a difficult decision to take a stand in one arena, to the detriment of the other. A man who had been loved by his kingdom, though he had not been so by his son. Emotion choked his throat. He had seen the longing in his father's eyes. He had not known then what it meant, but now he did.

By God's grace, he would be as good of a king and a better father to his children. A man who, by God's grace, could rise to the occasion in both arenas, protecting them both and showing love where it was due.

But for now, onward. *Lord, protect me.*

He stepped around the corner, head held high, and strode with confidence toward the heavily plated wooden doors that closed off the entry to the courtroom. *Give me strength.*

Malcolm was at one door. Another guard he did not recognize was at the other. Malcolm made a slight nod and motioned to his counterpart. "Open the door."

The kingsman obeyed, and the door swung inward. Elgon's knees trembled at the sight of the long throne room, the red carpet marching toward the throne. The columns and windows on each wall let in a foggy gray light from the rainy world outside, throwing the room into darkness. The shadows from the columns resembled tree trunks in a forest, and Elgon felt as though the same eerie stillness that had met him in that

254

woodland place waited for him here. The glass fixtures that shed their golden light upon the gloomy room were larger than his torso and suspended at the edges of the room between each pillar. Some other guards and nobles milled about, though Elgon recognized few of them.

Except here, the evil beasts that lurked around corners waiting to devour prey were of the two legged sort.

"Who goes there?"

Enguerrand.

The man on the throne had on his father's circlet, and Elgon clenched his fists at his side, continuing to close the distance between them. The man who occupied the throne had a comfortable air about him which reeked of a thief who reveled in the pride of his sin. His dark hair and salt-and-pepper beard covered an angular face, and his brown eyes were somehow warm and…inviting? Elgon's shadowed recollection of him had been colder, darker, and more menacing than this man before him. Enguerrand had sought to be a friendly counselor in the days of his youth, always sidling up to Elgon with suggestions of how to have a good time or a way to escape the demands his father had started to put upon him in the way of learning to rule. His had been a voice that had always sought to be congenial without the forethought and responsibility of actual friendship.

Well, no more.

"Enguerrand, by order of the king, I demand you give up the throne, declare yourself a usurper, and give the scepter and crown to the rightful heir." His voice bounced from the walls, and it was almost as if the shadows shirked away from the tones.

255

A pause, then a mirthless laugh echoed back at him, taunting him with its carefree nature. It was only when Elgon drew close to the throne that Enguerrand's laugh stilled in his throat and a look of surprise flitted across his face. Only for a second, and then it was gone.

Elgon knew he had recognized him. Though it had been months, something in him must still look of the boy Enguerrand had sent out with his kingsmen. The boy who should be seated where Enguerrand was now.

"And who might you be? Why is a random kingsman demanding the throne?" The voice was schooled, restrained, held in check with perfect finesse and dripping with humor. Elgon remembered well that reined-in voice that knew exactly what it wanted and how to achieve it.

"I'm not a kingsman. I'm a man who doesn't want to be king but fears he has to. You know who I am, as will the entire kingdom of Elira within a short amount of time. But for those within this room, I am Elgon of the city Niran, son of the former King Indulf, and I appear here today to claim the throne and remove the former Lord Chancellor Enguerrand from his usurped position."

Silence met his ears as the last echo of his declaration slowly settled in the room.

Enguerrand's piercing eyes did not once leave his, no mirth within their gaze as he burst into a warm and charming laugh, drawing similar reactions from the other men in the room—some kingsmen and a few nobles that Elgon recognized, though their names were not strong in his memory. He had hated the things of the court, except for what women and wine it would bring him. Now he paid dearly for not having cultivated those relationships when he had the chance.

The calculating eyes of his counterpart gave him a once-over that put the chill of confusion into his heart. "So you say. But what proof have you of this? Our beloved crown prince and ruler was killed on a mission, his body fodder for the wild beasts of the forest." Enguerrand's wave of a hand sliced through the air and seemed to flick away any reality to Elgon or his claim.

Elgon felt heat radiating from the medallion tucked against his chest beneath his armor. The room was turning, he could sense the mood shifting to side with Enguerrand, their perceptions sliding across the vast ornate floors like magnets, seeking the one who appeared self-assured and confident in his position.

"I need not proof of my rights, though you sit upon the throne with none of your own. I have here at my breast the medallion of the house of Indulf, the royal crest given to the king and his descendants." Elgon reached a hand beneath his leather armor and pulled on the string that was looped through the hole in the medallion, drawing it forth. The gold, now polished by his own hand, caught the light of the lanterns that filled the court with their golden glow.

The only betrayal of Enguerrand's face was a slight hesitation. It could not have been noticed by any of the other nobles or kingsmen, as it was so minute even Elgon had to strain to catch the wince about the eyes.

Without stepping off the dais, he reached out a hand as if to examine the medallion, grasped it in his hands, and before Elgon had any time to react, he pulled him by the cord toward him, throwing Elgon off balance. His brown eyes suddenly turned piercing, and there was a moment in his soul where Elgon felt that he was seen. The veil was lifted for a moment, and he saw that Enguerrand knew he was the prince. With that one glance, Elgon saw past the mask. He knew the chancellor would fight him for every step of ground he gained. But then the look of charisma and charm settled back in place, and with a rough tug that sent a sting to the skin of Elgon's neck, Enguerrand yanked the medallion, breaking the thin leather cord that was tied around his neck and removing it from his person.

"Guards! Arrest this man! I believe he has stolen the medallion from the body of the prince! I have it here in my hand." The shock in his voice was only fake to Elgon, but he felt the sting of it down to his very bones as he was suddenly rushed by the other kingsmen, two grabbing him on either arm while a third kicked out one of Elgon's legs, sending him to his knees. He heard another set of footsteps and looked up to meet the gaze of Malcolm, who had advanced to a position just off to his right. His head was inclined toward Elgon and his hand reached for the hilt of his sword, ready at the slightest warning to pull the weapon from its sheath and use it to defend his king and his friend. Elgon moved his head to one side with what he hoped was enough of a warning look to stay the man's hand without giving away Malcolm's allegiance. Malcolm was of more use to him free and in his position of leadership than he was in a jail cell beside him. Though, they had escaped many a snare together as boys.

"I am no thief!" Elgon's voice boomed through the room, shutting down the chaos and confusion, the rustle and chatter that had ensued after Enguerrand's declaration.

Stillness met the echoes of his voice that still bounced around the room. The tone had commanded an audience...and he would use it as best he could.

"I was on the envoy with the Kingsmen, as you had mentioned. It was upon that expedition that I was injured. I know not how, as I was ill for weeks after with my injuries. I sustained a broken leg and a head injury that left me with no memory of my previous life."

Enguerrand had the mental clarity to scoff at that. He was playing his part well, that was certain. "And how did you survive this dire state?" His voice was full of disbelief, and Elgon could almost feel the room's opinion sway with the tone of the speaker. It was as if a battle between actors was taking place upon a stage, and the one who held their attention held their court...and their belief.

"I was cared for by villagers who were kind enough to take me in, despite the fact that I was dressed as a kingsman."

"Dressed as a kingsman, but not a prince." It was more of a statement than a question, and Elgon gritted his teeth, pressing against the strong hands that held him back, meeting Enguerrand's gaze and returning it with a steely one of his own.

"You would know, Enguerrand, counselor of my father, how I was sent out into that forest. It was you who recommended that I dress as a kingsman so as not to draw suspicion or undue attention from those who may wish me dead." As those words left his mouth, Elgon had a sick feeling in his stomach. Something wasn't right. Enguerrand hadn't just sent him on an errand like a lackey boy to obey his whim. There had been a motive. He knew this man to be depraved

259

the minute he saw his father's crown upon his head…but to go that far? "But perhaps I should have been dressed to hide myself from your own men, Enguerrand."

If they had been any farther away from each other, Elgon would not have seen the regent's reaction, but as they were, he noticed a flicker of the eyelid and a bringing of the hands together to hide the goosebumps that could be seen upon his forearms. Elgon's words had met their mark.

There was an added sting to the words that came from Enguerrand's mouth next, further proof to Elgon that he was rattled, if even partially. "If you were the prince as you say, do you not think I would know you? But I do not recognize you from the boy that I sent out."

A double-edged observation. Elgon was no longer the boy Enguerrand had sent out, but he also looked different upon his return. He could not bring it upon himself to cut his hair in the short military way or shave his beard. He knew he looked different. But a watchful eye would have still recognized him, unless it did not want to.

"And what of these peasants that 'cared' for you while you were ill?" There was a sneer when he said the word 'care.' "Why would they have not turned you into us immediately if you had been in possession of this medallion as you say?" He held it aloft, and it swung from the leather string in a pendulum, further mesmerizing the hearers.

"Who are these folk to whom we owe this debt of gratitude for saving the life of our 'prince'? Perhaps we should ride out and thank them!" He was playing to the crowd now with sarcasm, an amused smile upon his face. His gestures were broad, theatrical…and full of deadly wit.

An overwhelming sense of protectiveness washed over Elgon as Violet's face swam before his mind's eye. He saw her brown hair, curled with perspiration and ruffling about her face in the breeze, and her green eyes alight in the afternoon sun, taking on its golden hue.

"Well, who is this peasant? I must thank them for returning you to us safe and sound."

The medallion still swung from Enguerrand's hand, and Elgon felt it keenly. It was as if it were winking and mocking him from the hand of his usurper. All he wanted to do was reach out and snatch it back from his hand. Anger filled the outside of his vision with a haze, and he felt the fire of his temper rise from his gut, starting to squeeze his throat. "You will never touch her." The words were out before he could stop them. Sudden panic set in. Had he just inadvertently revealed enough of Violet's identity to betray her?

"Her?" The sneer on Enguerrand's face made Elgon's blood run cold as ice, the fire quenched from his veins in one fell blast. "A woman. I would not have thought it." The regent swung the medallion up and caught it in his other hand like a ball upon a string, staring off out a window. "Perhaps I did not give these peasant folk enough credit. We ought to have a discussion with this…woman who seems to have caught your fancy." He reached out a hand and trailed the signet ring that rested on his index finger down Elgon's face, dragging the cold metal against his skin and making it crawl. The signet ring matched the medallion with the roaring lion on his haunches in the center of the crown of Elira. The kingdom of freedom that had become enslaved under this man in a few short years. It was high time he claimed it back from the hand

261

of evil that held it tight within its grasp.

With a sudden surge, Elgon stood against the restraining hands of the kingsmen, catching them off guard and standing nose to nose with Enguerrand.

"Try as you might, your time here is short. Know this." His words were a harsh whisper, wrenched from a throat tight with restraint.

Those brown eyes flickered, and the corner of Enguerrand's mouth twitched before a punch to his gut sent Elgon to his knees and another sent his head to the floor as he gasped for breath.

Enguerrand grasped him by the hair and lifted Elgon's face a short distance from the ground as he stooped. "You have picked the wrong players in your game, boy. Perhaps you should have stayed dead in that forest."

The words were so quiet, Elgon was the only one who heard them. But the chill they sent through his body was the last thing he felt before another kick descended upon his ribs.

# Twenty-Four

## WHERE FEAR BELONGS

VIOLET BRUSHED a lock of hair from her forehead as she pounded some herbs in the mortar with the pestle. She mulled over what on earth she was to do. The chances of getting a home built before snow flew this year was nearly impossible. Harvest season would shortly be upon them, and she would save as much as she could from the sale of her produce to put toward building it in the spring. She sighed. The loss of her home, her childhood residence, while hard for many reasons, also set her back farther than she could have ever expected.

The week the kingsmen had given her to pay the lacking taxes was long up, and she prayed they did not know of her location. There were few people who knew where she resided, and so far, they had not come looking for her here. She had not been much out of the house and hoped that her absence from the streets had kept her whereabouts secret, at least for the present.

She was grateful that Fendrel had been kind enough to let her and Granny share an extra room in his home. He would have one less room for patients, but should the need arise, she would take to the floor without a second thought. They shared the smallest room he had and split a tick mattress between them. He had offered for her to stay in one of the spare patient rooms, but she couldn't bring it upon herself to take up a spot that he would need in an emergency.

Marcus entered the house and threw off his cloak, keeping his armful of bundles balanced in one hand while he used the other to hang the cloak upon the peg by the door. He nodded at Violet with a welcoming smile. She returned it, but apparently not joyfully enough, because his smile immediately dipped. He set his things from the market on the chopping block next to the dishpan and looked over his shoulder at her, leaning his cane against the counter and angling his hips against it as well to hold himself upright. "Did you get much done?" He nodded toward the herbs she was grinding and storing in the correct tins. She had been able to harvest many herbs from her garden, and while she had hung many bundles in the rafters that had burned with the house, she had been able to rescue these from the herb beds. They would make a nice contribution to Fendrel's stash.

"Quite." She nodded her head toward the rows of tins, standing at attention on the kitchen table as if ready to do their duty. It was hard to fully smile still. It was as if there was something missing within her. A piece that she had grown accustomed to, ripped out forever.

And this just wasn't her home.

Obed…*Elgon*. His presence missing from her life was more than she could allow herself to think on. She had taken care of herself and Granny on her own all these years and yet...when it came down to it, she had grown quite used to his being there and helping. And perhaps a little fond of it.

Marcus poured some water into the basin and pulled a sack of potatoes from his pile of produce from the market, taking them out one by one and placing them in the water to clean the dirt from their skins. His back was to her, and he didn't turn while he worked. "You miss him, don't you?"

Violet froze. She didn't even know the beatings of her own heart, let alone what they meant, and yet Marcus seemed to. "I—I don't know." The words felt empty, as empty and lonely as she was. How could she ache for companionship when she shared a house with three other people?

She saw Marcus' blonde curls bob with his short nod.

Her heart broke. Fendrel had finally told her that Marcus loved her. And now she could sense it in every tortured look she caught when he didn't know she was looking. The whispered prayers and eyes lifted heavenward when she was around. She didn't know why there was a halt in her mind and spirit in regards to Marcus. He would make someone a fine husband, but her heart lay elsewhere, and she had no idea why. Tears rose to her vision. A peasant girl would never marry a prince. There wasn't much room for hope.

"Richard! *Richard!*" There was a loud shriek from the other room.

Violet stood so fast that her chair toppled behind her. Her feet felt like they were moving through mud as more terrified screams came from the room she shared with Granny.

Her grandmother, who had been asleep on the bed, sat bolt upright, her salt and pepper hair awry from its bun and her face covered in a look of pure terror, her eyes wide.

Violet took the old woman's reaching hands, but Granny's tense and terrified look did not change.

"Granny, Richard is not here. It's okay. Calm down. Nothing is wrong."

"They have come to take him away! They are coming! We must hide! We must stop them!"

Violet's heart was beating in her ears, drowning out Granny's shouting. Marcus had hobbled into the doorway and then hobbled away again, hopefully to get Granny a draught that would calm her. Violet felt fear clench her throat. Unnerved by Granny's shrieks, she hoped that this woman who had been with her through every single down-trodden moment of her life would not be taken from her. She looked so frail, and Violet worried over her heart and how it would take the shock of the last few weeks.

Granny's mind was broken; Violet knew that. But she had never reacted like this.

"Granny, shh. Nothing is happening. No one is coming." She rubbed up and down the old woman's arms, trying to soothe her.

Granny only gasped for breath and turned her head to look deep into Violet's eyes. The bluish tint to them had faded to gray, and she grasped her granddaughters' upper arms in a frail, claw-like grip and shook her with more strength than Violet knew she had. Tears filled Granny's eyes, desperation joining the terror on her face. Her shaking increased as did the strength of her grip on Violet's arms.

266

"They *are* coming. They are taking him away." A tear fell down her sallow cheek, the wrinkled skin holding onto the drop. "He's never coming back. I won't get to see him again. My son. Oh, my son. Richard." A mother's keening cry escaped her, and she rocked back and forth as sobs shook her frame.

Violet stared, unable to move, nothing in her able to react or comfort her granny. Her pulse raced, loud, throbbing, thunderous in her ears. She could barely breathe. Marcus was there, giving Granny a draught, coaxing it past her lips even though she was still crying and wailing.

Violet still didn't move as Granny slowly quieted; it was horrific to watch the old woman let go without relaxing, seeing the tension and pain still clinging to her in a drugged sleep, almost as if no rest could come to her in any state.

She still didn't move or react when Marcus stood and grasped her by the arms. He guided her from the room, leaning on her with every other step on his bad leg.

She felt cold, as if there was no feeling but utter horror in her.

Marcus was shaking her. Why? Why was he shaking her?

"Violet?"

"She knew. She has never known before." Tears fell from her eyes unchecked; she almost didn't feel them till they were cold, leaving trails down her face. She wavered on her feet. "Marcus." Suddenly her gaze snapped back to focus, and she stared into his blue eyes. "She knew."

Pain stared back at her from those depths. He made no move, just stood there in her pain with her, and she felt the support and warmth from his hands on her arms.

"Why? Why now? What if—?"

"Shh…" His thumbs rubbed circles into her forearms.

She drew a shuddering breath and blinked hard. She shook her head and took a step back, staring at the ceiling and trying to gulp in a large breath of air. "I don't understand."

Marcus shook his head. "I pray she will be all right."

Violet rubbed her arms, trying to warm the frigid skin that suddenly hurt all over with the shock. Pray. Not *know*. Not *hope*. Pray. Marcus didn't have much hope for Granny.

Who knew what this meant to her health, for her to deteriorate to such a point? Granny had lived her life on the belief that her son would return. When that hope was removed, could she survive the shock?

A commotion pounded outside, and they both started and looked toward the door, then each other.

The door slammed open, hitting the wall behind it with a resounding thud and flinging back toward the entrance. Violet gasped and jumped, her knees suddenly knocking together. *God in heaven.*

Fendrel had blood pouring from his nose and lip, coating his beard and dripping onto his tunic, one eye already swollen shut. The scruff of his tunic was held in the hand of a kingsman. She recognized him instantly…the one who had threatened her at her home before the fire. Ice ran through her veins, and she thought if she moved or breathed she might crack.

A slow smirk spread across the kingsman's face, and Violet thought she might vomit as Marcus took a step toward her, his arm going out in front as if to protect her. She was grateful for his attempt, as useless as it would be.

268

"Well, well, well...the wench. Guess who has orders to bring you before the king?"

Her heart thudded once, then again, a bit of air entering her lungs. Had Elgon made it to his destination? Hope suddenly died before it had taken flight. He had once again become the evil ruler she had initially thought him. Why else had he sent this man knocking at her door?

"What king?" The words were so clear she almost wondered if they belonged to someone else.

"King Enguerrand of Elira."

*Oh, Elgon.*

Violet's knees finally gave out under the pressure, and she hit the floor hard. The sound of chaos met her ears.

Violet's knees ached with the bruises from her fall. Her hands bound in front of her, she brought them both up to push a fallen lock of hair from her face. She wasn't used to riding, and this horse wasn't used to such a light rider. He seemed to think she didn't exist, and her hands being bound gave her no control. She squeezed her legs in a backward motion, trying to warn him that his jumping ahead was not permissible. He calmed for a second, but the minute she let up her grip around his midsection, the jumpier he became.

If only she had his spirit.

But two days on a horse through rain, hail, sun, and wind with nothing but a kingsman's cloak over her bodice, chemise, and skirt to keep her from the elements had done nothing but take the spirit right out of her. Her bound hands left her unable

269

to do more than tug with futility at the cloak in an attempt to huddle closer within it. She needed to save what little strength she might have for whatever encounter lay before her.

She had counted the costs.

She had known when she took in the kingsman, who had later turned out to be the prince, that she was opening herself up to persecution and perhaps even an execution. She had lost her father to it. Perhaps it was but the destiny of the Frell's.

To die for doing the right thing.

She slumped over her mount's withers. She was so worn out that she almost felt it would be easier if they would just kill her now and put her out of her misery. The kingsmen had not answered her questions when she asked if Elgon was still alive. Perhaps they did not know, but their silence did little to reassure her.

They crested a hill, and she squeezed her eyes shut against the cold, a shiver flooding her being with its icy blast. The air smelled...salty. It stung her nostrils.

She lifted her head, and far off to her left, the seas bluish-gray hue blended in with the mountains in the distance. Never had she thought she would see the ocean again. It's deep and broody blue was atoss with white when she squinted to get a better view. A seagull swooped overhead, its high-pitched squawk bringing the smallest of smiles to her face.

Had her father witnessed the sea on his march to Niran? Was she too to be executed after the journey of a lifetime? She shuddered and felt a harsh burn rise in her throat, her empty stomach clenching. She slumped over and rested her head on her horse's neck. With eyes squeezed shut, the image of him walking away bound as she now was, his face turned toward hers over his shoulder and tears cascading down his cheek before he was jerked away through the crowd, was imprinted on the back of her eyelids.

"Papa, I'll see you soon."

"What was that, wench?" A nasty whisper sent another shiver down her spine, and she jumped at the closeness of the lead kingsman. The bane of her existence. By God's grace, he had somehow always been distracted and had not touched her on this journey. She knew it was no accident. He could have had his way and wrecked her if he had been given the slightest chance. Which, clearly, the Lord wasn't allowing.

She lifted her head, her spine and seat aching with the effort as she glared straight into his eyes, evil as the day is long. Not a word left her tongue.

Annoyance flashed in his eyes, and their locked stares fought one another for supremacy. Her teeth hurt from clenching them, and his malevolent gaze crackled with electric energy, then frustration, and finally, a flash of anger. Not once did she waver or scarcely even blink.

He flung the back of his hand, catching her on the side of the face, and throwing her into the horse's neck, but with her hands bound she could not catch herself, and she crumpled to the ground. Her bare foot splashed in a puddle—she had lost one of her shoes along the way and had been unable to stop and retrieve it. She couldn't catch a breath, every bit of air having been knocked from her body. When she finally snatched half a gulp, her ribs, still sore from when the kingsman had kicked her more than a week ago, throbbed with the pain. Tears joined the rainwater in the road to make more mud.

They hauled her up, half of her skirt now soaked. Their roughness made her wish they would just kill her now in the street. She knew it was her fate. She had accepted it. Better to meet the Lord face to face with at least some dignity intact.

The rest of the journey into Niran left her completely void of energy, and the sun did not once show its face as they approached. She looked up through the rain and mist as the walls rose high. They should have been gleaming in the sun. She wished she could have experienced that warmth and light upon the capital city of Elira. Instead, it was shrouded in mist, and the clouds in the sky blotted out the light that should have lit up the shining city of freedom.

It was cold and dark. The ocean tossed its waves with loud crashes upon the beach and the cliffside on the west side of the city, the roaring of the water a protest against the tyranny and oppression that weighted down the very air in this place.

She gulped. There was something upon this city. It felt like a sickness. Much like the malaise Granny often complained of. It was sick in the mind. While the fear in the outlying villages was prevalent and sweeping across the land like fire, it lay heavily in the air here, thick, almost unbreathable.

It threatened to choke her as she entered the city and was taken through the streets. But something within her rose to combat the feeling trying to lay heavy on her shoulders, fighting it off. She knew what it was that fought within her. It was her King.

Her true King. The One who stood beside her and in her. The One she represented. The One she staked her life on, and the One who said that this way of life was wrong in His book. She drew in a deep breath, feeling the oppression shrivel in

His presence. She sat up straight, her back tight but strong, her head held high as she rode through the streets of Niran, looking fear in the face and putting it where it belonged. At her feet.

# Twenty-Five

## THE HALL OF THE KING

ELGON GLARED at the back of the kingsman who stood guard over his cell. He needed to remedy the dungeon's conditions and also sort out who was in charge of the army the minute he was out of this stinking hole. If he ever was. The cell was decent enough, but the straw on the floor hadn't been changed in who knew how long, and it smelled rank enough to rival the chamber pot in the corner.

The man tasked with guarding his cell was a bit timid, seeming to have gotten the short end of the stick. The poor lad needed some proper training. His wiry frame and hesitant patterns of action wouldn't last five minutes on a battlefield.

Elgon had tried to talk to him and tell his story, hoping that another kingsman swayed to his side would be a help in the future. The man had simply ignored him at first with an increasingly frustrated look on his face. When his timid shouts at Elgon to "shut up or else" had failed to produce the intended

275

result, he had glared at Elgon with a look of defeat mixed with frustration and had marched off down the hall, looking quite put out. With the soldier having come back and now ignoring him, Elgon had no one to talk to. No one, that is, except the Lord.

Elgon shook the chain that was attached to one ankle and kicked at it when it felt just as tight as ever. His back to the metal grate of the cell door, he let his head fall back, the cold steel biting a bruise but otherwise soothing him. One could get lost in these halls. Feeling something, anything, but boredom was welcome. "You really could have helped out a little more back there," Elgon prayed, throwing his head back toward the entrance and exit of the lockup as if to insinuate his conversation in the great hall. "I don't really see why I'm here at all, honestly."

Thoughts swirled in his head. The Enguerrand he had known had been a kind one. He made sure Elgon had everything that he wanted. He was a man who had always smiled on him benevolently from a chair at his father's right hand. He shook his head. How is it that a man could do such a thing after being trusted so implicitly by his ruler?

He wracked his brain, trying desperately with all his might to remember something that would point him in the right direction or give him a new understanding of the situation. It was a new feeling, being able to remember. By all intents and purposes, Enguerrand appeared to be a man who had simply taken over after the death of his father, filling a need as the regent while the heir apparent was sitting, wasting his hours trying to become a man.

But the mission he had been sent on made Enguerrand's

motivations clear. He had been sent out with the intention to tax the people. Enguerrand had told him it was simply a trust-gaining exercise; it would benefit the kingdom and the coffers if the man who was about to rule showed his face, pressed the flesh, and made an attempt at gaining their trust. He could almost hear Enguerrand's voice as he directed him, a smile upon his lips and an encouraging lilt to his voice. "Be personable, but be firm. Don't make them feel like you don't want to be there. You *do* want to be there, and you want them to know that you deemed them important enough to show up in their midst, but despite that, you are more important than them, and your visit should be considered a great honor." He had patted Elgon on the shoulder. "You will be a great ruler one day. Don't let them forget that."

Elgon shook his head and pulled up his knees to lean upon them. How could that man be the one who had usurped the throne and thrown him in here? What did he have to gain by being such a turncoat? Why so suddenly? How did the man who had been kind to him suddenly plot an assassination?

An image started to take place in Elgon's head. A glass. Enguerrand handing it to the king, and the king refusing that he had had enough and demanding Enguerrand drink the draught instead of him. Enguerrand had not done as directed by the king, and Elgon remembered wondering why he caught him pouring it out into a vase of summer roses instead of drinking the draught. Now a feeling of dread pickled the contents of his stomach, and a sickening darkness crawled up his spine, the hair on his head felt like every root was squeezing with the pressure of the chill. His father had seemed to decline rapidly, but it had been tempered. A man who had been in his prime, full of life and wisdom, suddenly feeling ill daily, worsening further and further till one day he could not get up from his bed...

Elgon gulped back the fear that threatened to choke his throat. Why had he not talked to the doctors at the time? Why had he not fought to know more? To understand? For all he had known in his drunken stupor, his father had just gotten sick, quickly declined, only to die shortly thereafter with little to no explanation.

Elgon jolted to his feet.

The draught.

The one Enguerrand would not drink for himself.

The one that had been intended for his father.

The only thing that could explain such a death so suddenly.

Poison. From the hand of the man who sat at the king's own right hand.

His heart beat heavy in his ears as he turned.

"Guard!" The voice rang down the halls with panic, but authority sparked off his tongue like flint about to light a forest fire. "Get me the captain of the guard this instant or your bones will rot in this cell when I finally take back my father's throne!"

Violet was dragged from deep within the recesses of a stable, up and up. The amount of stairs made her head swim. Down one hall and another. She had entered at a doorway from the stable into what must have been the kingsmen's quarters. The men milled about in varying degrees of full dress or void of their leather armor. There had been many whistles and shouts as she was led through them, her eyes spitting daggers and her head so high her nose might as well have pointed at the ceiling. If the room burned as hot as her soul did, then they would all burn in hellfire.

The halls grew more ornate as she was led through them, her eardrums popped at one point, and she started to feel the altitude affecting her. She knew the capital city was set against the face of the Ilias pass and sat with a westerly stare into the ocean. The back of the castle itself was set against the upper cliffs of the mountain. Between the water, salt-heavy air, and the height from the mountains, it was entirely a new sensation for her. She shook her head to clear her ears.

"Lord, help me withstand whatever I am about to meet. Don't let my story end in defeat. Even if someone comes to know you and your freedom, let them see it in me before my last breath leaves my body." The words fell from her spirit and dropped in a whisper down the hallway, getting lost amongst the boots that stamped the stone floors.

She was pushed into a large room, larger than any she had ever seen before. Her jaw dropped at the large columns marching down the room, each window looking in shape like the stained glass one that hung above the vestibule of the little chapel in the neighboring town back home. These weren't stained, but instead were clear and rose far higher than the little pointed window in the church. They gleamed with a soft glow from the dusky light outside, the cloudy day casting gray shadows dancing across the floor and the columns sending harsh black shapes atop them. The diamond pattern beneath her feet seemed far too clean for her muddy boots, and she stepped carefully and with reverence.

This was the hall of the king.

A room she was far from worthy to enter. The grandness of it all made her feel small and insignificant. There was something in this room that made the shadows close in around her and push toward her as if to swallow her whole. If she stepped upon one of the black shadows on the floor, it may just engulf her. She swallowed against a dry throat and felt her knees start to shake. *Give me strength, Lord.*

A lone figure stood at the far end of the room upon the dais, his back to her. She could sense the heaviness that weighed on him, and she felt herself recoil from it. The burden he bore was not a Heaven-ordained one. Something was amiss. Almost as if she were being led down the executioner's walk.

It wasn't a far-fetched idea. She wouldn't live to see another day. Of that she was quite sure. Tears rose to her eyes as she prayed that the Lord would heal Granny. The only soul that mattered so intensely to her was far away, and Violet prayed with all her might that no matter what happened to her, it would not affect Granny the same way the loss of her son had. *Lord, if I go, don't tarry in bringing her along. She needs to see Your face. And without mine to get her through the lonely days here...I don't know what hell exists for her on earth. Don't let her suffer. I don't want her to die alone, broken and miserable. Heal her mind or bring her to Your streets of gold where it will be.*

Just a few more feet now. Why was the room so empty? It was just her, the kingsmen who held either of her arms as if she were a threat, and this man upon the dais. Her heart throbbed as her pulse ricocheted through her veins. Her feet stopped of their own accord as her mind struggled to catch up with what her soul already seemed to know. This was Enguerrand.

The man who had ruined a kingdom of the ages. The man who had been responsible for the death of her father. The man who had let good people die for the sake of his own selfishness. Who had forced a living hell upon his people for the sake of his own evil schemes. This was the man who had lurked in the shadows of her mind, always to blame for what had happened. A man who had taken what was rightfully someone else's.

*Elgon*. She had once hated him. Had once despised him. Had blamed him for the deeds she now ascribed to this man.

And he had stolen it all from her prince. Her heart stopped, realization filling her mind as the kingsmen forced her feet forward and then pushed in her knees from behind until they gave in and she sank to a kneeling position on the wood floor. It all made sense now.

The chancellor had sent Elgon, her Obed, out to the woods. To die.

"Well, the maid who dares to hide a kingsman and detain him for her own purposes. Surely you did not think you would get away with hiding him from me?" It was a statement more than a question, and she kept her mouth tight until the man turned. He chuckled at her response to his direct gaze. "You seem surprised."

Violet tried to school her features, but he was right. She was surprised. The man who looked at her was not the cold, villainous, calculating killer she had imagined. Instead, eyes of warm brown, an enigmatic smile, and a handsome face met her gaze.

"Don't worry, you may speak in my presence."

She opened her mouth, to say what, she did not know, but her dry throat rebelled, and she choked on the air, lowering her head with a cough that startled her with the echo in the room.

"My dear, you must be parched. Here, drink this." Violet took a swallow of the goblet that he held to her lips, her eyes catching his so close to her own.

The moment felt surreal. Odd. Unfit. As if it were happening to someone else as she drank from the cup he held for her. She wanted to spit it in his face, but something else held her back. There was something there. Something in the eyes that made her stop. Confused.

He was an evil man. She knew this. Then why on earth did she feel as though he was a man who could be trusted?

"There, you must feel better now." He took the cup and placed it on the small table.

Dread filled every bone in her body. She knew this was the end. She knew this was the last stop for her before death. She could feel it, deep down; she saw it in his eyes. She was his toy to play with before he disposed of her in boredom. But...

The thought of light, warmth, everlasting goodness and...her father. The thought of experiencing those things under the smiling countenance of her Savior gave her comfort at the thought that she might die. Momentary pain and torture in this life would lead to the most beautiful, blissful experience of her soul.

Peace settled over her. She felt the tension in her shoulders abate and they slowly dropped. Either way, she would win.

She rolled her head to clear out a few of the kinks. The floor at her knees was burnished to the most beautiful honey gold. She smiled. If she died, streets of gold would be beneath her soon. Her heart started to sing.

But first…

She raised her eyes to the man who stood in front of her, the one who might usher her into her greatest joy, and a tear swam in her vision. This one would not enter after her, and the thought pained her. Would that he knew of the love that died to set him free.

Enguerrand seemed slightly taken aback by her reaction, but with a half-shake of the head, the look of charm and wit was back upon his handsome features. He stepped forward, his hands clasped behind his back. Not only was he standing and she kneeling, but he also stood upon the dais, giving him about a foot of extra height. She had to lift her head back quite far to see his face.

Holding his head high, he perused her, his eyes drinking in every detail of her face and dipping toward the ground and back up. "You certainly look as though you have had a difficult journey. I do apologize if my men have been…uncouth."

She swallowed back the preponderance of words that waited on the edge of her tongue. *Bide your time. Wait it out.*

An amused smile pulled the corners of his mouth up lazily. "You aren't prone to talk, are you?"

Tired of holding it so high, she dipped her head and took in his leather shoes instead. The black and silver buckle holding them on was tiny.

"Look at me." The words were peremptory in tone, stiff, as

283

a hand came down with a royal signet ring and grasped her chin, the ring pinching the delicate skin near her jaw.

Anger filled her chest. This man was used to having his way. She looked into his eyes, taking in a deep breath through her nose.

"You, a peasant maid. Taking in a kingsman. Surely you knew of the dangers, knew that hiding him from his own was an action that would land you in a position unsavory at best."

She still did not speak.

The hand on her chin squeezed harder, and she winced. "When I speak, you are to answer, wench."

"I did not discern a question, your grace."

Anger flared on his face, then gave way to mirth. He let go of her face hard, sending her, unbalanced as she was, down to the ground, catching her fall on an elbow, her hands still tied.

"You think you can play with me." His voice was cold.

"I do not wish to make this a game. But I find it far from serviceable to dance around a topic when shooting straight to the heart of the matter saves so much time." Well did Violet know that Enguerrand seemed to be a man of the game himself. Except he was the one who usually knew all the moves. Her silence and gathered composure made him an equal player instead of the victor who knew the entire play and was merely stringing along his weaker opponent for the sake of sport.

"If you do not wish a game, then perhaps we ought to understand one another."

"Let's."

He turned to face her again, the muscles in his jaw working as he talked and listened to her responses. "You willingly held a wounded kingsman against his will from returning to his battalion, and yet you stand before me as calm and cool as a summer breeze. How is it that you do not know or care about the import of your actions?"

"What actions, my lord? Those of a woman who put her entire family at risk to care for a man of whom she knew nothing? How is caring for a man who has no strength to walk and no memory to tell him where to go if he could, 'holding him against his will'? Aye. I knew the import when I chose to care for one as I would my own brother or father with little hope of anything in return save a clear conscience."

"Yet you did not report his whereabouts to his superiors at the fort in your town. You did not tell the men who were out looking for him who he was and where you had acquired him. You even lied, as my commander has told me, stating that he was a cousin who had traveled to work your land, if I believe? Correct me if I am wrong in any of these details, my lady." His words held scorn and derision, layered and tempered with a quiet reserve behind the soft-spoken words that had more bite than the sharp sting of a fire ant. "But how is it that you can excuse such negligence under the guise of caring for a man?"

Violet felt fear grip her throat. She should have known that the kingsmen would have told of her involvement. It would have taken little digging to determine that her newly found "family member" had joined her household in suspiciously close timing to that of the missing prince. The memory of her father again pressed in at the far corners of her mind, filling her with the fearful memories that plagued her every waking moment. She swallowed back the pain and fought the images and sounds of screaming that threatened to choke her in their tightening grasp. "Because of you, my lord."

"Me?" He spun from his pacing, the hem of his embroidered brown robe spilling out behind him in soft billows. "What could I have possibly done to be to blame for your negligence?"

Fire rose in her belly, and she stood against the restraining hands that sought to push her back to her knees. They stopped when Enguerrand flicked a hand at them.

"You are the cause of the fear and pain that your people suffer with. Do you have no compunction? Do you care not for the ones who have been abused, beaten, even beheaded under your rule? You were entrusted with a kingdom that you let go to ruin. Then you willingly turned a blind eye as your people suffered, were tortured and abused, forced into labor, starvation, and death under your very nose. Do you not have any care within you? Any compassion in the heart that beats in your chest? You are a coward."

The end of her words was cut off with a slap across the face that set her ears to ringing and her eyes to watering.

"A coward?" The man before her had changed into another. The composure was gone and a wild look entered his eyes, pain lurking behind their brown and glimmering gaze. His face was near hers, and she could see the flare of his nostrils with his sharp intake of breath and the red around his eyes. "I may be many things, my lady." He sneered. "But I am no coward."

"How do you figure?"

A sharp intake of breath caused his eyes to narrow, and she saw his Adam's apple move up and down and the veins in his neck stand out against the skin. The muscles in his jaw tightened.

"You took over the kingdom from a man whom the people loved, who stewarded well, and was respected and served by the people, and in a few short years, the people have been forced, coerced, and abused into labor, heavy taxation, and suffered from broken borders. What of that has *not* been a result of cowardice?"

He turned from her, and she saw him jerk his head to the side as if to shake off the tension and anger that was roiling from his form. She could almost see sparks on the hem of his robe from the intensity that burned from his tight shoulders, bulging veins, and tense fists. "I took the kingdom over from a coward. You think my rule has been cowardly? I have taken a kingdom, bent on destruction under the hand of a weak king who had nothing within him to make this kingdom greater. He scoffed at alliances and broke off treaties, all in the name of "preserving our integrity." I have made alliances, implemented changes that have made our country even greater, brought about the necessary wealth to build it even greater, and the needed strength of arms to fortify us from enemies for years to come. Cowardly? Weak? My rule has been anything but that, and the people know it. They now know that a man of strength and power sits upon the throne, not one who held a weak, slovenly allegiance from peasants who know not how to govern themselves. I am the strong one. I am the one worthy of this dais and scepter and with not only the strength, but the intelligence to wield it well."

"You think it takes strength to rule with greed?" Her voice rose with her passion. "Or intelligence to command the loyalty of your people? Loyalty cannot be bought, and integrity should not be sacrificed at the hand of tyranny."

"I sacrificed nothing, wench."

"You sacrificed much. You have bought your alliances and your power on the backs of people who will owe you nothing but their disdain for the way you have treated them. You have treated them as commodities, to be bought and sold, sacrificed on the altar of success and greatness. You are not great. You are weak, and your need for more only proves your weakness, not your strength."

His hand flew toward her face but stopped mere fractions of an inch before it caught her cheek. Then it dropped to his side, and she saw him visibly school his features. She glanced to her side, somehow suddenly aware of the kingsman who held her in her bonds. The one to her right had a face that looked like it had seen a ghost. As if the man in front of her had suddenly sprouted horns...or perhaps just revealed his true identity.

Enguerrand cleared his throat, his shoulders set back in their straight line, his hands tucked neatly behind his back. She could see the muscles in his face were still tight, but the mask of control and charm was back in place.

"You think that you, a peasant wench from the village of Padsley, days away from the capital city, used to farming, with dirt under your fingernails, knows anything about ruling a kingdom?"

Violet could sense the scorn in his voice that was heavily cloaked with the charm of his demeanor. She suddenly felt self-conscious, as if he could see every flaw, every fleck of mud upon her skirt, and every blemish.

He continued in his charming voice, "You know nothing, and if you did, you would know that your loyalty ought to lie with this kingdom, whoever rules it. You cannot pick and choose who will rule over you, and you ought to serve to your best ability. You think you can manipulate me and make me out to be the evil one in your scenario? You know nothing but the dirt you till and the animals you tend. What could you know of state and commerce and the affairs of men? Serving at the will of the king ought to be your entire life. That is what you exist for."

"You are right. I exist to serve the king. But that King is not you."

His face turned gray.

"And I serve at the behest of a Kingdom higher than that of Elira."

"Guards!" His voice was louder than it needed to be, and she startled as it ricocheted off the stone walls of the great hall, its echo falling and slithering at her feet. "Fetch the prisoner. I am done with this wench."

# Twenty-Six

## THE PRICE OF POWER

ELGON'S BREATH caught in his throat when he saw Violet. She was alive. She was here, the gleam of the light from the windows casting its gray hue upon her pale and dirt-stained face. He could not wait to see those green eyes again, as bright as a forest a-spark with sunrise.

Enguerrand waved a hand, and Elgon's heart chilled. If that man had dared to lay a finger on his Violet…

"Ah yes, the young prince, was it?" Sarcasm bathed his voice in ash. "Guards, leave us. All but you, Malcolm."

The room was suddenly devoid of any others, and it was just the four of them. Malcolm at Elgon's shoulder, Violet standing, her shoulders straight, but he could sense the weariness in her form. Enguerrand stood as he seemed to like, upon the dais, a head taller than the others in the room. There were no nobles for Elgon to appeal to for their compassion and sense of duty.

But nor could Enguerrand.

This did not bode well for them. Enguerrand thrived off of an audience. It gave him the stage to compete and shower them with his wealth of superiority, all while degrading others and picking apart their story like any skilled actor would.

But divesting himself of his chance to shine could only mean one thing.

What he intended to do would be done without witnesses.

Elgon swallowed hard. *Lord, help us. If this is Your will, give us the strength to stand for the truth, regardless of the consequences.*

"Come, come, come. You do not need to stand so far away. Come! See the woman you owe your life to; surely you could do no less!" Enguerrand's broad gestures and oratorical voice seemed out of place in the empty room.

Elgon drew closer, and Violet turned, her eyes bright and full of sudden unshed tears when she caught his gaze. The relief that caused her to drop her shoulders was as evident to him as it must have been to Enguerrand. Her ragged appearance stilled his feet in surprise before he swallowed up the remaining steps in what felt like one.

Her eyes were underlined with dark circles, weariness in every feature, but somehow supported with an inner strength that held her upright and tall. A red mark on one cheek was starting to swell and already made one eye look puffy. He held back a growl. The man who bestowed that mark upon her beautiful face would pay for it dearly.

"Obed!" fell from her lips unbidden. "I mean..." She looked somewhat muddled. "Elgon."

292

"Obed? Elgon?" Enguerrand's eyebrows were as high as the sky. "Well now, this is a new development. Which are you? Elgon or Obed? Because it seems to me that only one claims the prince's name."

Elgon tore his gaze from Violet's pleading eyes. "As I said before, my name is Elgon, prince and rightful king of Elira."

"Yes, so you said. Now listen, children, as I see it, there are two options before you, so let me lay them out carefully." He was still performing, his fingers steepled in front of him as he paced the dais.

Elgon swallowed, trying to eliminate the dryness of his throat. His stomach sank, and he felt sweat on the palms of his hands. He sought and found strength in Violet's eyes, their warm green depths alight with a fire from within. He straightened his shoulders. He knew now where that strength came from, and it was just as much his for the asking as it was hers.

"One." Enguerrand waved his fore finger in the air, making his point of number. "You may both be killed; all you need do is say the word. A deserting kingsman and a rebel peasant are as easy to dispose of as..." He snapped his fingers. "Well, as that."

Elgon's blood ran cold, and he sensed a slight tremor in Violet. He caught her eye only to see a sadness upon her face that he did not expect. She drilled him with a look he didn't quite understand. As if she was begging him to stay the heat that was suddenly coursing through him. Begging him to do the right thing, no matter the cost. He caught himself shaking his head. She seemed to be asking him to do the right thing, even if that mean losing her. No, he wouldn't do it. No amount

293

of sacrifice was worth losing her.

But still that gaze, solid as a tree trunk. Stalwart in the face of any wind, no matter how harsh, and just as deeply rooted as the oaks that filled the forest. He started to shake. He didn't know if he could do what she was asking of him. Leadership required sacrifice. There was something in him that sank at the very idea. But then a verse sprang to life in his memory. He had heard Granny read it to him many a time from the old Bible as he lay in bed, his leg beyond use and his mind on fire. It was a miracle it had even come to his recollection, let alone perfectly played through his mind. "Therefore, my beloved brethren, be ye steadfast, immovable, always abounding in the work of the Lord, forasmuch as ye know that your labor is not in vain in the Lord."

Her lips moved, and he realized it was in prayer. There was a glory that lit her face as the light from the windows fell across her form, illuminating the wisps of hair, forming a halo that caught and reflected the golden hues.

The sight both ate at him and revived him all at once.

"Your second option is that I release this farmer's daughter. There is much that a girl of your position can do to serve the kingdom yet. We have no need to snuff out such a life so soon, if only Obed or Elgon, whichever you may be, would release this foolish idea to take the throne and be deemed unfit."

Elgon stood taller. That was the first time that Enguerrand had admitted, however surreptitiously, that he was actually Elgon, the prince. He gathered that was also why the regent had sent the rest of the attaché into the outer hall. He did not want his petty show to be on display before the entire court. Someone was bound to recognize Elgon or start questioning

Enguerrand's story if they were but close enough. It was a small wonder they trusted Enguerrand implicitly. Elgon had been the spoiled prince, royalty that was used to getting his way and little else.

But now, instead of standing in this throne room to ask his father a favor or argue his selfish point, as he had been wont to do in the days of his youth, he was well aware of the fact that he stood upon authority that was God given. Authority that was meant to be used and would reign again by God's might. He drew a breath.

If Enguerrand wanted a show, a show he would get.

"You seem to think that you have authority to make such decisions. A chancellor is only as good as his king or prince allows." Elgon matched the tone and broad movements of his nemesis, but there was a difference. Elgon had a fire of righteousness that burned within him. Having been washed clean by the water of the Word, he had emerged victorious over the selfishness and greed that this man still clung to. It would be a battle of the Spirit of God against the spirit of this world.

Hardly a fair fight.

Enguerrand perused him from a distance, almost as if measuring what Elgon might have against him.

"You see, my father placed you in charge of an allotment, and I seem to recall that the decision you made with your new-found authority was not to the liking of the wise minds of the court."

Enguerrand colored, and Elgon was almost surprised. The tight rein the man had over his emotions only went so far, and clearly, he had struck a chord.

295

"Your father was worthless when it came to ruling. His authority was wasted." He spat.

Malcolm moved a hand to his sword hilt, and Elgon drew a breath, hoping Enguerrand would not notice. Their plan would never work if Enguerrand sensed that Malcolm was unfaithful to him in any way. Elgon watched from the corner of his eye while the hand slowly slipped from the hilt of the sword, all the while keeping an eye on the now red and seething Enguerrand.

"So, you admit now that he was my father. Your charade is up, Enguerrand."

The chancellor was upon him in an instant, his hand buried in Elgon's long hair and pulling it back with a force that caused Elgon to feel the muscles in his neck tighten in protest. "You think you can trick me, boy? I have been in a position of power since you were born and know far more of the ways of the world than you." The words were a harsh whisper, and behind the sneering face of the chancellor, he caught Violet's worried eye. "Why do you think you were petted with everything you could ever ask for, as we watched you sink into depravity and distrust? Your eyes lusted after anything and everything, and your desires were gratified at every turn. It's hard to learn how to rule a country while you are drowning in cups and any woman you could want. Does this wench know of your former conquests?" He released Elgon and instead walked to Violet, trailing a finger down her face in a way that made her flinch and set Elgon's teeth on edge. His hands strained against the chains and fetters they were bound in. Now was not the time to make his move, but everything in him fought against the tight grip of self-control that still held him in check…for the moment.

"Does she know of the women you seduced and courted? Or is she blissfully ignorant of the ways of the world in which you walked?"

Elgon didn't see a flicker of disdain in Violet's eyes. Her lips still moved in prayer, but he felt only acceptance and love from her. He knew. He knew she lived by the scripture that said, "Behold, I am a new creation. It is no longer I who live, but Christ who lives in me." He smiled. Enguerrand could not bring up the works of his dead flesh to haunt him. The old Elgon was dead. A new one had arisen in his stead. And this one was ruled by Christ, not man.

"You may have distracted me for a time with the pleasures of this world, Enguerrand, but you will distract me no longer. I am a changed man."

Enguerrand scoffed. "Changed? How can one change overnight? You are the same man you have always been."

"With Christ, all things are possible."

"Christ!" Enguerrand laughed outright at this. "You think you can convince me that worship in one of these primitive village churches has made you into a new man? When I sent you out, I didn't for the life of me think you would have been killed by religion."

"No, you only intended that I be killed by the very hand of one of my own men."

Enguerrand stared unmoved into Elgon's eyes. A smile pulled at the edge of his mouth.

"You killed my father as well, didn't you?" Rage started to simmer within Elgon, but remained, as yet, hidden within his breast. His heart beat heavy in his ears, and pain started to tear through the muscles of his neck, tense with his purpose. This thought had been filling his mind ever since he had the realization that the power to kill his father was within this man's hands. Their long, attractive, and expressive fingers perhaps being the very vehicle by which his father's death had been hastened.

"A weak man invites death."

The words fell from Enguerrand's lips, and their echo slithered across the floor and constricted Elgon's muscles from his feet to his neck, cutting off his air supply. He gasped for a breath. "How?" was all he eked out as a whisper.

"He was insane."

Elgon remembered every moment of his past recollection when he had seen his father. He had sensed the decline, and while his father had grown weaker and more saddened and depressed, Elgon had never once seen an ounce of insanity. "You lie."

"Think what you like, but your father was losing his mind. The decisions he made put his country at risk. But I righted the matter. I was able to right his wrongs against the people of Rusalka and reunite with their ruler. There will be no more border attacks from Rusalka. They have guaranteed me an army to defend our borders. There will be nothing that will stand in the way of Elira with their army at our disposal."

Elgon still hadn't breathed. The dread that overwhelmed him spread from the top of his head down to his very toes, rooting him to the floor like a tree searching for life giving water.

A treaty. That was what this had all been about. It explained the infestation of Rusalks within their borders. The raids amongst the outlying villages, the lack of resources, and the sudden surge of taxes and demands upon the commerce of the land. It was where all the food had been going, the produce, the sheep's wool, the goods made by every villager on the outskirts. It was why the mines had been filled with men, the shifts doubled, every rabble rouser and disturber of the peace, rightfully convicted or not, sent deep into the mines to draw forth iron and the coal needed to forge it.

Niran had yet to experience the hunger, the strikes, and having their sons and husbands sent out to the mines, but it was only a matter of time before an entire people was enslaved in the name of ambition. Borders would continue to weaken as their army merged with Elira's, and then the country would crumble from the inside out, their wealth of resources ravaged by Rusalka's indelible greed and ambition. There was a reason his father had disdained any form of treaty or offer of assistance from their king. Their country was a lawless one, run by rugged mountain men who forced its people into servitude, their children into service to the country, and bled their resources dry.

He gaped at the man in front of him who would dare destroy the kingdom that his father had worked and sacrificed for. The man who had ruined every single safeguard his father had toiled his entire life to put in place to protect his people from the ruthless country of the north. Anger hot and fast burned within him, and fire filled his bones. Not on his watch.

"You may think my father and I weak, but when God is on our side, you have only to watch, as your plans will crumble and fall. Not one of them will remain the minute I am king." He stepped forward, every ounce of passion in his being directed at the man who represented the demolition of an empire of freedom and prosperity.

Enguerrand pulled a knife from his belt and in one quick motion stepped behind Violet and held it to her throat, her hair caught in the grasp of his other hand. "One step and I'll end her life." The words were sharper than the knife that now threatened Violet's slender throat.

Elgon stopped dead in his tracks, and they all stared at one another, willing the others to make the first move.

Elgon's heart had ceased to beat, and he stood, frozen to the ground as the fire in Violet's eyes grew brighter instead of being clouded with fear as he would've expected.

She shook her head in the most imperceptible of movements.

"I know where I'm going," she mouthed.

Horror filled him as he realized she was not the least bit afraid of her death.

Then why was it that he was?

300

# Twenty-Seven

## THIS SIDE OF HISTORY

VIOLET FELT EVERY second of this impasse with agonized slowness. The breath suspended between them all filled her with dread that perhaps she would not make it through this moment. But then peace overcame her. Final prayers filled her spirit as she locked eyes with Elgon. There was fear frozen on his face, eyes wide, and lips parted as if the shout he desperately desired to free her with was stuck someplace within his lungs. The horror that had spread over his face at her words hadn't been the feeling she had hoped to fill him within that moment. Her heart pounded in her ears, and her mind was blurred and slowed with the sound of it.

The knife slacked at her throat, and suddenly she was on her knees. She did not know if perhaps she was alive, or maybe dead. The wood beneath her hands was cool and smooth to her touch, the golden hues imprinting on her mind and the pattern of the inlays in their swirl and interwoven

301

patterns burned upon her memory. The grit of some hidden dust upon the floor dug into her palms, and that was all she felt.

Distant shouting was muffled, and a loud bang reverberated through the floor beneath her hands, but it was the hands suddenly grasping her arms and pulling her to her feet that shook her from the malaise.

This was not heaven, and she was still within the king's courtroom.

She looked up into Elgon's brown eyes, a honey golden hue filling them. Creases around his eyes spoke of worry and concern, and his voice echoed in the distance.

He shook her by the grip he had on her upper arms; she wasn't sure if he was holding her upright or simply supporting her. Then his voice rang clear.

"Violet! Are you all right? Can you speak?"

She blinked hard and swallowed against her dry throat, dragging in a reluctant breath. Nothing came from her voice, so she nodded, suddenly looking around her.

Kingsmen had rushed the room. One with brown hair, a few strands dangling in his face, stood with a sword at the throat of Enguerrand, looking down his nose as he stood over him, both arms straining and the outline of his muscles pressing into the linen sleeves of his shirt with the tension. If Enguerrand's look could manifest in the physical world, he would be spitting flames, and the room would be engulfed. The rest of the kingsmen stood about, looking from Enguerrand and the head kingsman who held him captive, to Elgon and herself, confusion on their faces and their hands on the hilts of their swords. Some even had them drawn, unsure how to act.

"Take him down you fools!" Enguerrand spat.

"No!" Elgon's voice was the loudest she had ever heard it, and a new timbre of authority filled it.

The men still stood, frozen, but now looking to Elgon, some with curiosity and some with suspicion.

Elgon released her and she stepped back toward the shadows and colonnades, her legs trembling beneath her and bent under the weight of the stress. She gripped the column for support and watched from a distance.

"Some of you know me. Others may not wish to know me. I am the Crown Prince Elgon Indulf of Elira. I am here with my father's medallion, ready to take my throne."

Violet stood in awe, seeing this man in a new light. No longer was he the farmer who knew not his purpose. The man who had been broken and battered, without identity, weak, and disillusioned in her home. No longer was he the man who had helped at her farm, relying on her for food, but also for comfort.

Here was the man she had seen in the market, defending the life of a young boy.

And suddenly, that scene made perfect sense. That identity had flown from some deep place within him that he had not even been able to identify at the time. But here it was. Perfect and utterly divine.

He stood with authority. His voice was large and commanding, and it was as if he had been intended for this his entire life. Born to it. As indeed he was.

The men paused at his statement, taking note of its tone and command. The confusion slowly melted from their faces as if a spell had been lifted.

"You have seen what this man has done to Elira. The way our borders have weakened. Our trade and commerce given to those on the outside. Our people starved, taxed beyond reason, and their lives forced into servitude for the sake of its rulers. What have we gotten out of the reign of such a man? Dare I say it, a tyrant, who wants nothing but his own selfish gain. What use have we for an alliance with a kingdom such as Rusalka, one that we know exploits its people and reigns over them with terror? Do we want that for Elira? A country that is known for its freedom? Elira has always been the most prosperous country on the continent—would we really give that up at the expense of our people?

"Enguerrand has made a treaty with Rusalka, a country that has been our sworn enemy for decades. A country that has no concept of honor. Do you think for one moment that they would reign with a lenient hand? That they would not go back on their promise to protect Elira the minute that it inconvenienced them? We all know them to be a government without honor. They want Elira for its access to the western seaboard, the gain they can ensure from our natural resources. Why should we fill the coffers of a kingdom that has offered us nothing but pain and control?

"My friends, even if this treaty was a good one, what would be its cost? At what cost would we sell our country into the hands of our enemies, all because of one man who has taken the throne by dishonest means? Would you do so at the cost of your sisters? Your wives? Your mothers, brothers, fathers, children, and friends? Who would you give up for the sake of such an alliance? No one! My father always fought for this

304

land like no other. He fought to keep it out of the hands of men who would see it go to ruin. Out of the hands of our enemies, and out of the hands of countries ruled by tyranny.

"It will not be easy taking what ground we have lost back from Rusalka, from King Zuko and his raiders. But it will be worth every sacrifice.

"What side of history will you be on? The side of a usurper? The man who arranged for my father's death and then ran me out in the forest to be killed like a dog? The man who plotted to take the throne from those who rightfully ruled?

"Or will you side with me, the true king who wants what is best for Elira and her people? I have learned about the God who gifted us with Elira, a country of freedom, and that we must stop at nothing to see His purposes come to pass.

"Choose this day whom you will serve. Either stand with the man who wishes only success for himself, or with me, who desires freedom and success for all of Elira?"

Elgon raised his fist, the royal medallion concealed within and the leather cord dangling around his wrist.

Violet felt the tension in the room heighten. When she dared to look at Enguerrand, the kingman's sword still at his throat, and a blazing fierceness in his eye, there was something else that she saw. There was still defiance in his face and the set of his shoulders, but there was also defeat. There was a desperation that was growing on his countenance as his eyes met those of one, and then another, of the kingsmen.

They all stood about; those who had drawn their swords had lowered them, and others stood staring at Elgon, as if he was an oracle. Some looked around at the others.

"It is true." The kingsman guarding Enguerrand spoke for

the first time. His voice was one of strength, but gentleness, and she liked him immediately. It might have had something to do with the fact that he was holding Enguerrand at bay with a sword to the throat and his other hand wrapped in the back of the man's collar. It made her feel safer, but there was something about him that spoke of comfort, stalwart faithfulness, and outstanding loyalty. He wore a bronze shoulder piece over his leather armor with the king's crest pressed into the metal. He must have been a trusted kingsman, or of higher rank, as he had been the only man Enguerrand had let in the room when he spoke with them, and most of the other kingsmen looked at him with respect.

"Speak, usurper. Let us not be too hasty in our judgment of you. Let only truth pass your lips." The kingsman pressed the sword tighter to Enguerrand's neck, and the man cringed.

"Clearly, you can see that this man is not fit to rule. He may be the prince, but he has the same weakness as his father. His is a rule of all talk, while mine is one of action. He is merely a boy, born and bred in the lap of luxury that was always taken at your expense. What reason have you to trust him?" The sword cut off his words as it pressed at his neck, a little drop of blood from the sharp blade dripped onto the metal. Engeurrand's face contorted in anger, but he said nothing.

The man's voice was sharp in return. "You have one last chance. Your words of slime are not welcome here. Did you or did you not send the prince out to die with orders to your men to kill him in the woods?"

Enguerrand clenched his jaw, and the kingsman leaned in. "Speak! And I might let you live a miserable existence." Sharp as the sword he carried and as commanding as Elgon, he was not putting up with anything from this man who had ruined their lives.

Cowed and with his life on the line, Enguerrand took a breath, and with all of the scorn he seemed able to muster under the blade, he straightened his shoulders. "I did."

Violet's knees gave way, and she sank to the wooden floor. Exhausted and with all the fight gone from her very bones, she lay her head down on the coolness of the honey golden inlay. It was over. Elgon would be king. She knew it deep in her heart without watching the shift of power in the room.

He would be king. King of Elira. A ruler worthy of the people by the grace of God.

And she was still a peasant girl.

The loneliest in the land.

# Twenty-Eight

## TO GREET A KING

THINGS HAPPENED WITH a suddenness that left Violet reeling. The announcement of the change of power was made to the city of Niran and would be sent out by herald to the outlying towns. She had been taken under the wing of the kingsman who had defeated Enguerrand and saved her life. She had learned his name: Malcolm. He alone had been responsible for ensuring her safety at the direction of Elgon. Malcolm had chosen the very best of his men, those whom he trusted the most, to care for her. She was grateful that she was able to trust him, for there was, as yet, still much turmoil amongst the Kingsmen as loyalties were sorted out.

She now sat in a castle room, the window overlooking the sea that was now dancing beneath the golden rays of the sun. She hadn't seen it so sunny, bright, and beautiful until this morning, and her wish was fulfilled. She couldn't seem to take her eyes off it. The golden light highlighting the whitecaps that danced upon the waves and the sound of them hitting the cliffside filled her heart near to bursting. Something about the sea called her, spoke to her, and filled her with strength and rest. She wished with all her might she didn't have to leave it.

To think that the One whom she worshiped could command even the powerful wind and the ever-changing, strong sea with a mere word from His mouth. Her Savior was the one who could speak and command their going out and their coming in. She closed her eyes as she ran the comb through her hair and leaned against the window frame, breathing in deep the scent of the salty air that tickled her nose and filled her lungs with life.

Wearing a dress that was far more beautiful than anything she had ever seen, let alone worn, the olive-toned linen was finely woven, not coarse like the threads that they spun and wove back home. She had fingered it before putting it on, marveling at the tightness of the weave and the softness of the threads. She hadn't seen the clothes that she had worn on the journey here since a maid had taken them to be washed when she had bathed.

After the showdown in the throne room, she had been brought to a room, and she had forgotten much for hours as her body finally succumbed to some sleep. She had been so exhausted, having hardly slept on the journey that was fraught with worry. The sun was now up, but she was unsure if this was the first or second sun since collapsing on a feather mattress, the likes of which she had rarely seen.

The dress laced up the sides and the bodice that she placed over it was of heavy, emerald velvet with mustard sunflowers embroidered about the edges. She brushed the yellow with a finger, and it was soft as silk. Perhaps, it even was.

A knock at the door startled her from her revery and made her jump, a hand flying to her chest at the sudden increase in heart rhythm.

"May I come in, my lady?" A soft, feminine voice from outside drifted through the heavy wooden door.

"Of course." Violet rushed to the door, pulling it open, just as it was pushed open from the hall. A young maid stood outside, her tan bodice, brown skirt, and white apron, while of similar quality to Violet's usual garb, was far cleaner and prettier than anything she had ever worn.

"I have come to fetch you, my lady. The prince—erm, king wishes for your presence."

Violet's heart skipped a beat, and she drew in a breath, biting her lip. "Please don't call me a lady." She placed a gentle hand on the young woman's arm; her brown hair was tied up neatly in a kerchief, and her eyes were bright as diamonds. "I'm only Violet."

The girl smiled for a moment, her blue eyes brightening at the gentle look on Violet's face. She dipped her head in a nod and dropped her eyes to the floor, the smile still painting her pink lips in an attractive line. "The king wishes it, my lady."

Violet sighed, but her lips still pulled upward at the corners. He may be king, but he had also been Obed once, and she had taught him how to plow a row, harvest a field, and milk a cow. Turning her into something she was not, despite the reasoning, would never do. She would resolve this later with him.

"Thank you. What's your name? I apologize, I was quite tired when I last saw you."

The maid dipped into a curtsey. There was an energetic air

about her that Violet warmed to. It was as if the girl's very spirit was alive within her, dancing and whirling constantly, even when her physical form was still. "Zehra, my lady."

That 'my lady' business would have to be dispensed with. The sooner the better.

"It's a pleasure to meet you, Zehra. Lead the way. Let us see what his majesty wishes." Violet followed Zehra down the hall, her soft shoes barely making a sound on the stone halls and stairs. An urgency started to rise within her, and her heart steeled itself. All she could think about now that death was no longer impending was of Granny. Was she all right? Did she need Violet?

She choked back a lump in her throat. The idea of Granny being so desperately upset over her granddaughter's disappearance filled her with dread of what she might find when she returned. She loved her Granny more than life, and the idea of her suffering so under such fear made her heart stutter in her chest. Granny's mind was as fragile as fine glass, and Violet just hoped and prayed with her whole heart that it hadn't shattered. Cracks could be repaired, but she feared it might have been more than that.

The heavy oak doors of the throne room suddenly stood before her, and she realized that she had completely forgotten to keep track of where they had turned, getting hopelessly lost in these majestic stone halls. She touched Zehra's arm as the two kingsmen guarding the entrance moved to open the massive doors. "Please, do wait. I don't know that I would be able to find my way back."

Zehra nodded, a solemn and respectful look on her face as she stepped off to the side, her back to the wall, hands folded

312

in front of her, and her head bowed in homage.

Violet gathered herself, lifting her head and standing tall. She was no longer meeting a lowly farmer boy, rescued from the woods and unable to fend for himself.

Now, she readied herself to greet a king.

Elgon paced the dais, the crown heavy on his head. It was the lightweight circlet for everyday use that his father had worn without seeming to notice its weight, nor did he seem to even notice that it was on from day to day. But to Elgon it felt unnatural, yet fully and completely his at the same time.

Likewise, these stone walls were welcoming but frightening. They didn't fully feel right yet. As if he were simply not used to them. Like a new pair of boots that are stiff and may produce a few blisters before softening with time and wear. How he longed for the farm fields, the soft breeze whipping through his hair, making it stand on end, and the soft, cool feel of the fresh air on his face. He closed his eyes, pausing in his walk. The breeze, the sunlight glistening off the long grass as it swayed, moved by an unseen hand. Lifting Violet's long, brown curls, the ones that always escaped from the kerchief that bound her hair back. Her green eyes trained on him, rimmed with lashes that were dark and long.

The sound of the doors pounding and falling on the hinges as they opened startled him, and his eyes flew open as he turned, his robe falling behind him. He still wore the more relaxed kingsman uniform from yesterday; somehow it made the men more at ease, but he did have on the long blue cloak of the monarch, falling from the pauldrons at his shoulders.

There she stood. His heart stuttered in his chest, and his stomach turned over. His jaw fell. Violet was one of the most beautiful women he had ever seen, but with freshly washed hair, her curls sprang to life even more than usual, almost seeming to have a life of their own as they moved and bounced with her stately walk across the courtroom toward him. The dress she had been given made the green in her eyes darker, like the deep shade of the forest, leaves shimmering with the slightest sliver of light that brightened their tender surfaces. They were so deep… He could almost hear the soft rustling of the trees.

And then she bowed, dropping to her knees before him like a willow bending beneath the weight of some unseen hand. It was beautiful, but oh, so wrong.

"Violet." He lunged forward, grasping her hand in his and drawing her back up to her feet. "You do not need to kneel before me."

She took her hand from his and dropped her eyes to the floor, her head slightly bent. "Your majesty, you are the king. I am merely paying my monarch his due respect."

Elgon pursed his lips. Why on earth was she acting like this? Had the months where they had shared a roof and the work of the field meant nothing to her? He had lived in her home, eaten her food, helped her care for the livestock, and been nursed back to health by her and Granny's hands. Why was she treating him like a stranger?

"Surely, we have been through so much together, we can make do without formality."

Her eyes did not leave the floor. "You are my king, and as

my king, my lord, you will receive the same respect I would give to any monarch."

"I—" His voice caught. He had no idea what to say.

"Thank you for your hospitality, my lord. I am grateful for your shelter after such a trying experience."

Aghast, he could not even respond. What had happened to the Violet who had stood by his side, who had been shooting daggers from her gaze in the throne room before Enguerrand, and whose soul had touched his in the moment where he thought he would lose her forever? He still felt the panic rise in his throat at the mental image of a knife to hers. He was in awe of her bravery in the face of such catastrophic consequences. She had stood up for him. Stood in the gap and poured forth flame from her tongue upon the man who had taken his place on the throne. Malcolm had told him all that had transpired before his entrance into the throne room.

There was an awkward silence. Elgon had no idea what to say. All he wanted to do was wrap the Violet he had known into a hug and take all of the tension that was sitting on her shoulders, but for some reason, she repelled him. Not in anything that she was, but in some unseen way, tone, and manner she had about her. It was weighing on her, he could see it, but somehow, he could not approach her.

"Why have you summoned me, my lord?" Her words were so aloof they sounded as if they were far away.

He shook his head to clear the fluff from his brain. "Your wishes?" he blurted out. The stupidity of his words echoed back at him from the depths of the cavernous room.

She looked up then, her green eyes full and shining like crystal with what he believed to be unshed tears. "Home.

Please, let me go home. I must tend to Granny."

His heart sank clear into his boots.

"Of course." His mind took a minute to catch up with what she had said. Requested. A hope that had flown at the back of his mind for quite some time but that he had not been able to name until now fluttered and dropped within him. She did not wish to stay.

Oh, how he had wished she would.

"I can send you with herald and protection to the village of Padsley."

Her eyes caught on his face.

"Don't worry, I will have Malcom ensure that they can be trusted. You will be well cared for. I promise."

"Thank you, m'lord." She bobbed her head and bent in a slow bow.

He stepped forward on impulse, his hand reaching out with a mind of its own to tenderly touch her elbow, the linen soft beneath his now calloused fingers. "It's the very least I can do. After everything you have given me." His words were soft, a mere whisper that seemed to sink into each of them, pulling them closer.

She looked up, her eyes nearly brimming, and his breath caught. She was so close. Everything in him wanted to kiss her trembling lips, her elbow resting gently upon his fingers, her breath warm as it feathered his neck. It was as if he couldn't pull his eyes from hers, his whole body straining forward to meet her.

Her breath hitched, and she stepped back, a tear falling from her eye, and she quickly dashed it away with a hand, almost as if to ignore the tears' very existence. "I only did what anyone ought to do."

"But no one would." His voice had still not regained its full strength yet and the husky tones made him swallow hard to coat his throat.

"Thank you for your protection, m'lord." The words changed tone, and she was suddenly in control again, the tears lessening, but her eyes still watery as she blinked rapidly.

Short of taking a step back, he could see her desire to leave; her entire being was begging it of him. He reached a hand to pull at the collar of his shirt. It was suddenly incredibly warm in this room, the cold stone pressing inward.

"Of course. You may go, if you wish." The last bit sounded too forced and rushed, as if it was the one thing he couldn't wait to get off his tongue. As if, for some far-off chance, she actually did not wish to go.

But with only a low bow, her eyes on the floor, she was gone, and he stood staring at an empty room.

As empty as his heart now felt.

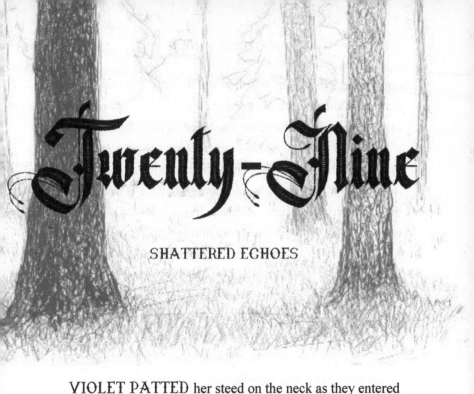

# Twenty-Nine

## SHATTERED ECHOES

VIOLET PATTED her steed on the neck as they entered Padsley. There was the same dour outlook on the town; nothing had changed in her absence. But along their journey, it had been a wonder to behold, sensing the change in people as the herald had proclaimed the change of authority over Elira to each town, village, and ford that they passed through along the way. The entire mood would shift. From oppressed and dark, to a slight hopefulness seeping into everyone's weary bones. She started to see smiles, hopeful looks on their faces, as if they hadn't smiled in some time and were suddenly trying it again.

Her heart ached when the children playing in the cobble streets would run at the first sight of the kingsmen, their faces full of the fear the adults tried to hide, but could only disguise. Her people had been in bondage for far too long. Slaves to the fear, chained to their trembling, and held hostage by their oppression. No longer. But then she would rejoice when they learned of the news, and she saw their fear lift. The relief set in, and the joy of freedom exploded across their faces in shock. They were slaves no more, and her heart danced at the prospect of her townsfolk being filled with joy at the news.

It would take some time for them to believe it the way she did. She had seen Elgon in a way none had—as Obed. The man who had stood in the street and fought for justice, who had torn through a burning building to rescue the one that she loved on her behalf. The man who had been beaten rather than allowed her to be hurt or treated unfairly. Her eyes started to fill again. There had been a void within her that had grown larger the farther from Niran that they traveled. There was a wall within her heart. She knew it now. So much loss. So much fear. So much hopelessness had built up brick upon brick until her entire heart was walled off from those around her. She couldn't let the drawbridge down, couldn't let anyone in. If she let her guard down, she worried what would follow.

The pain, emotions, and fear that she had held at arm's length for years would come tumbling over, swallowing her whole in its tempest and leaving nothing in return. A tsunami, drowning her with the impossible.

But someone had snuck over the wall. A thief in the night upon a heist to steal entrance to her heart. She could feel the bricks giving way, as Elgon's sudden departure had left holes, and they were tearing open from within, a torrent ready to explode at any second. She swallowed. She would be strong. She always had and always would be. There was no need for that to change now.

She caught sight of Everard. He was a welcome sight

indeed. Familiarity and safety cloaked in a giant of a man.

Their gazes locked. His face drew back in surprise, and his eyes widened. Moving toward her, he then stopped at the sight of the kingsmen. Without a second thought, she slid from her horse and hiked her skirts, running across the street and dodging the herd of sheep that were being guided toward the other edge of town. Her hurried steps grew faster as she flung herself at him, and he caught her in his arms.

Pulling back to look up the long way to his face, a few tears escaped her eyes. "It's all right. The Kingsmen are on our side now. Obed…the prince is now the king. The chancellor has been deposed."

His eyes, wide and troubled, stared back and forth between hers. Then back up at the kingsmen, who stood with hands on the hilts of their swords and their watchful eyes on them as if Everard would do anything to her. "You mean—?"

She nodded. "We will be saved."

After another long look into her eyes, as if he didn't think she was serious, his shoulders relaxed more than she had ever seen before, and the line on his forehead she had thought was permanent was suddenly gone. She was almost shocked at the change.

He gathered her into a hug before she had time to react, and the tears she kept desperately trying to repress leaked out where no one would see them, mingling with the grease on the man's leather apron.

"Saved," he whispered, his breath rustling the hair on the top of her head. "Praise God."

When he released her, she smiled sadly up into his face. "How is Granny?"

His face immediately fell, and her heart dropped clear to her toes. *No.*

She turned and ran.

"Violet!" Everard's voice called after her, but she evaded it as she did the sheep in her path, dodging around them and hiking up her skirt as she did so. With a mad dash between traffic and down the street, she hurried to Fendrel's house. Oh God, let her be on the mend.

"Violet!" The call was distant now, and she spared a thought to wonder how Everard had not caught her with his longer stride and powerful presence that could push a way through any crowd. She hoped the kingsmen weren't holding him, thinking he had meant her ill, but that would have to be sorted out later. The soldiers under Captain Malcolm's orders had been the most attentive and overly protective bodyguards a person could ask for.

*Granny.*

The word raced through her mind, panic and prayer all at once.

She flung open the wooden door, her heart racing in her chest and the blood pounding in her ears as if desperate to escape. Marcus was there and almost fell over at her abrupt entrance. He snatched his crutch as it started its descent to the floor.

Her gaze was fixated on the door to the room she had shared with Granny. It was ajar, and the light was dimmer, but not dark. If it was not in use, it would have been dark. Her feet led her across the common room before she even knew where she was going.

"Violet! Wait!" Marcus's voice was urgent, full of pleading

and some note of panic, which only fueled hers.

The bed. It had a figure in it. A sigh the likes of which she had never experienced leapt out of her lungs with relief. Suddenly gasping for breath from her run, her shoulders collapsed forward in release. Granny was just asleep.

Violet stepped forward to the bed, grateful just to see her granny. But her heart, beating fast from her run, stopped. Something wasn't right. The sheets were barely moving.

God, please, no. She reached out a trembling hand and laid it on the sallow, wrinkled hand that rested upon the bedclothes, hardly making any impression in the soft fabric.

"Miran?" The whisper from the pillow made Violet jump. It was soft, as if the speaker was exhausted.

"It's me, Granny. It's Violet. I've come home."

The eyes that met hers were pale and seemed to look right past her. "Miran, don't you let Violet play out in that rain."

Violet bit her lip, all of the emotion in the world suddenly choking her, pushing at her from the inside, threatening to explode. Granny had not once mentioned her mother's name since Miran's death long ago. The distant eyes forced her to her knees beside the low bed, still holding her hand.

"Granny?" Violet's tortured whisper tore from her lungs like a knife.

The eyes lit up, and for a second, the grief in Violet stilled with anticipation.

"Richard?" Those pale but seeing eyes were fixed on the ceiling above the far wall. "Your robe. Why is it so bright?"

A sob wrecked Violet's throat as it exploded from her. Not yet. Not again. Not one more time.

"Is it because you are with…Him?" The awe and reverence

in the faint and weary whisper tore at Violet's heart, and she turned to look where Granny's eyes rested, almost expecting to see some heavenly apparition. *Dear God*...

"No, I'm coming. Tell Violet I love her. My darling baby girl. I'm coming Richard...I surrender."

A sallow hand reached toward the ceiling, barely making it off the bed before it fell again. Granny's eyes closed.

Violet heard a far-off ringing in her ears, and the hand that touched her shoulder was the thing that shattered her from the echoes she was trapped in. She collapsed under the touch, realizing that the ringing was her own agonized scream. The floor met her with its welcome blackness. She swam in it, the darkness, drifting between awake and unconscious. She desperately wished for one or the other.

The walls had caved. The tsunami had come. She was drowning.

Elgon reached out a hand, his fingers brushing the Bible that sat upon a chest of drawers in his father's room. The large, canopied bed, with its heavy draperies that kept out the cold in the winter months, stood on the opposite wall, and the window overlooking the sea was open, the air crisp with the first taste of autumn and the smell and sound of the sea spilling into the room, echoing off the stone walls.

This book. He had seen his father read it. He could remember it now, but he had thought nothing of it. He hesitated, almost afraid to pick it up, feeling utterly unworthy of it. But Granny had spent many an hour reading to him from her own tattered version, though far more inexpensive and cheaply made than this parchment and leather tome.

His heart stirred within him. So many of these words had sunk into his mind, deep into his spirit, and done a work that he had not been asking for, but had been granted to him nonetheless. Perhaps, to prepare him for this moment, this time, this opportunity that he had before him…and that he felt utterly unworthy of.

He picked up the book and flipped it open, his eyes falling on the first right-hand page. "And I thank Christ Jesus our Lord, who hath enabled me, for that he has counted me faithful, putting me into the ministry. Who was before a blasphemer and a persecutor and injurious? But I obtained mercy because I did it ignorantly in unbelief.

"And the grace of our Lord was exceedingly abundant with faith and love which is in Christ Jesus. This is a faithful saying and worthy of all acceptance, that Christ Jesus came into the world to save sinners, of whom I am chief." Tears started to his eyes and burned. They were not familiar to him, but somehow, they felt as if they sprung up from some deep well within him that had yet to be used. "Howbeit, for this cause, I obtained mercy that in me first Jesus Christ might show forth all longsuffering for a pattern to them which should hereafter believe on him to life everlasting." His chest heaved.

He had been that sinner. The one who had flown in the face of everything that he knew to be good, holy, and just. His own father had been ashamed of him, of who he was becoming. The voices of others had tugged at his mind, offered him many things that in the moment had been his deepest desires. He had been in pursuit of his pleasures, but they had never filled the aching holes within him. The places that had desperately cried out for a loving father, a caring mother, and the wise counsel that he so desperately needed. The heart that longed to be accepted, even in the midst of heartache.

Yet God had reached down into his tiny universe, had plucked him from the life of sin he had been born to and fed with, had placed him in a place that had stripped him of everything. And instead, he saw two women, living out the words of this book the best that they could, offering to God their every waking moment as a living sacrifice to protect, nurture, and care for the land, animals, and people that God put in their lives. Even at great cost to themselves and great danger to their persons.

Through them he had first experienced Christ's love. He didn't know it then, but it had laid the groundwork for him to understand what it was like to receive love, care, and nurture at the hands of those from whom he least deserved it.

These women had poured out their everything to serve and treat him as they would a brother. But it had been him, his family, his rule that had taken the things from them that they loved best. Their son and father killed at the hand of his leadership.

He gulped back at the scratchy feeling in his throat and used a spare hand to brush away the tears that fell from his face.

He so desperately wanted to go back. To experience that simple life on the farm. Rectifying the mistakes that had been made while he slept at the helm, his kingdom and rule being drained away by the man who he had allowed to be in charge. He could have stepped in, said anything, taken over the rule of his father, long before he did. Learned of the circumstances and put in the time to better prepare himself for the legacy of his family to care for the country of Elira. But instead, he had left it in incapable hands and had wasted his life away in temporary pleasures.

The one woman who had made him see differently, who had lived an example that was worthy of following, who had stood in the strength of her true King, the One who ruled from His seat in heaven. Who had taken every risk and every punishment to serve that King and had borne every loss to do what was right. The woman who had lived her life in a manner worthy of the call that was upon it. Who had stood up to evil at great cost to herself.

He had let her slip through his fingers.

His heart ached. He so desperately wanted to be worthy of her. Worthy of the throne. Worthy of the responsibility of ruling a nation. Worthy of protecting the people…his people. The ones he had sold out for cheap, momentary happiness. The ones he had given up responsibility for. He was so empty. So useless a vessel.

Yet…God.

"Lord, why have you put me here? What have I done that makes you think me worthy of this call? I have no strength within myself to stand up for my people, to give them the protection that they deserve. To stand in the gap and shore up the holes that have been made in our safety and freedom. Why should they trust me? A man who has taken every opportunity to do the right thing and squandered it away for cheap pleasantries? What have I to give that you would choose me? What have I to use that will strengthen this nation to the life and light it was before?" He dropped the book upon the chest

327

and buried his head in his hands, rubbing them vigorously through his beard and squeezing his eyes shut against the hot, burning tears...the first he had shed since he was a boy. His fingers bumped into something cool, and before he could catch it, the light circlet fell from its place upon his head and clanked as it hit the stone floor, spinning in a circle on one end before it fell flat.

*What strength you have, I give you. You will live a life worthy of the calling which I have placed upon it. But it is by My strength you will be worthy of the call. It is My blood which makes you worthy. I have chosen you. I have breathed My life into you for a purpose greater than you. I filled you with My Spirit that you may rule with decisions from My throne room. Your throne will model Mine because I have asked it of you. I have saved you for this purpose...that you may save the earthly kingdom of Elira and restore it to its proper birthright of freedom. My peace I give to you, and My peace I will leave with you until I return. Until such time as I see fit, you will rule in My name and by My hand. Do not despise the life you have received. The second chances you have been given. Do not throw them in My face and say that you are not worthy. I have called you worthy, and My words are the only ones that are true.*

*Now live by them and fulfill the destiny I have called of you and your family. You serve a higher calling and a higher purpose. Do not set your sights too closely on this earth, but look to My kingdom. Look to My example. Out of them you will pattern your own rule. Show mercy and grace as I have shown it to you. Your legacy is far reaching and will be one that will change the course of the nation. Do not let your past mistakes or failures assuage you any longer. Have I not saved you from them? Redeemed your life from the pit and crowned you with lovingkindness and tender mercy? Do not look any longer to your old ways, for that man is dead and the new one has been risen by the power of My Son. Follow My ways, for whom I have called, I will not abandon.*

Heart full and a sob choking his throat, Elgon sank to his knees, reaching out trembling fingers to pick up the circlet that had fallen from his head. So much meaning existed in that small circlet of silver. Its shininess seemed almost heavenly, and its weight heavier now that its purpose was so defined. Holding it in his hands, the responsibility of it burned in his palms. "God, give me strength." The words came out as a harsh whisper, and with a shuddering breath, he lifted the circlet to his head and settled it again where it belonged. Where God had placed it.

He still felt wholly inadequate. But his heart burned with a new purpose. This was not just something he would take on for his earthly father's sake. For the people outside of these walls who so desperately needed one who could discern and rule with wisdom and insight. But for his Heavenly Father who had seen fit to use the circumstances of his life to pick him up, turn his life completely around by His grace, and set him on a wholly new path with a new purpose, identity, name, and destiny. He would strive, with all his might and with all his days, to be worthy of that call. To live by faith and grace. He stood and reached out a hand to the book upon the chest...and by these words.

# Thirty

## ALWAYS MINE

VIOLET SWUNG THE sickle, using every ounce of her muscle to pour into this harvest. There wasn't much of the wheat left, but what little she did have left, she intended on seeing to the finish. So much had been poured out of her this year. So much work, effort, suffering, and pain. She could reap little from it, but she would savor every last morsel and grain of this wheat. The image of Obed swinging behind her was almost so vivid it caused her to turn around. Nothing but waving wheat and a freshly cut swathe met her eyes. She drew in a deep breath, stretching her neck to the opposite side to ease the muscles that were pulling hard and starting to tighten with soreness from the one-sided motion of swinging the sickle from right to left.

She choked and coughed on the chaff that blew in the air and paused to catch her breath, raising a hand to her face to

331

push back the errant strands of hair. Averting her eyes from the place where a fresh pile of exposed dirt and a headstone rested under the willow tree at the back of the blackened pile of the remains of her house, she ducked, picking up the scythe once more, fitting her hands into the familiar and worn handles, the wood smooth from heavy use and worn from the oil of her palms.

Little had changed for Padsley in the last two weeks. The people whom she had grown to love around her still looked over their shoulder expecting to be spit upon or berated for any little thing that might be construed. They still clutched their purses and pockets close, hoping that the authorities wouldn't see how much they had made to feed the starving mouths at home. But the kingsmen who had escorted her from Niran had taken charge of Padsley and announced that his majesty, Elgon Indulf, was soon to be officially crowned king of Elira. While Elgon had assumed the throne, he would officially do so in a public manner. The border kingdoms would be made aware of the new ruler, and Rusalka would be notified of the nullification of the treaty that had been put forward by Enguerrand's treacherous hand.

She hoped there would not be too much violence, but King Zuko of Rusalka was said to be a volatile man who had an especial hatred for Elira and her monarchs of generations past. She knew not what had been the cause of such animosity, but it was definitely not something she hoped would be ignited. It had been a few months since the last raid into Elira from Rusalka, and she hoped it would be the last. But the dread in her heart told her that perhaps a time was coming when there would be battles, perhaps even war.

She prayed that it would not be so and that the people would be spared from this. They had already endured so much.

As had she.

Her heart ached, even more than her muscles, as she swung with vigor and marched steadily across the field in a shuffling maneuver, cutting the wheat that would then be picked up and beaten for the grain and sifted till the chaff was separated. She was grateful for the work and grateful that it was left to her. So little remained of her life.

She was still residing under the hospitality of Fendrel, but being inside of that house was painful in many ways. She was grateful that Everard had offered her his help in cleaning out an apartment for her above the smithy. His house was a few doors down, but the large and roomy attic above the stable and smithy was mostly unused aside from old harnesses, tools, and a random assortment of boxes that lay about covered in dust. They had some time before the snow fell, but he had promised it to her by then.

Much needed to be done in the space, aside from cleaning to make it livable, and she hoped that she would be able to create a place that would at least be comfortable and that she could call her own for the time being. As much as she loved Fendrel and Marcus, it wasn't the best place for her. They were generous enough, but they had need of the space, and she did not want to get in their way, nor be constantly tormented by the memories and trauma that lurked within those walls, seeping out from corners like shadows, waiting to pounce on her without moment's notice and putting her through the memories again and again.

She shuddered. The overwhelming weight of the emotion

that had collapsed into her had left her reeling. But through God's grace, she had made it outside. Her consolation was the sunlight, fall breeze, and the field full of wheat, ripened on the stalks and ready to be harvested. She had gotten through half the field in three days, spending every waking second working the land, feeling the wind in her hair, and raising blisters on her hands. If she hadn't had anything to do with her hands, she might have been tempted to shake a fist at God. While she knew where Granny was and how much better off she would be on the streets of glory...Violet still felt broken. The only one remaining in her life had been taken from her. But, as it was, the open air gave her a perspective she would not easily shake.

Granny's last word of surrender had stuck in her heart, and she had realized the grip of control she had tried to hold onto in her life. Every emotion in check. Every action made with an effort to hold and command her destiny. But every vestige of that control had vanished, and with it her desire and strength to hold onto it any longer.

God had walked beside her in these fields. His hands on her heart as she had swung her scythe. His touch had floated to her on the breeze, His comfort toying with her hair on every gust of wind. His tears had fallen with hers in the rain, and the clatter of the leaves in the forest had signaled His presence, and the voices of the trees were His voice, whispering His promises and words to her with every breath. His presence had met her and been with her while she worked, restoring her mind in ways she had not known possible. He had carried the grief with her as she carried sheaf after sheaf, laying them within the unburned part of the barn for storage from the elements while He reminded her again and again of every word from His book that was stored within her heart.

She drew in a breath and closed her eyes, halting for a moment as her chest heaved and her back muscles screamed from the exertion, taking another short break. There were two rhythms, that of the back and forth swinging of the scythe, but also the burst of hard and focused work, and the moment of rest for aching limbs and straining lungs.

Without the sound of the swishing blade and sliced stalks, there was another sound that met her in the stillness. Someone was coming down the road. Fear ricocheted into her chest at the sound of hoofbeats, nearly every other horrific moment in her life preluded by the sounds of a kingsman's horse. She turned sharply, gripping her scythe like a weapon, her hands tight and the knuckles bursting with the strain she was putting on them. She couldn't make out the rider, but the tall black horse with flowing mane and tail looked familiar.

The man who pulled up to the edge of the field dismounted, and she tightened her grip. His kingsman's garb was not hard to mistake, even from this distance. She squinted but didn't want to take a hand from her potential weapon to shield her eyes from the late afternoon sun. Her breath came quick and fast, every muscle at attention.

"Violet?"

Her knees almost gave out, and she relaxed her grip, dropping the scythe to the ground and leaning heavily on it for support instead.

"Obed." The name slipped from her tongue, and she hadn't the strength to take it back.

He stood before her. Cleaner, healthier than she had seen

him last. And there was brighter light in his eyes than before, but there was something about the way he carried himself. He wore the kingsman's green uniform, the light leather vest of the riders, and the spaulder of a leader, the king's signet pressed into the darker-hued leather. His cloak hung off his shoulders, fastened around his neck with a pin in the shape of a bow and arrow. He was no longer a boy in his father's cloak, but he stood as if it fit him. As if he wore it, instead of it wearing him. There was a confidence to him she hadn't seen before, and he stood with shoulders steady and a small smile on his face.

She looked harder at his upturned lips, then back up at his eyes. Those amber depths, the warm color of a sun-washed tree trunk. She couldn't remember if she had seen him smile before.

The implications of who was standing in her wheat field suddenly struck her, and she fell to a knee. "My lord. Your majesty." *Good God Almighty, give me grace. The king is standing in my field.*

He took hold of her elbows and helped her up, the smile lighting up his eyes. "It's only Obed just now, I think."

She held her breath; he didn't release her elbow. Why was he looking so deep into her eyes? Tears welled in them, and she tore her gaze from his to stare at her feet.

"Violet? Fendrel told me about Granny."

A sob forced its way from her throat. Suddenly, she was pressed against the wool and leather, the smells of leather oil, horse, and...strength met her. Surprise at the unexpected movement, and a reminder of her lowly station filled her mind, but something forbade her from pulling away. The starving child within her that had not received one touch of love or comfort in days begged for solace, and she forgot herself in the pure and utterly filling embrace. Tears chased each other down her face and were dried on the wool sleeve of his shirt, her shoulders shaking beneath his arms.

He wasn't Elgon; he was only Obed, the man who had weeded this very field at her side and who had fought through every demon in her, now held her, and it felt completely right in that moment.

The torrent of emotion that welled within her breast wasn't the overwhelming wave of a storm-tossed ocean, it was the gentle cooling and healing of a mountain stream, running over the drenched and war-torn land of her heart and healing the cracks and crevices that had formed.

After a long moment, when the tears had ceased, she stepped back from his embrace and looked up. Tears hung in his eyes as well, and she brushed at her lashes to clear away the ones that still clung there.

"What are you doing here?" she asked in what she hoped was a polite, conversational tone. He had said he was here as Obed, not as her king, so she hoped her question was taken in the casual way it was asked.

His hands looked empty and useless in front of him, as if he didn't know what to do with them now that she was not occupying them. She shook her head at the thought as if to clear it from her mind.

"I needed to see you."

The words held emotion cloaked in meaning, and she wasn't quite sure what that meaning was.

She didn't even need to ask but only looked up quizzically,

and the look that met her from his face made her heart stop.

Was that…love?

His eyes had warmed, growing wider and his face held a confusing mix of longing, compassion, openness, and…reverence?

She took a slight step back on instinct. She didn't know what that look meant, but it was too much to hope for. Her heart leapt in her chest, fluttering in the most annoyingly inconvenient way. She didn't want to hear what he was about to say, right? What on earth was wrong with her?

"Violet…I…could not stop thinking about you for the last few weeks. You have shown me so much about myself that I never knew was within me and…oh hang it all, I want to ask you to marry me." The words tumbled out of his mouth as if he couldn't hold them back, and she reeled from their impact. Had she honestly heard him say those words?

She felt her mouth gape but was completely helpless to rectify the matter. Marry? The king?

He rushed on. "I'm sorry, I should have eased into that. But, Violet, you have shown me what it means to be a child of God. To stand in the gap for those less fortunate. To stand up for what you believe in and what His word says, no matter the consequences. You have put your life and everything you had to offer on the line again and again in service to your King and…would you be willing to do it in service to this lowly farm hand? I know I am not in any sense worthy of the woman that you are. Of the woman who God created you to be, and if you could not love me, just send me away at once, and I will obey.

"But what I feel for you has been grounded in what I have

experienced of the fierce love you show to that which is yours. You are a woman who has shown me what it means to be called by destiny at the hand of God and walk in it. I have fallen in love with who you are and who you will become, and I could not rest until I had asked if you would be willing to take me, a man who is not worthy of you but is striving every day to be more so by the hand of a merciful and loving God."

Elgon stood, his heart laying raw and vulnerable in his hands as he offered them to Violet. The breeze rustled in her curls, a look of complete shock on her face. Her vibrant green eyes were shedding tears that chased each other down her face, the freckles beneath them shimmering in the golden light of the late sun. His breath caught in his throat, and he couldn't look away, but now that he was here and he saw her again, working with a heart so pure in this field of wheat, he felt so utterly unworthy of her, and he knew deep down to his very toes that nothing he could ever do could make him worthy of this woman who was already a queen. Marrying him would get her no farther than she had already come, formed and molded by the very hand of God and carrying the heart of a queen and the conviction of a saint. His shoulders dropped. He could not ask it of her.

"I know I am unworthy of you in every respect. I was a man no one could respect and honor for the things I have done. Just say the word and I will leave you in peace."

"But you are!" Her words were soft, nearly a whisper, and her hand darted out to rest on his arm. "It is I that am not worthy of you. A lowly peasant girl with nary a house or family to her name. What dowry would I offer you or lands to add to your domain? What have I to give you that you could possibly view as an asset? Surely you must marry some princess who will be worthy of your love and contribute to your purpose."

He stepped toward her, taking the hand that had been on his arm and looking down into those eyes as green as the fields after a spring rain. "Contribute to my purpose? My beautiful flower, have you not done so? You have only ever pushed me to discover the purpose for which God made me, shown me a hope that has made me serve a higher calling and propelled me to pick up the destiny for which I was created. It is you who has shown me what my purpose was. To live out the calling which He has placed on my life and, Lord willing, do some good for Elira and her people. To set to right the wrongs that were allowed to happen on my watch. Violet." The words came out bursting with emotion, and his chest was heaving with it, every breath a labor under the intense weight.

He touched a hand to her face, tenderly stroking back the wayward curls that clung to her wet cheeks. "You are all the dowry that I desire and all the wealth I could ever possess. Nothing else compares to the wealth of your spirit and the strength of your heart. I love you with all that is within me, my flower. Only let me show you and I will cherish you for all of my days."

It was as if all of creation held its breath, them included, their hearts beating close to each other. He could feel her breathing beneath his fingers on her chin, and with a slight gasp of air that caught on a sob, the words he so desperately desired to hear escaped from her lips in a breathless whisper.

"I love you with every breath that is in me."

The sun burst forth in a glorious flame across the sky as it set and his arms pulled her close, her head resting just beneath his chin, and he caressed her hair with a kiss. His flower queen.

The orange and red rush of light across the sky, brushing every cloud with its elegant colors casting gold and pink light across them both. She was nestled beneath his arm, her hand caught in his other one and her heart beating in tandem with his. They walked together toward Sigeric, their steps slow as they basked in the moment. Love had come hard for them both, and much loss had been endured. But she could not remember the last time she had felt happiness overtake her. It was as if the summer sun had illuminated every single shadow and crevice within the forest of her heart, its warm rays touching even the most broken and vulnerable places and filling them with the growing rays of a thousand lights.

His fingers brushed hers, and she stared at them. The long, elegant fingers, worn, rough with scratches, scars, and callouses. It was hard to believe that they had once not been this way. Once white, soft, unused to the work and toil of his current life. Their fingers danced together, a slow movement, feathering and soft, interlacing then unlacing. She turned her hand to fit against his more securely. His fingers were gentle, tender. He ran his thumb along the back of her hand, looping it down and caressing the inside of her wrist.

341

"It's so soft," he whispered, his eyes warm as he looked at her. She thought…perhaps, if he asked her to, she could kiss him now. Her heart melted beneath the thought. She knew she was ready. After all this time, this short amount of time in which they had lived so much life. The days becoming years and feeling as though they knew each other inside and out, despite the fact that it hadn't been very long at all. It felt…right. Like it was meant to be. Their lives together were filled with such purpose, destiny, and calling. She knew beyond a shadow of a doubt that not only were they meant to be together, but that they were called to walk together, stepping forward and changing the course of history. Changing the world. For the better.

Once she knew that, there was no turning back.

# THE END

# WANT TO READ TWO
# BONUS SCENES?

Follow the QR Code to subscribe to my newsletter and receive two bonus epilogues!

https://mailchi.mp/f8bf74b2ca49/once-i-knew-landing-page

# ACKNOWLEDGEMENTS

THANK YOU first and foremost to my Savior. The One who seemed to take hold of the pen and lead me through this story. The One who gave me words in the first place and is THE reason that I write. For His glory, from His glory.

To my dearest girl, Alex. Sister. You are the reason this book was finally born. Your encouragement, fangirling, and being an absolute blessing of an alpha reader gave me the courage to push on, the joy in continuing, and the shoulder to cry on when I became a mess in need of comforting. You were the only ear I could turn to, and I am so grateful for who you are and the sister and partner in crime that God gave me in you! Thanks, Captain X, for all the adventures! Can't wait for round two.

To my family. The ones present and the ones not so much. I love you all more than words can say, and I can't wait to see the goodness that God has ahead!

To the beta readers, Abby Elissa Johansen, Helen Adams, Kylie Hunt, Jenessa Anderson, Sydney O'Rear, Morgan Giesbrecht, Emily Knowles, Virginia Burford, Cherith

Bradley, Beth Buckles, Flora, LaCara Boothe, Marissa Archibald, and Morgan Smith. You all are a treasure and gave me the confidence that there was something special here. Thank you for all of your cheerful, helpful, and fangirling comments! You made this book better, and I'm so grateful for your help! Don't worry, Marcus shall have his own story soon.

Micaiah, you are a diamond! Thank you so much for your patience and hard work on polishing this book within an inch of its life! You pushed it over the edge and gave me the confidence to push the publish button! So grateful for the work and heart and enjoyment that you spilled into *Once I Knew*!

Beth: Thank you for being a faithful encouragement who I can trust with my writing voice. You are the one who gets it. Your words of encouragement, gentle and sweet as honey, have always been a blessing to my heart. Thank you for being a friend, a writer, and a reader who knows my voice and my heart and sees all the hidden threads that others might miss. <3

To the readers and Instagram community. This one was for you. Your joy and excitement to glimpse my writing gave me all the fuel to keep going, to continue writing, and to get this story into your hands as soon as possible. Thank you for the encouragement and joy you have been to me! You bless me beyond belief!

To the Glory Writers. Your sprints in multiple cabins kept me going, and your hearts ablaze with stories for His glory give me hope for the future of stories and of publishing. I can't wait to see where God takes us. Together.

To my King. I serve You and no other. For my King, I would traverse all of Elira, dive into the depths of Rusalka and lead the prisoners home. I will sail my boat upon the high seas at your command and for your Kingdom. I pray I set captives free, heal the sick, and speak life and hope to the brokenhearted. I serve at the behest of your kingdom.

Till next time,

VICTORIA LYNN

# SECRET VAULT

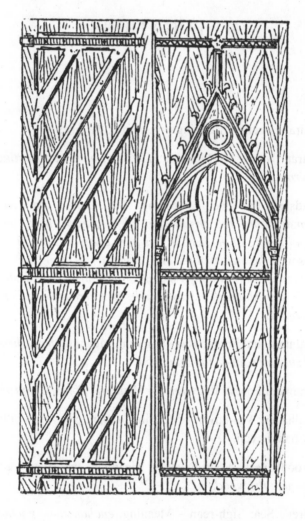

Do not open until you have finished the book.
Spoilers inside.

# GLOSSARY:

## LOCATIONS:

Elira: El-eera – Meaning: *freedom, to be free.*

Niran: Nee-ran – Meaning: *The high place, everlasting and eternal.*

Padsley: Pad-slee – Meaning: *The name is derived from Parsley and the inspiration of medieval times and the significance of the herb. It has been cultivated in Europe and fits with the medieval feelings. Parsley was thought to remove bitterness and although medieval herbalists recommended it for a sour stomach, it was also thought to remove bad or bitter emotions.*

Raintamount Forest: Rain-ta-mount Meaning: *from the mount of smiling rain or laughing rain*

Pranvera Forest: Pran-ver-a – Meaning: *Forest of Spring*

Valhaven: Val-haven – Meaning: valiant or a worth of haven. Valiant haven.

WoodRiver: Wood-River – Meaning: *the river that cuts through the wood.*

Sirene Sea: Sigh-rean – Meaning: *enchanter or enchanting, like in terms of alluring sirens*

Illias Pass: Ill-ee-as – Meaning: *Yahweh is God/the Lord is my God*

Rusalka: Roo-sawl-kaw – Meaning: *Infested with demons and water filled with evil.*

Izevel Mountains: Eye-za-vel – Meaning: *Hebrew origin,to exalt or to dwell. Usually in the context of exalting evil.*

Pavlin: Pav-lynn – Meaning: *Small or humble. Of little consequence.*

# CHARACTER GUIDE:

**Violet Frell:** A farmer in the south country near Padsley. Name meaning: *Purple flower of royal valor. Frell means Free or freedman.*

**Richard Frell:** Violet's deceased father. Name meaning: *powerful or brave valor*

**Miran Frell:** Violet's deceased mother. Name meaning: *worthy of admiration and peaceful one.*

**Granny:** Miran's mother and Violet's constant companion.

**Obed:** The Kingsman that Violet takes in. Name meaning: *servant of God*

**Master Fendrel:** The medicinal of the village of Padsley. Name meaning: *Future minded, always looking ahead.*

**Marcus:** Fendrel's assistant and apprentice in all things medical. Name meaning: *hammer, shining or polite warlike.*

**Drake:** the Kingsman who was in a fight with Richard. Name meaning: *dragon or snake*

**Galeron:** Woven goods merchant. Thin, usually jovial and with a witty joke for everyone. Name meaning: *knight.*

**Everard:** The village blacksmith. Name meaning: *brave or hardy: wild boar. Strength of a wild boar.*

**Enguerrand:** The Chancellor and usurper of the throne. Name meaning: *Raven. Ravens are intelligent creatures, often solving complex problems with ease. Plotting and calculating. Will prey on baby animals of other species. Ravenous for power. Hungry for control.*

**Elgon:** The prince and true heir to the throne. Name meaning: *noble or white, worshiper of the Most High. High minded.*

**Malcolm:** Commanding kingsman of the palace guard. Later, the first knight to the king. Name meaning: *follower of peace [dove]*

**Zehra:** Servant girl in the palace. Name meaning: *beauty.*

VICTORIA LYNN has an insatiable desire for truth, light and beauty.

Traveling to destinations of beauty created by our Heavenly Father, reveling in creative pursuits that fill her with joy, or pouring her heart into words of life are some of her favorite things to do.

She seeks to bring the life giving words of the Savior to a dark and broken world that desperately needs to know of His sacrifice.

A writing and publishing coach, author, journalist, seamstress and creator, she loves spending time with any of her 8 siblings, exploring her native state of Michigan, and sewing gowns fit for a princess.

@VICTORIALYNNAUTHOR

RUFFLESANDGRACE@GMAIL.COM

WWW.VICTORIALYNNBLOG.COM

@VICTORIALYNNAUTHOR

Marcus is tired of losing those he loves. With Violet's marriage to the king of Elira, the last shred of his childhood has been uprooted and he feels alone... again. When Elgon's new policies take effect, the anger of the Rusalkan mountain king is unleashed upon the borderlands. With refugees streaming into Elira by the hundreds, the stories from the wall are horrendous.

Marcus joins a convoy to lend his medical skills to those in need at the Eliran border. What he finds there is about to change his life forever.

Dilara's life as a slave in Rusalka was anything but idealistic. Consumed by a system that was designed to use, abuse, and discard the likes of her, she has been taken through the very depths. Carrying a traumatic secret and wounded in her frenzied escape, she finds herself with an unlikely protector and an even more confusing relationship. Can she traverse the waters of this new life and make it her own?

And can Marcus overcome his own deformities to find the one missing piece? Or will his life forever be marked by suffering and sacrifice?

# Enjoy these other works by Victoria Lynn!

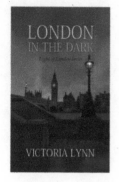

## London in the Dark

With a sudden death in the family throwing a brother and sister together, there is bound to be some conflict when one is the leading detective in London. When a string of thefts suddenly seems tied to their family legacy, can Cyril and Olivia find the answers to their questions? And their struggling relationship?

## Bound

When two children escaping abusive families encounter each other at the same lonely train station in the middle of the night, throwing their lot in together seems to be the best option for them both. But when injury lands them in the hands of their worst nightmare - foster care - will they be encountered with the love of God or dragged back into their broken lives?

## When Beauty Blooms

Marjorie Kirk is a woman with no fortune, no prospects, no family, and no skills. She is awkward, shy, and the farthest thing from any semblance of a society lady. The new minister keeps turning up in the most awkward of places and she can't help but feel that her life is doomed to one of embarrassment.

A story of a young woman with social anxiety and how she learned to bloom.

Enjoy these other works by
Victoria Lynn!

## London in the Dark

With a murder to solve, the Inspectors have a problem to
solve on their own... Sophie is lost in London. Having never
left the English countryside for London, When Sophie's
parents send her away to visit a city family friend, she
and herself thrust into the mystery of the question... Just
what lies in the dark?

## Bound

When you are a slave, you have nothing. Only oppression
exists... But one man has seen in the mud of
the battle slaves more to it all just seem to explain...
to himself what he does, but he must stand firm in
his purpose. Can he accomplish all? How can a slave
have freedom? And yet, perhaps he does in the most unusual
way of all, to be...

## When Beauty Blooms

When a family's fortune has gone from them so deeply
for hope, and something they they can find themselves
and belonging in a world... when a family and
find themselves in a struggle in the most unusual
way of all, to be...

When a family's fortune has gone from them so deeply
so upon them to...

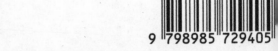
9 798985 729405